THE UNFLINCHING ASH

ANGELA ARMSTRONG

NORSOU BOOKS

NORSOU BOOKS

Text copyright © 2021 Angela Armstrong
Illustration copyright © 2021 NORSOU Books Limited,
Aotearoa | New Zealand
First Edition | Printed in New Zealand
Cover illustration: Kerem Beyit
Title design: Sarah Gauntlett

ISBN 9780473578343 (paperback)
ISBN 9780473578350 (POD paperback)
ISBN 9780473578374 (Kindle)

www.angelaarmstrongbooks.com

To my daughters

ASH

There was a man with a gun and everyone knew someone was about to be shot.

Ash made a quick study of the pistol. It was studded with unnecessary domes and had a wine-red, bulbous grip. The muzzle was excessively long, trumpetish even. The whole thing was flashy, like its bearer.

Ash stood with her brother-in-law, a quince-throw away among the gathered crowd, but close enough to see the man who held it well enough: Banyan.

"You'll see. He'll surprise you." Wynn whispered beside her, rubbing his hands together. Ash stilled her brother-in-law's anxious tell, capping his hands with one of her own and lowering them out of sight with a sigh. She pulled her hood further forward.

"Sorry," Wynn said, wincing.

Ash nodded in acknowledgement but kept her eyes fixed on the man with the gun. Banyan was about to address them.

"Who would like to pull the trigger?" Banyan scanned the assembly, Ash and Wynn among them. "You? You?" He offered the ornate Flintlock, grip first, to one, then another.

"You're wrong. He will *not* surprise me." Ash spoke through her teeth.

Wynn nodded his head eagerly.

Ash narrowed her eyes.

"You, sir." Banyan dipped his head towards a man near the middle of the night's throng. Not just any man. Someone Ash *knew.*

"No!" Ash whispered her disbelief. She schooled her expression as Mórlough's burliest falconer was chosen from the crowd in the square. Hallam Falconer clutched his chest and answered Banyan with a gaping, speechless mouth.

"Yes, you." Banyan confirmed, flashing a smile.

Not Hallam. Impossible. Yet there Hallam was, shrugging out of his mantle, passing it to his curly-haired wife. This could not be happening. Hallam Falconer, chosen by Banyan – a gull Ash and Wynn both knew. Hallam took the three stairs to the raised platform in a single stride.

Ash wasn't the only one who knew Hallam. Wynn was beaming, for a start. A wave of jostling sent a tremble through the group as others recognised the falconer. A cluster of young ploughmen in front of Ash and Wynn changed position, forcing Ash to crane to see the platform. She kept her eyes on Banyan's hands. Always on the hands. Banyan passed the pistol to Hallam, whose large paw swallowed one end of the barrel.

Banyan's hands now appeared empty. "Your name?" Banyan asked, loud enough for all to hear.

"Hallam, sir. I mean, *Hallam*." He projected his voice the second time, realising his answer was for the crowd as much as it was for Banyan.

"Are you here with your wife, Hallam?" Banyan raised his brow.

"Uh, yessir." Hallam's forehead began to bead with sweat. Banyan cast his eyes back expectantly into the crush of those looking on. Hallam gestured towards his curly-haired wife, Peony. A pillow of lamplight tinted the night's gathering a soft yellow. At its heart, Peony gave a modest wave. Hallam's face at seeing his beloved and her delicate response was a perfect contortion of nerves and pride. Banyan's voice boomed: "Please, come join your husband."

Peony did – taking the steps one at a time – sidling up stiffly beside her falconer spouse. She held his mantle tightly across her mid-section as though it might serve as a shield against all who watched.

"Your name?"

"Peony."

"And what is your favourite colour, Peony?"

"Yellow. Sir." Peony blushed.

"Something like this?" Banyan swiftly drew a swath of amber silk from beneath the mantle Peony clutched. Peony's eyes flew wide. Hallam locked his arm around his wife's shoulders.

Peony answered, "Well, I am more fond of the colour of buttercups... but that sure *is* yellow, Mister Banyan, sir." Soft laughter rippled through the assembled party. Peony's cheeks burned brighter.

"Peony, would you be so kind as to hold this yellow silk, like so... " Banyan stretched an edge of the fabric between his fingers, allowing the square to fall in a thin wall.

Peony passed her husband's mantle back to him, along with a look of uncertainty, then took Banyan's proffered silk between pincered fingers.

"Ah, the angle is right, but if you please..." Banyan placed his hands over Peony's and adjusted her grip so that her full hand held the silk in the air. Hallam bristled at this display of familiarity before quickly checking his posture. "Hallam, before we get to the business," Banyan nodded towards the pistol Hallam still held, "Would you do me another service?" Banyan retrieved a small lead ball from a pouch at his side.

Ash wanted to roll her eyes. She opted for squinting harder.

"There's more," Wynn whispered. He half-lifted his hands to rub them together again before thinking better of it and dropping them.

"Please etch a symbol onto this – any mark of your choosing." Banyan held the gun's ammunition aloft between his forefinger and thumb. His voice easily pierced through the crowd's whispers and the muted coos of a mother soothing a babe swaddled in a sling.

Hallam offered the pistol back to Banyan to free a hand. Banyan displayed his palms, "I'd rather not cast any doubt that I have tampered with the gun – someone else should assist you." Hallam froze. Banyan turned to the crowd. "Who has some experience loading a gun?" A few hands raised in response. "You, there, please, take it." Hallam handed the piece to a man in the front.

Ash smiled.

With the gun out of the way, Hallam retrieved his knife and took the lead ball from Banyan. The large man then knelt on his mantle and worked his tool across the ball's surface before standing and sheathing his blade.

"Hallam, if you please, ensure the pistol is loaded with the ball bearing your mark." Banyan's voice rang out. He offered Hallam a patch of cloth and some powder, which Hallam took over to the volunteer holding the gun. Banyan directed Hallam through the steps – loading the powder down the muzzle, wrapping the inscribed lead shot in the wad of cloth and adding it down the shoot as well. The volunteer then swiftly rammed, primed and closed up, and offered Hallam the gun.

Now Hallam was ready to shoot somebody.

Ash couldn't see these smaller activities well at this range, but she didn't need to. She'd seen enough.

"Hallam, please take your place on the white fleur de lis." Banyan's gestures were flowery. "Forgive me, I've neglected our aides! Peony, please, rest a moment," Peony gratefully lowered the yellow veil and released a sigh. "And thank you...?" Banyan extended his hand to the man who had assisted by holding the pistol when Hallam's hands were full. The helper supplied his name.

"Thank you, *John*!" Banyan gave John a firm handshake of introduction and thanks. "Where were we?" Banyan squeezed his own jaw, extracting his train of thought. Peony raised the silk in answer. "Ah yes, the lovely Peony. So we were." Banyan strode over to stand upon a black fleur de lis on the far side of the stage, so that he and Hallam now book-ended Peony. "Hallam, are you familiar with how to fire your weapon?" Hallam nodded. "How is your aim?" Banyan donned an expression of faux-terror for laughs, which he received. "I want you to aim for my mouth, as best you can. Then, a lead ball bearing your mark will pass through Peony's favourite colour...well, almost her favourite," more laughter, the crowd had become his butter, "and I will catch that ball between my teeth." Banyan turned to Peony but spoke for all to hear. "Now Peony, it's understandable if you drop the silk after your husband has fired. It's normal for some sparks

ANGELA ARMSTRONG

to spray and I don't want a single hair on your lovely head to be singed." Banyan shifted one foot back as a brace, then spoke to Hallam, "Now, aim for my mouth!"

Hallam's hand shook slightly as he released the safety lock, which was fair – he'd never shot a man, much less through a veil held by his wife. And that was the rub; why Wynn had brought Ash here – her brother-in-law surely thought Banyan was a bona fide illusionist if he could do all this using a trembling local.

That local fired solid and sure.

Peony released the silk soon after the bang and Hallam rushed to stomp on the smoking fabric and clutch his wife close.

Ash's eyes were on Banyan. His head had shifted slightly and he now stood on tiptoe. He slowly lowered himself to flat feet and pulled back his lips. Between his teeth, he held a small ball of lead.

Ash nudged Wynn and made a move to leave. "I've seen enough. Let's be on our way."

Wynn gaped in reply. "Wait, you haven't seen if it's the marked bullet."

"Oh, I know it is."

"Then why are we leaving…didn't he…?"

"I've known for a while, but I stayed in case poor Hallam fired early – that might have been diverting. He's alright Wynn, I'll give you that, but he's no great magician – "Ash's hood inclined towards

Banyan — "you've found a fair Manipulator maybe, but nothing we need worry about."

Wynn remained fixed on the spot, looking to the couple on the stage, still embracing, and back at his hooded friend.

Ash began to slice her way out through the crowd, ignoring open mouths and the impetuous press towards Banyan's prestige.

"Is this," dramatic pause, "your mark?" Banyan offered the lead ball for Hallam and Peony's inspection. The falconer nodded, wide eyed, with the promise of tears glinting. Banyan recovered the silk with a flourish and held it up on display to confirm the weapon had indeed fired, leaving a charred hole and a spray of smouldering evidence across the fabric.

Ash shook her head as she moved into the shadows and out of the perimeters of the night's chicanery.

The crowd was still clapping – marks that they were – or *gulls* as they were more commonly called around the Lough. Ash forgave them their applause, they knew no better.

Besides, the gulls were hers to woo as well.

Wynn came at her heels, "How did you know? I was sure this 'Breath-stealing Banyan' was the real deal. He's pulled a different local every show, but a local every time – they can't *all* be in on it, Ash! And the marked bullet means it was the same bullet…"

Ash bumped Wynn playfully and tugged on his sleeve. "Not here. Come with me. Then we'll talk."

ASH

Ash perched across from Wynn at a knotty inn table, resolve and fire etched on her face as she mapped the room. Wynn knew her well enough to wait before he spoke, that she'd listen better when she was finished. That was one of the things Ash liked most about Wynn – that he let her be in her head when she needed to be.

Ash counted her exits (one – through the window beside them, two – out the front entry door, three – through the kitchen and out the back door, four – up the stairs then through a window on the landing, and five – *down* the stairs and a tight-squeeze through the slim cellar window, provided she still fit) *then* she turned her gaze towards her childhood friend. "I'm done."

Wynn began. "What did I miss? I was so sure I'd found someone worthy – someone you'd at least class as fair competition. Banyan chose *Hallam*, Ash! There's no way Hallam is in on the act – that brute's the kindest, most *honest* guy this side of the lake! It's what *you* do – call a known gull from the crowd…"

Ash bit her lip to hold back a laugh. "Yes, I saw *Hallam* fire that ridiculous gun. Honestly, what purpose did all that decoration serve?"

"I didn't promise a *humble* contender, merely a competent one!" Wynn protested. "And you're still not answering me! Hallam's no inside man, and yet he did the firing. He somehow got a *signed* ball into Banyan's mouth without bringing anyone harm. The same bullet he'd signed – into the man's mouth, Ash!"

"The very same one."

"So you admit it! Banyan accomplished it! With a gull!"

"I didn't say Banyan accomplished anything."

"Release me from this torture. How did he do it?"

"Do you know a 'John?'"

"What does this have to do with Banyan?" Wynn was flustered, but indulged Ash nonetheless; "I know a great many Johns. John Fletcher, John Wood, John Webb, John who used to line up all the shoes in pairs while we swam past the docks – what's he now? Something awfully dull and pious…"

"John Godfrey."

"Are you sure?"

"Quite."

"Your point?" Wynn paused. "OH. OOOOOH. Of course." Wynn raked his hand through his sun-bleached hair and then down his face.

"You've realised that although Hallam took the stage as an unassuming, impartial, non-colluding assistant, our dear friend *John* – what *was* his last name, Wynn? – had his hands on the gun for the most pivotal of moments in our parlour magician's act. And that 'John' did some very assuming, partial, colluding things in his pivotal moment."

"John loaded the gun."

"Yes, John did."

"Wax?"

"Most likely."

"Banyan got the actual bullet from him…"

"…when they shook hands."

Wynn resembled a stringed Mystic puppet, suddenly dropped by its master; "Oh, it's so obvious now... Banyan employs a shill after all."

Ash leaned in to give him a commiserate shoulder squeeze. "Don't despair! When he called up Hallam even *I* thought things looked promising. Just for a moment I thought you'd found something – *someone* worth worrying about. But how he held that angular chin of his in melodramatic thought… *that is* how he popped the marked bullet into his mouth like a bonbon!" Ash released a deflating sound of exasperation. "His sleight of hand is fine, his misdirections are awful. Really, who clasps their jaw in thought?"

It was like Ash's Papal had always said: *Everything was in the hands.*

"So he merely opened his mouth after Hallam fired wax to reveal a lead ball he'd been holding there for the past few minutes...?"

"Oh the talent."

"I've done nothing to shrink your ever-growing head then?"

"Not a thing." She smiled. "But you're a trier, and triers are keepers – especially loyal ones." Ash nudged Wynn's hand with hers, causing their table to tip slightly.

Wynn slouched in exaggerated defeat. "I've failed to find a Mystic worthy to be named your rival yet. But that doesn't mean the path to receiving The Queen's Seal is straight."

"You mean the pesky matter of how half the Lough would rather see me hanged, burned or drowned first?"

"Yes, that."

Ash shrugged. Her attention snagged on a stranger. The stranger was both strange *and* suspicious. The flags he sent up were three-fold; one – his clothing, two – his posture, three – his expression. He wore a dark, winged vest cinched with a silk cord. The design was unfamiliar. He sat with a symmetry and stillness that made Ash wonder if there was a ripple in time in the tavern's corner – perhaps they were all moving on to tomorrow while this man remained anchored at eternal, peaceful union with his stool.

But it was his expression that made her check her exits. Side-window, Front, Kitchen, Landing, Cellar (hopefully).

The motionless stranger was looking at *her*. One of his mouth corners tented. His eyes were sharp and dark, his skin warm brown. The stranger had seen a great deal more sunshine than had shone in these parts, or perhaps his skin was always darker.

"Ash?" Wynn sing-songed.

"Mmm?" Ash reluctantly turned her head back to her friend.

"You'll do it in your first year. I can feel it. With the Seal, you won't always have to hide, and then – Mysteries permitting, my beloved wife will rest her delicate heart and I'll not have to reassure her every time you perform that... " Wynn broke off.

Ash had unleashed a smile, which gave anyone who saw it pause, her current companion no exception. She was looking behind Wynn, and whatever she saw there had made her grin.

From Wynn's face it was clear he knew what must be behind him, or rather *who*, and so said, "Grete Appleby, are you sure you're no Mystic? Your knack for appearing when your name's fresh on the air is supernatural." Wynn kept his eyes straight ahead, but spoke louder so that his wife, Grete, behind him, could hear full well.

"A Mystic born, but an Appleby chosen." Grete answered, leaning forward and squeezing her husband's shoulder. "Now, what of my 'delicate heart?'" Grete pulled up a stool and joined her husband and younger sister. It put her on the side of the closest exit, but Ash decided if it was required, the time lost thrusting her sister beneath the table to shield her from any raining glass was acceptable.

"I was just telling your sister here that her days of skulking about the alleys of the Lough must soon be at an end – I've failed to find a rival that could stand between her and winning the Seal…"

"That's not the same as winning the Seal."

Grete wore caution like a crown. Although Ash and Grete were both born from the same Mapa and Papal, the sisters were antipodean enchantresses. To Ash the Mysteries had dealt passion, grit and tireless intent, which she carried like a loaded quiver on her strong, lithe frame. Grete's appeal was no less, but instead came by way of caution, calm and censure – an attractive safe harbour expressed in her soft edges and soft speech. Both young women had thick dark hair and the blessing of symmetry on their side. Both could sneak.

"So I take it tonight's show has failed to convince you to retire and find a suitable husband? Or at least a suitable occupation?" Grete leaned against Wynn, but eyed Ash across the table. "Wynn was saying this Breath-stealing Banyan fellow has the crowd in rapture at show's-end."

"Gulls. He has the gulls. The Seal is given by someone more discerning. The queen wants the best. Banyan is not the best." Ash downed the last of the

Lough-ale and upturned her tumbler to mark her
tab's end.   A barmaid was quickly at her side and
took her coin.   Ash noticed then that the unusually-
motionless stranger was gone.

"But Banyan may very well be the best the
queen'll *see*, come Queen's Day."   Grete allowed
some sympathy to paint a small frown.

"But that's the trick I'm about now, *oh delicate
heart*," Ash almost smiled, sardonically echoing
Wynn's words about her *resilient* sister "— for *the
best* to be numbered among those seen." Now she
smiled, and even Grete repositioned herself in
response.

"It's madness."

"But the best kind."

No female Mystic had ever been numbered
among those performing at the pleasure of the queen.
Female Minstrels – yes, Minnesingers too.   The
Troubadours – and even Acrobats had females
among them. But a female Mystic had never
rendered her talent as part of Queen Valencia's
celebrations. Not for lack of female Mystics, no. It
was because female Mystics were given another
name around Mórlough – a name they didn't ask for.

Witch.

The ability to commune with the Mysteries was
something to which both priests and Mystics made
claim.   For the basilica, All Untold and Unproven
unilaterally meant "God and His will." God and His

will were accessed by way of prayer and sermon, and only by a few.

For the Mystics, what All Untold encompassed was open for exploration – and by anyone.

Both groups appeared to deal in matters not of the *physical* world, having some access to the unseen and spiritual. This shared area of interest between the church and Mystic circle was proving... problematic.

Even devout worshippers at the basilica paid other dues to All Untold one way or another; a sprinkling of salt here, a hushed blessing answering a sneeze there. Then there were the basilica-attending believers who became gulls after the sun's setting; night-goers who dared to seek diversions through the witching hours – despite all the basilica's warnings.

And the Mystics? They made those witching hours and All Untold their business.

If only the devout, the daring, and the Mystics were all who dwelled in Mórlough. It was the others that were the problem – the ones who led tiresome campaigns against women who did more than pay dues or dare diversion. Campaigns targeting women like Ash.

But with an unwed queen on the throne – the first of her kind in many years – Ash felt certain that change was brewing about the lake, even if a coven of zealots was fighting it. If anything, the zealots' fervour only gave Ash pluck; she wasn't imagining progress loomed – all could feel it. For her opposition, the sense of impending change invoked anxiety and...irrational behaviour.

The solution to the conflict, for Ash, was both simple and timely. The Queen's Seal – an endorsement none in the realm could ignore – ensured patronage and immunity. The Queen's Seal would usher in the looming change. This year, Ash would be freshly old enough to receive a commendation to perform for a Seal.

And Ash *needed* it.

She spoke her need aloud – "I'll get in. She'll see me. And this year, *I'll* be the best." Ash shrugged at the seeming simplicity of her plan. To perform, Ash only needed to receive a commendation from a lord or lady – which only meant appearing and earning respect from some while avoiding assault from others. *Easy.*

Grete managed to marry a smile with a sigh of defeat. Ash rose to take leave, and Grete unfolded from her position at Wynn's side, gently placing a hand on Ash's shoulder as she spoke; "May the Mysteries untold share your will."

"Mysteries willing." Ash and Wynn dipped their heads with the ritual reply.

As Grete sat again, Ash saw the peregrine stranger had not gone, simply moved. Ash found him now, wedging a wood chip beneath a short leg of a table behind Wynn. Odd. He hadn't been seated there, begging why an imbalance of *someone else's* table would call him to action. As the stranger stood, he brushed against Wynn before spinning to say, "My apologies." His voice was smooth and low.

"No matter, unmet." Wynn smiled. He turned slightly to better see the unmet to whom he spoke.

"You could use one too, yes?" The side-smile again, as the unmet offered a wood chip from within his sleeve.

Wynn returned a look of confusion. The chip wasn't edible – the kind of offering Wynn was more likely to see need for.

"It's for under our table," Ash's whisper to Wynn came out with harder edges than she'd intended.

"Ah! Many thanks." Wynn took the chip and held it towards Ash. He then presented his hand palm-up and honest, to shake hands in thanks. That was when things blurred. The unmet released Wynn's hand while somehow also moving to pass Wynn. Wynn bumbled. A tumbler fell on a table. A server blocked one of Ash's exits. The stranger gave a parting salute by way of his infuriating grin, then left.

Something had happened, in his passing.

Ash stood there squinting, confused. Wynn and Grete exchanged shrugs. *Something Ash missed. Something Ash knew but had not entirely seen.* "Wynn, check your purse."

Wynn grasped at his side. The whites of his eyes shone in answer. "It's gone." Grete gripped her husband's sleeve in silent alarm.

"A moment." Ash made a promise with a single finger, then strode after the side-smiler. She hadn't caught it. How had she failed to see? She scanned the tavern, then the muddied approach beyond the door. She caught no sight of the thief's distinctive vest or bearing. She groaned in disgust. How had he managed... ?

"Ash?" Grete said. Wynn and Grete joined Ash at the door, where she stood weighing the best direction to take. Grete slung her arm like a belt around Ash's side, intent on ending her sister's pursuit.

"He's gone... I... " Ash was unsettled.

"Ash?" The second time Grete spoke, she drew out her sister's name with a note of apprehension. Ash felt a tug at her side and looked down to see its cause. Grete had tugged at Ash's waist and now held a bag of coin...just like Wynn's. "Funny Ash, very funny." Grete passed her husband the purse. "I didn't think sleight was your style."

"It isn't... I... "

"Is Ash the Unflinching... stammering?"

"What I mean is: I didn't take your coin. The supernaturally-still-man took it, and then..."

"She *is* stammering. Are you saying the unmet offered us a courtesy, stole my coin, then *latched it to your belt*?" Wynn's dubious expression spoke as loudly as the unlikelihood of his words.

"*I* didn't take it." Ash gave pause and mentally replayed the scene, then an idea lit her face. "Check it." Ash gestured towards the bag. Wynn had been in the process of securing it at his side, but obliged, releasing its drawstring. He withdrew a small card, frowning. Ash smiled. "Now tell me, was *that* there before?"

"I think it's for you," Wynn stretched forth the card. It bore only two things in fine script – a place and a time.

"What makes you think this is for me?" Ash asked, tipping her head, one eyebrow raised.

"I doubt the unmet has invited an obviously-married man so clearly in love with his wife to go courting in the Western tract."

This time, Wynn was right. Men seeking male company – married or otherwise – went to Delian's Wash, The Chalice, or Seb's Cup... and anyone could see Wynn was a poor mark for such a match. No, this was about Ash. The unmet had somehow eluded Ash's detection, but eluding her had *got* her attention. A slow smile lit Ash's face. She was rolling this peculiar irony around on her tongue.

Grete's crumpled brow was no surprise. "You're not going to go, are you?" The suggestion of how ludicrous she found such a consideration was all in the 'go.'

"Now, *who* was it that begged I'd find a suitor and retire a mere ale ago?" Ash tapped her chin, as Banyan-esque as she could muster.

Grete's lips puckered in irritation, although her eyes smiled.

"I'll not flinch from a challenge now. Besides, it's hardly ladylike to leave a man waiting!" Ash smiled and drew up her hood for her skulk home.

Tomorrow at noon then. At Bess's Fry.

REN

The fresh linens on Ren's bed almost masked the dank smell from the musty window-frame and rotting wall beneath it. Ren had been shuffling cards for hours in his loft room. The cards riffled and slapped to an unsolicited inward chant;

> *The Unflinching Ash*
> *After vanishing lingers*
> *Long in a man's mind*

Or so it was in the Lough tongue – in his own it bore intermingling notes of mockery and anguish, for which he had found no perfect translation.

The first time Ren had seen Ash, it had been night and she had been upon a stage. Like everyone watching, Ren had been enchanted. Ash was elegant in her movements, focussed in her performance and achingly passionate in her speech. These all added upon her physical beauty, which alone could drive a man to poetry (and it had for *this* man, but that came later).

Ash had invited the crowd to hide an object of their choosing anywhere amongst themselves while her back was turned. Once the item was hidden, she faced them once more, and through watching the crowd (though they were sure she was reading their minds), she successfully located the hidden item. Four times. On the fourth round, the audience had hidden a ring. Ash won a hefty sum from a fool who'd bet against her. The betting man assumed most ladies would blanch at naming the ring's hiding place. Most ladies would have. But Ash was not most ladies and so declared, unflinching, that the ring lay sandwiched in a certain crevasse of a certain gull.

Ash made a hasty departure with her winnings – in what Ren soon learned was her modus operandi – vanishing without further praise.

That had been the start.

Although he had willed the Mysteries to bring a crossing to their paths, it had seemed pure coincidence when he saw her again a mere two nights later. Ren had been scouting further talent in the Western Tract – an Illusionist named Banyan was showing – when his eyes hitched upon Ash among the gulls. Although cloaked and quiet, she failed to hide her elegant bearing and boundless confidence.

It fast became difficult to watch Banyan's show – what with intrigue assailing him, as The Unflinching Ash made her exit. He had observed she preferred discretion, and so opted to wait for the show's end to introduce himself – a thing he felt compelled to do.

He longed to speak with her. He must be prudent, he knew. She was flighty, this one. Private, elusive by default. He also held then that a *professional* alliance would benefit them both. Maintaining professionalism with such a... wonder... would be difficult.

But he lost her in the throng.

He had retired for a consolatory tumbler of a beverage the keeper called *hum* beneath his rooms, but The Mysteries Untold must have shared his will, for Ash serendipitously appeared there – where Ren was lodged.

Ash lowered her hood across the room, and the inn-lamps withdrew in reverent answer. He need not find her – the Mysteries had brought them together.

It was in answer to inward caution that he took some time to ascertain exactly what kind of relationship Ash shared with her company. If she was already married or otherwise committed, Ren needed to know from the outset. Management of expectations was paramount. If she was not so joined, espoused, or otherwise attracted, well...a man could dream.

So Ren had pick-pocketed and planted her friend's coin-purse. His diversion had been feeble at best, but he had worked with what he had observed – the tables had all seemed off-kilter that night – but had not everything?

The discovery of a woman such as Ash was re-writing everything he knew of women.

Having established Ash's companion was indeed her *friend*, Ren had come to the decision that a simple introduction would be insufficient. That would not gain her attention. If she enjoyed flattery, she would stay after her shows, would she not?

He needed to *earn* her attention. Demand it.

He hoped he had done enough.

If not, he would keep a respectful distance. And if from that distance he became a rival she could not ignore and so sought out? Well, he would bear her attentions with humility and good manners...and a touch of hopeful grooming.

ASH

When Ash was a feisty 14 years of age, her mother Pabla conceded they could no longer keep her from the family act. Ash had joined her parents on stage before of course – delivering props and mechanics, making the final bows – but for the most part her parents had succeeded in keeping Ash, a knot of precocious energy, confined to warming the wings during their actual stunts.

Until the year she found her name. Or rather: it found her.

For in Mórlough all were born with a name they wore until they found another – their new name to match the path they'd chosen. Many simply adopted second names that beat the drum for their wares; the Brikendens (bricks), Coopers (wooden buckets), and Fletchers (arrows) all did the like. But Ash was born to Mystics, and knew since reaching the height of a pedlar's wagon wheel that she was partial to no such name. Mystics were prone to theatrics and bore names to match.

Within the cloth walls of their own pageant wagon, her parents were simply Papal and Mapa. To those wide-eyed souls who braved their night shows, they were Alexact (her father's name had been carried on whispers) and Pabla la Precisa (her mother a raven-haired wonder to the gulls of the night; a witch to the rest).

Mapa and Papal bore witness to their daughter's naming. Ash forced them to. She'd sent her elder sister, Grete, with a message that bade them come with haste – and they had quickly done so. Pabla la Precisa and Alexact followed Grete until they found their youngest daughter and dear old Wynn, behind their own wagon at the lake's edge. They were met first by the tang of rotten quince on the air. Wynn, Ash's right-hand man in the curated spectacle, stood next to a wooden cask. The cask was confirmed as the source of the sweet odour by a grist of winged pests hovering above it. Upon seeing Ash's parents arrive, Wynn took a series of disciplining breaths beneath a veil covering his nose and mouth, then took aim. With quinces for missiles, he fired. Ash was his target. Grete watched through splayed fingers, her shoulders snapping with each pelt. Stains had bloomed across Ash's clothes as Wynn's fruit found their target again and again. One struck Ash's cheek and left a bright streak of juice down the side of her face, though it slid down her neck and lodged there.

Pabla and Alex worked their mouths silently in turn as though about to question or challenge the display before them, but barred themselves each time. Wynn, encouraged by their silence, armed both hands and emptied the remains of the cask with renewed vigour. Ash's hair became slick with the juices of the fruit. Pabla placed a hand on the crook of Alex's arm and the two exchanged a look of pride, tinctured with pain.

Wynn flipped the empty cask, placed one boot on top and spread his arms in presentation. Few quinces had missed. One that had struck Ash's forehead had raised a small welt there. She was a mess.

Only then had Ash moved. (And then it was only her jaw, she'd not so much as *blinked* through it all.) "Mapa, Papal. I am ready."

There, behind a wagon circle near the Western tract of great Mórlough, at 14 years of age, Ash the Unflinching had been born.

A smattering of arguments had sharpened the days between that day and the first night Ash joined her parents on stage, but none of them changed the course that had been decided before her bravura against rotten fruit.

And so it was that the Mystics, Pabla la Precisa and Alexact, began throwing knives at their youngest daughter. Well, mostly Pabla had done that, Alex was more of a juggler.

ASH

The peregrine stranger arrived early at Bess's Fry.

He took a seat at a table in the corner, his back to the wall. The air around him appeared frozen, complicit in his state of calm. The stool opposite was empty, until, with a belch from the wooden floor it was dragged across…the stool was filled.

"You are not who I was expecting."

"Oh? You put a note in *my* coin purse, did you not?" Wynn replied. He looked large on the stool. Smug.

"You speak true, but I think we both know whose attention I sought."

"That we do. And you've got it – to a point."

"Yet she is not coming?"

Wynn smiled. "Woah there, unmet, first we establish whether or not you're mad."

"Is she not capable of doing that herself?"

"Mysteries, yes! But she likes to let me feel important now and then." Wynn winked.

"So, how are you going to establish whether or not I am crazy?" His words were easily understood, although formal and consciously formed. Ash – concealed but looking on – knew then that the peregrine stranger wasn't speaking in his first tongue.

"I have some questions." Wynn paused. "She wrote them."

"Why am I not surprised?"

"Let's start with your name."

Ash could see and hear most of this exchange from her place behind a kitchen screen, her hair tucked within a borrowed cook's cap. She gnawed on a skewered eel with one hand and shook a frying pan with the other. The stranger answered Wynn in time with a clang behind Ash, intercepting her eavesdropping. By All Untold, no! What was the man's name?

"*Ren*, you say? Hmm. You're not from around here, are you Ren? Or even the far side of the Lough..."

Ash wanted to hug Wynn. Gull that he was, he got some things right.

"I am from here now," Ren answered. His voice skimmed through the hollows of the Fry's clamour and, like his posture, was measured and refined.

"And what is it that brings you here?"

"To Bess's Fry? Or Mórlough?"

"Both? Yes, both." Ash resisted rolling her eyes as Wynn's cracks began to show. He was enjoying the defensive brother-in-law act, yes, but unsure of anything outside the script she'd fed him.

"The Queen's Seal brings me here."

"To Bess's or Mórlough?"

"Both."

"Are you from a foreign court?" Wynn asked.

Ash stopped chewing. They hadn't gotten this far in their role play – she hadn't known what motives the stranger would supply for his appearance last night – Wynn had done well to ask. This Ren could be royal, *should* be royal, for his air.

"No," Ren answered.

Ash emptied the fry she'd been shaking into a bowl and tossed the pan into a cask of sand to be scrubbed.

"Not a royal...so how do you think you'll get in to watch on Queen's Day then?" Wynn asked.

"I am not here to watch the fight for the Seal. I am here for the taking of it."

Ash's jaw locked. A competitor. The peregrine stranger wasn't a spy from the basilica hoping to flush her out; he hadn't smiled at her at the inn because he'd found a prize to report to a zealot horde – as he might have been, since Ash had been working the Mystic circuit in earnest, of late.

If this meeting was no snare, what *was* it?

Ren was a Mystic, and either he was very good...or very deluded.

Ash's gut lurched its answer and the air about Ren concurred.

"Well, I'm out of questions." Wynn put his hand in the air, the signal call for food. A server came promptly and stood at Ren and Wynn's table, then noisily drew up another stool.

"You mean to win, yet I've never heard of you," Ash said upon joining them. She placed the bowl of fry she'd filled in front of Wynn.

It had been more than three years since Ash's day of naming, and much had changed in her countenance and manner. As a child she'd smiled even when she was alone, skimming stones or sorting baskets of veils. Not so now. Now her eyes were hardened at the flex from pain and over-thinking, her hair fuller, her smiles hard-won. Her magnetic resolve and fire, however, were unchanged.

"Ash, you are late," Ren spoke through his smile. Sitting this close, Ash could better see the mischief in Ren's eyes that his smile had blinded her to at their first meeting. Ludicrous as it was, she was tempted to smile in return when she was trying to be serious.

"Late? I was here before you." Ash answered, removing her cook's cap and dropping it in her lap. Taking all of Ren in, Ash thought his chest and shoulders filled his vest very well.

"Ah." Ren looked to the screen behind them and the kitchen beyond. "I understand. Then you know why I am here."

"I heard you *say* why you are here."

"Is that not the same?"

"I'm not sure yet."

"I have come to win The Queen's Seal."

"To Bess's Fry? That's why you've come to me?"

"Yes."

"Why? I'm not in the business of dispensing Seals."

"No, but I believe you could win one."

"That much I already know."

"But I think you cannot alone. It is hard for one to receive a commendation if they are scarcely seen. I understand why it must be so – it would seem people... do not much like a woman performing illusions."

"People are changing. And I don't perform illusions."

"I am not sure how you can deny what I myself have seen – I saw Ash the Unflinching perform three nights ago. You are she... "

"I didn't say I didn't perform, I said I don't do illusions."

"Whatever it is you do, I saw you make a very quick exit."

He had seen her before the night of Banyan's show then. Ash re-counted her exits from the Fry. Only four, but the first (through the kitchens) was a solid one.

"Until people are done changing, I make myself scarce. It's best to be gone before squealers for the church cronies come calling. Once I have the Seal, I won't have to do that anymore."

"*If* you get that far."

Ash swallowed. People *were* changing, but she was wise to number her exits, still. While the queen's thrall for Mystics of late had made Ash's caste more socially acceptable, magicians and illusionists still occupied a niche that caused many to bristle. They claimed to know things only deity or the church should; claimed access to All Unknown instead of subscribing to approved authoritative sources for such. This Ren – though peregrine – had learned something of the region, she gave him that. "What are you proposing, exactly?"

"An alliance," he said. "We stand a better chance together. I am new around here, and it is clear you know your way around. I am sure you are worthy of the prize, but I am not sure you will make it to Queen's Day without some attempt to...stop you. Join me; an act with us both would be...impossible to beat." Then he waited, ever-still. *Did he even breathe?*

"I don't know you. I don't even *get* you. What with this..." Ash waved at Ren's general person, "air freeze thing you have going on. Unmet or otherwise, the last thing I want to do is ally myself with *a man* to be seen before the queen – it contradicts everything I'm trying to achieve here. Don't you understand? Although I congratulate you on last night's sleight-of-hand — no thanks — I'll take my chances going it alone."

Ren's stillness was broken by one small nod.

"Bess?!" Ash called to the kitchen and the muscles in Ren's neck drew taut as he turned to watch for the Fry's owner.

"I hope you will reconsider," Ren answered. He turned back to the table to find Wynn, and only Wynn.

Ash was gone. A cook's hat sat upon the third stool.

Wynn wiped his mouth and upturned his tumbler.

"Does she do that often?" Ren asked.

"All the time." Wynn stood, then nodded in farewell. "All the time."

REN

Ren had first come to Mórlough by way of Adhmad Thoir. He had found himself serving as minder to a grieving mother in the same caravan. She was not long abandoned by the man who'd sired her stillborn child. The woman had warned him the further south she went, the greater the danger of travelling in her position. She had taken comfort in being seen with a man. Ren was thankful no moment of weakness on her part led her to seeking greater intimacy as consolation.

They had parted at Adhmad Thoir's edge, where the woman took leave to stay with a relative. He saw her to the relative's door. Her story left a tenacious ache behind.

Ren took his time with his next meeting. He didn't want to rush things.

He wanted this bond to stick.

Journey over, travelling companion escorted, Ren was ready to stop travelling – to *arrive*; to meet the lake at the heart of his new home.

He privately committed to giving his all to this introduction. He made that promise to himself, with his eyes closed. When he opened them, he imagined his chest cavity as a clean vessel – open, ready. He drew the view of the Lough inside his vessel. His eyes glanced over the lake's shore, docks, and circlet of dappled light. His eyes stilled on its horizon. He regulated his heartbeat until it tuned to the gentle tide.

He whispered the new acquaintance's name; "Mórlough." He closed his eyes and checked he could still see the vista there. He could. He repeated the name with his eyes closed.

Home.

After that meeting, Ren's appetite led him to Adhmad Thoir's cross-hatching of wharves. He weaved in and out through shanties, tethered houseboats, trestled stalls. A pair of children pulled wooden boats by strings behind them on the Lough, their feet adding creaking dock-boards to dusk's song. Every four or five leaps the children were tsked as they jumped a cook-pot or dove beneath a rack. The day's catch hung drying from wires and ropes, suspended in angled lines. Fish soup simmered, gruel bubbled.

Ren tugged with his teeth at eel from a skewer as he walked. He left the steam and tang of the serveries and found himself in the craft guild quarter.

"You look like a man who could use a gander into the Mysteries." A woman with long hair and long earrings leaned over her table, lacertine. Ren ducked to a crouch, making a closer examination of the objects for sale. The woman's face – then above Ren's own – looked considerably put out. She settled back onto her stool. "I haven't seen you before."

"I do not believe I have seen you either. Nor stones such as these." Ren's eyes remained fixed on the table's spread – an array of stones, all painted with a single eye, though the eye's shape was created entirely by intricate dots. "Did you paint these yourself?"

"Every one, yes. The plum-stones are three val, palm-stones are five."

"I am sorry, I think I misheard you. It sounded like you repeated yourself, only the price went up. Have I offended you?"

"I'll say it slooow for the slow foreigner." The woman drummed her fingers on the table beside the larger stones. "*Palm*-stones, five," she pointed to the rows of smaller stones, "*Plum*-stones, three. And the veils," she motioned to painted fabric flourishing from a wire above her, "Twelve val."

Ren smiled in thanks, meeting the woman's eye for the first time. "Thank you for helping me, I hear the difference now. And the price seems more than fair."

Impatience melted from the woman's face in answer to Ren's gaze. "How many will you take?"

Ren smiled at her phrasing. In his own tongue, the action would be specified as *purchase*, not *take*. He had learned with some embarrassment while travelling in the caravan that "taking" did not mean taking without payment. "Are they ornaments alone?"

"You haven't been here long, have you?"

Ren offered another smile, then shook his head.

"These are Eyes to All Unknown." She propped her chin on her hand and recited;

> *Two eyes upon eyes when all is done*
> *Two eyes in the purse when bets are won*
> *Two eyes in our shoes guide our feet to fall*
> *Two stones in the Lough should the Seeker call.*

Towards the end of her narration the woman's frown and rising inflection suggested she was still unconvinced anyone could be unfamiliar with the rhyme.

"Much more than ornaments, then." Ren raised his eyebrows apologetically.

"In truth, unmet."

"I am short on val. Do you trade?"

She raised an eyebrow of genuine interest. "What are you offering?"

"A Mystery."

"Oh? I'd not taken you for a Mystic."

"I am not sure that I am…" Ren considered the term, thoughtful. "But I have a Mystery for you."

"Mystery first, stones after. I decide how many."

"Deal." Ren drew a deck of cards from his vest.

The woman offered a side-eye in answer.

Ren spread the cards across the little space left on the table, then turned and took one step away, displaying his back to his audience – four further gulls had stalled to watch, in addition to the stone-painter. "Select one card, and touch it with your finger."

The woman rolled her eyes, but did as she was bid.

"Is it done?" Ren called.

Seven gulls.

"Aye."

Ren turned to face the stone-painter once more. "Please, gather up the cards."

The woman did.

Ren took the cards from her, appeared to stir the air above the woman's table in one slow circle, then flipped the cards, fanning them in offering to the stone-painter. "Do you see your card?"

The woman leaned forward, then stood. "No…"

"Are you sure?" Ren raised one eye-brow and freed his lop-sided smile.

"I know what card I touched…" she reached forward and pulled apart cards, checking none nested beneath those presented.

"Perhaps the Eyes to All Unknown saw where it went?" Ren nodded towards the array of goods for sale. He collapsed the card fan and sheathed the cards in one smooth motion. "I would recommend consulting your favourite of the palm-stones."

The stone-painter's face screwed up in scepticism. She lifted the palm-stone closest to her nonetheless, finding the table beneath it bare. She shook her head in self-censure. "That's enough, unmet, move along."

"But I have not yet given you the Mystery." Ren held his hands open in appeasement. The woman imitated his pose, but added a mocking tension that said, "Well!?"

"You did not consult your *favourite* palm-stone…" Ren trailed off.

The stone-painter dropped her hands and presented her cheek, wavering. Then she crouched, lifting the table's covering. Ren followed suit, peeking back at her beneath the table. Beneath the table sat a palm-stone, near to the side of customers, watching for quick-handed thieves. Tucked beneath it, a red queen.

The stone-painter retrieved the card, her movements slow. Her return to standing was drawn out with the same, protracted disbelief.

"Is she not your card?"

"She is."

"It is a Mystery how she found her way there, is it not?" Ren brought one eye so close to closing, it looked like a wink, but it fell short – a single-eye's squint.

"Aye." The woman held the card at eye-level, looking between it and the wharf-boards below. "Two palm-stones or four plum-stones. Take one or the other, they're yours."

"Many thanks." Ren plucked four of the smaller eye-stones from the table; they vanished within his vestments without ado.

"Wait, your card, unmet." The woman stood, stretching to return the red queen to Ren. One of her painted veils whipped across her throat in the wind.

Ren pressed the card back into the woman's hand. "It is yours, lady. A gift from *Ren*."

The woman grasped Ren's hand with her other as he made to withdraw it. "Ren, then. I'll give you free counsel in turn, since you're new to the Lough. Cards such as these are like the stones – best hidden in the company of many."

Ren had nodded and placed one hand to his chest in thanks.

Ren's name had carried on the whispers of more than twenty gulls as they scattered. *Good. Very good.*

REN

By the time Ren had reached an inn in Adhmad Thoir proper, he was considerably less short in val (though running short on cards).

He had drunk *hum* at the bar, arranging his eye-stones in a line before him. Most patrons slouched over their ales or bowls of fasels. Ren somehow achieved an aspect of pleasant rest at the same time as perfect posture. Bodies lurched, slouched, teetered and postured. Bodies talked. Ren was the circumspect listener.

Many outlined their plans for an approaching festival called Dawn's Veil – which dance they'd offer which person, which veil they had chosen for this year, where they'd stand when the sun rose. *Mildly interesting.*

Some spoke of a man who'd visited the wharves that afternoon – a foreign Mystic with flair. *Better.*

Ren honed in on one conversation, within a cluster by the fire to his right.

"Dawn's Veil's well enough, but it's Queen's Day that'll fill the sails this year."

"How so?"

"A she-Mystic."

"Isn't it always about a girl with you, Darley!" A harmless nudge. "You'll have misheard – or heard what you wished you'd heard. She'll be a minstrel. Cawlon's sister went in as a minstrel two Queen's Days past."

"She hasn't shown this side of the lake, but word from the south is she's won favour in the Western Tract, and that she's good. And fair."

"There he goes – spreading word of a pretty lass." The group laughed, goading Darley.

"Let me finish, would you? She's not just any fair lass. I hear..." Darley lowered his voice then, "...she's the spawn of Alexact...and Pabla la Presica."

"No. Their daughter settled down on a farm or some such."

"There's another."

"Farm?"

"Daughter!"

"Oh." Two in the group raised their tumblers for more *hum*. "And what came of her naming?"

"Ash the Unflinching."

"She's doomed."

"Aye." The group threw back more hum.

"So you think I'd have a chance with her then?" Darley sounded hopeful.

His friends' answering mirth was interrupted by a sudden dampening all around.

Ren was not visibly altered for this change in the air, but within it, his attentions sharpened. Without any introduction, Ren knew trouble had entered the establishment.

On the edge of his vision, he registered a portly killbuck of a man. His forehead, small beard, arms, and gut were his most prominent features. The man's hands sat propped on his hips. He dripped with haughty menace.

"Evening, all."

The man received no answer. The keeper of the inn stood as still as his patrons.

Three more men stalked in behind the first. The widest of the group held two sleek dogs by their collars. The dogs choked, their front legs making little contact with the floor.

The first – the killbuck – announced, "I've come to renew my protection!"

A woman at Ren's left buried her face in her husband's sleeve.

The killbuck continued; "The price has gone up. Dawn's Veil's approaching, you all understand. I have a family to veil, after all. It will be *two* val per sin." The group did well to conceal their agitation at this news, but Ren did not miss the minute extension of the keeper's chin. That chin extension told of discontent, a veiled temper. "Two val for every sin unspoken, should the Seeker ask how faithful you all have been."

Ren began bagging his newly-acquired stones, without a sound. He didn't want their paint getting chipped.

The killbuck held a purse open before a seated woman, close to the door. "For your sister..." He blinked slowly in answer to the coins being dropped into it. Clink. Clink.

"I was sorry to hear your daughter has taken to thrashing upon the ground," the killbuck said, moving to the next table. "But not to worry, your shame will remain untold ..." He held the bag out, its mouth wide.

Clink. Clink.

Some murmurs slipped from Darley's group, by the fireplace.

"Ah. Darley's here." The killbuck spoke across the room. "Spreading talk of she-Mystics I hear – that'll be four val."

"I told you," Darley hissed through his teeth to his neighbour. His fists clenched and unclenched. The killbuck approached Darley's group – leaving Ren's vision a moment before reappearing at his right by the fireplace, the purse presented again. Clink. Clink. Clink.

Clink.

Ren cricked his neck.

The killbuck turned, following the sound, noticing Ren for the first time. The dog handler craned his neck attempting to see who this man at the bar was.

Both of them turned their attentions to Darley, who'd stood, chest inflated. "Double, Segar? *One* val was enough – two is...well...I'll not say what I think it is. I will say this: It's not right I pay double what all else are payin'..." Darley took a step forward. His mate clasped his shoulder in warning. Darley shook off the restraint. "That's the last time I give you any coin. I'll take my chances with the Seeker before I pay a ransom and call it 'protection.'"

The killbuck – Segar – forgot Ren and turned all of his body to face to Darley. Ren heard him tie the purse to his belt. Segar answered, "Now now, Darley, I can see you're upset, but you're speaking fa-"

That was when bedlam tore out.

Glass smashed. A table overturned. Two men, once seated, now grappled with Segar's men while the dog-hand visibly weighed whether he should release the hounds or guard the door. He took a step forward, uncertain, looking to Segar.

Darley drew a mallet. The killbuck absorbed a blow from it with his forearm. The back foot that braced him sent a shock through the floorboards.

Ren finished drinking his *hum*, his posture unchanged.

The couple, with the child earlier accused of some affliction, began crawling through the legs of the fray, the wife emitting dull whimpers, her palms bleeding from the floor's debris. They stayed close to the wall, eyeing the doors and their escape.

Ren tilted his head to the left. A tumbler sailed over his right shoulder. He returned to his former pose.

A chair broke across the dog-hand's head, splitting his scalp and sending a ready rivulet of blood down through his greasy hair before he hit the ground with concussive force.

Ren retrieved his tanto, stabbed a piece of meat from a board behind the bar, and flung it long and level – out the door the married pair slunk towards. The dogs bounded after the prize.

Ren stood. Then turned.

He slid a chair out of one assailant's reach.

He kicked a blade back to one from Darley's company.

Segar and Darley crushed against the bar in front of him. Ren stilled. Popular Darley thrust a blow beneath late-comer Segar's ribs. Segar crumpled, staggering back.

Ren took another step towards the door while Segar advanced towards Darley again behind him.

The dogs were back and licking the dog-hand's face, confused, when the downed handler took a blow that sent his form belly-sliding against the wall.

The other two underlings were down and out of the fight.

The ransom mob was down to one.

Segar.

And Segar became aware of this when he next broke apart from Darley. He weighed his options only briefly, then hurdled over a collapsed fighter, whistled for the dogs, and bolted through the door and into the night.

Ren made a move to follow, but stopped short of crossing the threshold.

"That man Segar forgot something," Ren announced.

He turned and surveyed the motley victors – shirts torn, teeth bloodied, and at least one nose broken. The dog-handler groaned into the wood floor. The keeper held a towel to his eye, a bootprint stamped upon his exposed cheek. He raised one weary eyebrow in question.

Ren held Segar's purse aloft, unleashing a dashing grin.

"I believe this rightly belongs to all of you."

He treaded heavily and precisely on the leg of an upset table beside him, righting it, then dropped the bag of coin on top.

Darley spoke over a fat lip, "Wait, how…?"

"Who are you?" Darley's friend interrupted.

"Why didn't you take it?" the keeper had asked.

"I will be showing tomorrow night. You can throw your coin then – if you think I have earned it."

Ren had made a small bow.
Then he had left.

ASH

The gulls were out in force. The location of the night's performance had been passed in hushed tones from Cooper to Fletcher to Blacksmith until everyone who dared to brave the night for entertainment's sake knew of the designated hamlet for the Mystic gathering.

The crowd was tight tonight, their breath forming a visible opaque cloud above their heads.

Wynn took his place backstage, guarding Ash's fourth exit. But Ash was merely Ash no longer. Ash the Unflinching now stood centre stage in garments of blue-grey. They fell fitted and simple around her frame, without hidden catchments or billows to conceal dirty moves. Her sleeves were tight at the forearm and finished before her wrist. Her hair lay untamed aside from a few small braids in its mass, her shoulders were pulled back, her teeth shone. She was radiant, and no man or woman in attendance could look anywhere else.

She spoke slowly, "Welcome, discerning defendants of the Mysteries. Before we begin, let's get to know some of *you* better. After all, without you we would be without a show this night."

She watched them then. She took inventory of the first twitch from the fisherman she could smell at three paces, the chewed cheek from the man with a full quiver at his back – more likely a bowyer than hunter, given his age, and the clenched jaw – of a candlemaker Ash concluded, given away by the wax on her hem. A few others made moves worthy of consideration, but these three were the best.

"Do we have any fishermen amongst our number?" Ash called, knowing the answer full-well. She took in the same twitch in her peripheral glance. The man shifted his weight onto his other leg before slowly raising his hand. "Please, sir, will you come forward?" Ash's smile suggested the honour would be entirely hers and the man followed its promise to the stage. Ash shook his hand with both of hers and indicated where he should stand.

"Now, you there," Ash extended her palm towards the bowyer, "would you keep this fellow company here?" The bowyer chewed his cheek briefly, then dipped his head before joining for handshakes and positioning.

"We are in need of a lady." Ash swept her arms open wide. She took in jagged exhales, clasping hands, and bitten lips that almost pulled her from her course. The candlemaker's clenched jaw spoke louder. "Please, would you join us?" Ash's eyes were alight with playfulness, and the candlemaker of the waxy hem followed Ash's outstretched hand to the stage after only a brief squeeze of her husband's arm.

Ash paced behind the three gulls.

"One of you bears a small sore – one you considered fair payment for your trade." The fisherman's brow wrinkled, the bowyer folded his arms, and the candlemaker – bless her – clenched her jaw. "You sir," Ash brought her head close to the bowyer, "given your experience in your craft, I imagine sores are unlikely and unreasonable, by your standards?"

The bowyer nodded and permitted a small smile.

"But you," Ash led, "you've been stung, haven't you?" Ash's frown of commiseration was for the candlemaker. "Burned too, I'm sure, but no one talks about the stings, do they?" The candlemaker's mouth opened slightly. Ash smiled as she took in the woman's kindly face, and then her arms – always returning her gaze to her face. As Ash's eyes crossed the woman's left wrist, there came the woman's tell: jaw clenched.

"A bee stung you here, if I'm not mistaken." Ash pointed to the spot the woman had given away, then smiled at the crowd. The candlemaker's mouth opened in surprise. "I doubt these gentlemen knew you had knowledge of the bees for the nobles' candles." Ash gave the candlemaker a tight smile and wink of affection. The candlemaker relaxed.

"M'am, may we know your name?" Ash placed her hand lightly on the woman's back.

"Mave, Miss Ash. Mave Chader." The candlemaker's voice was melodious, and it escaped in a chirp that appeared to surprise even her.

"Mave, have you held a revolver?"

Mave blanched. Ash knew then she could not ask it of her.

The fisherman had *volunteered*. Ash spoke to him next. "And you? Your name?"

"Fischer, ya. Terril Fischer."

Ash was pleased. She knew his accent hailed from the near-East and the name was given to babes who proved strong. Terril Fischer could be her mark. She would confirm it first. And so she whistled. She saw Fischer's eye twitch minutely, before he twisted his head as though clearing it. She knew whistling was considered bad luck at sea for many, it seemed even on land the superstition was hard to break. "Forgive me, Mister Fischer, I didn't think the wind could harm us here," Ash said, knowing many sailors believed whistling a challenge to the wind itself – a storm's invitation. She had riled him some. Good.

"Mister Fischer, how do you feel about revolvers?"

Fischer shrugged. Even better. She could work with a nervous eye twitch and a man who revealed his nerves but held no excitement to hold a gun.

Ash placed her hand feather-light on Fischer's mantle, high on his back. "Will you assist me this night?"

"I can." The consonant N came out hard and decisive.

"Thank you, Mave, and you sir, for coming this night. You may return to your company." Ash ushered them back to their places below stage. "Defenders of the Mysteries, our thanks." The dazzled crowd followed her lead in gracious applause.

She turned to the one remaining of the three. "Mister Fischer. Here is my revolver." Ash crossed the stage, collected the simple piece, then placed it in Fischer's hands. "And here is its ammunition." She crossed the stage again and delivered the ordinance. "How many chambers has it, Mister Fischer?"

"Six, m'am."

"Thank you, Mister Fischer. Please, face your back to me."

She then talked him through loading the gun with a single bullet, but iterated loud and avidly, "Do not reveal to me which chamber you select, but be sure *you* note where it is." Fischer did as he was guided, following Ash's final invitation to turn back to face her. "Thank you. Now you recall which chamber the bullet rests in?"

Fischer nodded, then twitched faintly.

"So you know now if it rests in the first, fourth, or, say, sixth position?"

"Yes, m'am."

"You need not worry at all. I'll pull the trigger. Perhaps more than once!" Ash took the revolver, and placed it to her temple. She faced the audience square. Fischer twitched twice.

"I will ask that you count for me, Mister Fischer. And would you step forward?" Ash beckoned with a nod.

"May All Untold share your will," Fischer whispered. After an encouraging nod from Ash, he began his count, folding his arms and hunching in on himself. "One."

Ash pulled the trigger to an eruption of gasps.

"Two," Fischer tightened his arms.

Ash pulled the trigger. The gulls wheezed.

"Three." Fischer put his arm to his sides.

Ash's finger squeezed slightly and pressed the gun hard into her skin. She inhaled through her teeth, taking the heartbeat this theatrical stunt availed to check her exits. She saw this stunt caused poor Mave the candlemaker to wail and bury her face in her husband's sleeve. She'd made the right call, dismissing the sweet soul from the act.

"Four," Fischer pronounced. There. There it was. Ash saw Fischer's tell flicker at the corner of his eye. The twitch. She heard the subtle waver in his voice, albeit masked by calm.

"Vier. Or four, Mister Fischer, I believe, is the chamber you selected this night." Ash lowered the revolver from her temple. She'd detected Fischer's first language and delivered her pronouncement in the same to drive her Mentalism home. She continued, "Mave, will you witness as Mister Fischer checks my call?"

Mave lifted her head and hiccuped a reply over the murmuring gathering, "Oh, Miss, you made me suffer!" She gathered her skirts and returned to the stage. Ash passed the revolver to Fischer, who opened the cylinder for Mave's inspection.

Mave's hand flew to her chest and her jaw clenched hard. She wailed her confirmation: "Aye, it's there! The very next shot would've been her end!" Mave pulled at her lips and clenched and unclenched her jaw. She paused, then surprised Ash with a hug. Turning and descending back into the crowd she continued to buzz, "I don't know how she knew it, but she did! She did!" The gulls clapped, cast coin, and clasped shoulders in disbelief.

Fischer shook Ash's hand and she made a small bow of thanks. It was when she rose that she saw him. A man leaning against a fencepost near the back. In shadows that seemed tranquil rather than menacing for harbouring him. He inclined his head and an anchored torch lit his side-smile. That maddening smile!

Ren.

She surrendered to the grin's pull and smiled back. Ren raised his hands higher, displaying his applause.

A blush washed over Ash's face. As she bowed and placed her hand to her chest, the warmth on her cheeks muted the applause.

She was happy to see him there. Mysteries have mercy.

ASH

Ash left the stage quickly – as was her custom – and took a roundabout route to a quiet jetty, lakeside. There she'd meet Wynn, who'd come with the thrown coin and profits from wagers on the side. Most gulls who'd seen her shows knew that no amount of cheers for "More!" would bring her return, but they tried the routine all the same. She took that time to get away – a different jetty nominated after each show.

Predictable habits could see a female Mystic hanged. Ash did without them. Still, the revolver snug within her well-fitted show accoutrement gave some comfort, her blade even more. She'd retrieved her cloak from the weeping willow's lower limbs and wore it now over The Unflinching Ash garb.

Though Ash looked out across the water, she spoke to one approaching; "You best be Wynn, or I'll draw my weapon before your next step." In truth she'd already drawn the weapon and pointed it towards whoever drew near.

"Must our conversations always begin with concealments?"

Ash knew the voice, but it wasn't Wynn's. She smiled at the lake, then wiped the expression from her face before turning to face Ren. "You followed me."

"You gave little choice – what with your habit of leaving without the accepting of compliments and praise."

"So *I* asked for this impropriety?" Ash squinted in distaste, then continued after mentally replaying Ren's words. "Wait, you come bearing compliments and praise?"

Ren smiled but stood perfectly still.

A nocturnal water fowl broke the lake's surface nearby in a food-bound dive.

Ash took Ren in. He wore the same dark winged vest and the moonlight illuminated the way he filled it with dashing ease. His hair was almost lost to the night, for being so truly black. He was less a stranger for their meeting at Bess's Fry, but Ash could hear Grete speaking in her mind, begging her take caution. This Ren was very good – a call for caution on its own – Ash had not detected him until he was already on the jetty. There was also the small matter of her heart's leap upon sighting him by the fence-line after her act.

Her favourite of his tells thus far, was how he looked up briefly before he spoke long sentences – drawing down vocabulary from memory, no doubt.

He did it then, then spoke. "I will come no further. Impropriety is my last intention." He was still smiling and the heart leap returned, unbidden. "Well, not the very last intention, but I have bound and buried it deep."

"Compliments and praise will work at this distance, I'd say." Ash spun to face Ren, cross-legged, holstering her gun beneath the cloak. It wasn't far away.

"You did not flinch."

"Is that the best you can do? It's hardly creative, given my Mystic name. "

"You did not employ a shill, you called upon a local, the local loaded the gun, you never tampered with it, and you did not flinch."

"Getting better... "

"I see now you are not an Illusionist at all, but yes, you perform. And very well." Without meaning to, Ren had succeeded in paying her a fine compliment indeed. One she'd never been given. Her acts baffled the gulls and pointed to the Mystical and Mysterious most assuredly, but Ren – he could see there was no illusion in her performance.

For Ash did not read minds. She read people. There was no *illusion* of risk when in fact there was none (such as Banyan's face-off with a wax bullet with the real bullet betwixt his teeth).

Ren looked up briefly, so Ash readied for verbosity. "What I wonder, is how you fail to flinch; I am sure you watch their tells – but what of human error? Surely the risk of being wrong would give you cause to flinch *sometime*. Do you not allow for the possibility – however small – that you might one night read a mark wrong? That such a show…might be your last?"

"That's just it. I am perfectly ready for *every* show to be my last."

Ren tipped his head sideways a moment. He made a study of Ash that managed to warm her in spite of the morbidity of their exchange. It was the fascination she saw in his gaze. She'd encountered many who had eyed her with admiration, but this…this was for an answer she'd given, not her symmetry. She was grateful the dark and her hood veiled her appreciation of this novelty on her cheeks.

"That's why she doesn't flinch. She's not at all afraid, that one." Wynn called as he lumbered onto the jetty. "You didn't draw a weapon on my approach, Ren – isn't it? Are *you* so sure of yourself you do not allow you might be robbed or caught unawares?"

"I trust anyone coming to meet Ash is Mysteries-blessed." Ren answered without turning. He was still causing a commotion of colour on Ash's face with his gaze, though answering Wynn.

Ash broke their eye-gaze first, though it risked Wynn seeing she flushed. "He means to say he heard you a league away, Wynn! You jangle after every show. No matter how many times…"

"…you tell me, I know, wrap the coin in cloth before filling the purse. Sorry." Wynn finished Ash's sentence. He walked past Ren and took a seat next to Ash. "Are you joining us then?" He cast a call back to Ren.

"If Ash does not object…"

"You know who's in charge around here at least, I'll say that," Wynn answered.

"The jetty's not ours. I won't stop you," Ash said. Her blush was beginning to settle down with Wynn beside her. And she didn't want Ren to leave, she knew that much.

Ren lowered himself in silence to sit next to Wynn. Ash abruptly spun to face the water and held out a hand for Wynn's purse. Wynn swivelled towards the water too and Ren expertly manoeuvred with precision to follow suit. The three sat there, looking out across the lake – Ren and Ash with Wynn between them. The bird Ash had heard earlier bobbed and left bubbles that caught in the moonlight.

"What I won't give you…" Wynn picked at lichen encrusted on the jetty, crumbling and sprinkling it on the lake's surface, "…is agreement anyone coming to meet Ash is Mysteries-blessed. We can tell you're not from around here, and so I'll remind you not everyone honours a female Mystic."

"So I hear."

"Well the worst of 'em catch wind of Ash time and again and have very unsavoury plans," explained Wynn.

"And I'm always ready," Ash added. And she mostly meant it: she meant she was ready *now*. There had been a time she had not been. A time she'd underestimated the basilica's distaste for women who did not look to their husband and father as their patriarch and the church for overall governance and direction. A time she'd learned how certain people's fear could lead to force. And pain.

"Good." The sincerity of that single word from Ren brought Ash back to the present. He was pleased to learn she was prepared. Curious. He did not see her strength and independence as something to be reined in to the basilica's conventions. Refreshing.

"So what brings you to this jetty this night?" Wynn picked again at the wood.

Ash's wish to see Ren's face rose in equal measure to her relief she could not. She listened intently instead.

"No more proposals, I assure you," Ren answered.

Ash sensed Wynn tensing momentarily at the term then relaxing as he caught up – this had always been his loudest tell. The mysterious foreigner meant there would be no more proposals *he and Ash join acts* – not the sort of proposal Grete hoped would spare Ash the danger of continuing on with those acts. *Sorry Wynn, no development you can eagerly report to my narrow-minded elder sister.*

"He came to shower me with praise, if you must know," Ash answered, having finished counting the coin.

Wynn froze listening, before tying his purse back at his hip. He might notice it was lighter for Ash having rightly taken most of her winnings but, as always, he would find she'd left a share for him and Grete.

"I did come with praise." Ren leaned his head out past Wynn slightly so he could see Ash. "But news too."

Ash resisted the urge to pull her hood forward and look away, instead meeting Ren's eyes. They were dark in colour but warm in feeling.

"What news?" Wynn and Ash asked together.

"A warning. I thought myself your greatest threat to winning The Queen's Seal," Ren allowed Ash a brief scoff before continuing, "...me, and these people who would do you harm."

"I'm yet to see anything to substantiate this mighty claim of yours." This was a lie. She'd seen some indication Ren was good with this sleight of hand, and his uncanny stillness spoke "threat" to her gut. She realised she was leaning forward too, and noted Wynn had leaned back to allow his company a better line of sight.

Ren continued, "As I was saying, I worry there is more than me and more than them to worry about."

Wynn's head pivoted back and forth between them. He now watched Ash for her response.

"Is that so?" she said.

Wynn's head turned back to watch Ren ask, "Have you heard of The Luminous Collier?"

Wynn and Ash exchanged a look. "We haven't," Ash answered.

"He is coming, and he is good."

"Collier?" Ash's tone was incredulous.

"The Luminous," Ren replied.

"'Good' is fine. We could use some more good Mystics around here." She knew that's what this Collier's profession had to be, with a name like that. "'Good' is not cause for concern."

Ren's smile at Ash's proud reply did give her cause to pull her hood forward. "Be that as it may, listen out for him. He has been working his way over from Adhmad Thoir. I will be watching him. His act is…large."

"Large?" Wynn returned to the conversation.

"Excessive," Ren clarified. "I had better be going. I have detained you both long enough already, forgive me. Until we meet again – Ash, Wynn." Ren nodded very deliberately with each name. Ash took note he'd plucked and stored Wynn's name without being directly given it. She noted too, how Ren the Still (as she was beginning to think of him), had stood between her and one of only three exit points and she had not felt at all alarmed…and that was alarming.

He was not long gone when Wynn asked, "You worried about this Collier fellow?"

"No."

"You worried about this Ren?"

"No."

"Well then, neither am I." Wynn rubbed his hands against the descending cold. "How much was it then?" Wynn reached for his purse. Then patted at his other side. The whites of his eyes shone in the lakelight.

"You're playing," Ash glowered.

"I'm not. It's gone again!" Wynn was smiling with shock. He had to, that Ren was a smooth operator.

Ash of course checked herself, despite confidence Ren the Still could not have possibly managed...but he had. She found a second bag of coin beneath her cloak – one was her own, heavier for tonight's profits, but there was a second as well. How? Beneath her cloak? No one had ever...

"He didn't." Wynn's eyes were wide. He leaned back and clapped. "Oh, I know I should be worrying about his being improper, but all I can say is that you may just have met your match!" Wynn belly-laughed as Ash drew his bag of coin away from herself. Wynn laugh-spoke, egging her on. "Check it. Go on. Oh, truly, it's a gift to see you trumped."

"Mind your tongue or I'll be returning this minus tonight's share." Ash nudged her childhood friend. "Trumped? Hardly! There was talk of a threat from this Collier, and there's that bird bobbing incessantly, and it's dark..."

"And you were busy making moon-eyes!"

Ash let out an unceremonious sound.

"And?" Wynn leaned towards Ash and at an angle that would allow more light to fall on the bag of coin. "Did he leave a note again? Where's your next date?" Wynn was laughing again.

"No."

"What then?"

"Cloth. He wrapped your coin in cloth so it wouldn't jangle as you walked."

Wynn's laugh now startled the bird into taking a short flight to be further from them. "But he tied it to you, not me!"

"Yes, Wynn."

"Because he wanted you to be sure he knew what he'd done, and that he could."

"I suspect so." Irritation and admiration fought in Ash's chest. She bit her lip to realise admiration was winning. "That man! He scarcely moves, but when he does, nobody knows it!"

"Not even you." Wynn stopped laughing then, with an expression of borrowed caution reminiscent of his wife's.

"Wynn?"

"Ya?"

"It's time we saw this Ren put on a real show." For the first time... ever... Ash felt invigorated at the prospect of some real competition.

REN

Ren missed the mountains. Meditation for him had always come more easily with elevation. Today he had settled for a *tor* tall enough that he might pretend the morning fog was low cloud. His back against a tree, he closed his eyes and sent spidery fingers across the forest floor around him. The soft earth yielded easily to his exploration. No wonder hamlets crowded around the lake, with soil such as this.

Ready, he cleared his mind of all but the lake. He pictured it as it had first appeared to him upon arrival – its banks, added structures, how the light broke on its surface. Next he sought the memory of the lake's gentle tide and timed his breaths so that they lapped like the lake's shore from his chest.

Ash's face entered his thoughts, without his bidding. He washed it out with his next exhale. A wrench of thirst for The Queen's Seal came next, deep in his stomach, but with his next breath he dismissed it, edging it out with renewed focus. An image of Ash's hands stole in next. They came in a flash, and instead of washing them away, Ren dwelt on their neat cuticles, quickened nails and inherent strength. Then he washed this vision away too.

Easy, Ren, go easy.

A smile pulled at the corner of his mouth for half an inhale before Ren anchored to the lake.

The Western Tract basilica towered over the village – a hulking leviathan over the modest homes below. Attentively maintained topiaries sat within the recesses of its outer walls. Beyond, lay the rugged beauty of the surrounding wood.

Ren stopped by an edict affixed to the basilca's entry. According to a harried departing parishioner, congregations met more than once a week and some of the meetings were restricted to men alone. This policy applied to the "Patriarch's Council," recently adjourned. Considering the company Ren craved most, he could think of few things less appealing.

While Ren stretched, dusk fell. The lights from the basilica appeared as bright slashes on the night road. Few were out-of-doors – which he had learned was the norm – through hushed whispers of witching hours and children swept within houses like errant leaves in autumn.

The earth beneath him in the dark felt as sure as it had to him during his daylight meditations, so Ren resisted imitating local common custom. He instead shared the night with the few others unconcerned with such superstition – or more intent on the type of business night-time was better at bringing.

So it was that Ren found himself propositioned more than once (he always declined, with all the manners he would afford any equal). He was also routinely privy to shrewd murmurings of Mystic gatherings on private holdings, of which he took note. Ren's night-time jaunts oftimes gave way to another reoccurrence; that of many, many Lough-folk being startled silly. "Mysteries! I did not see you there!" or "Forgive me, you appeared from All Unknown!" It couldn't be helped; an unaccompanied Ren was a quiet Ren.

Ren considered Ash's vanishing from Bess's Fry and her predilection for the same night-time he now occupied – declining advances, snatching whispers and startling gulls. He measured Ash's determination to brave audiences who, by day, might attend councils about her, or send their family patriarch in to voice their concerns. No, determination to *brave* audiences was not accurate, she was determined to *woo* them.

And Ren was not immune to her ability to succeed in doing so. He did not want to be.

A couple hastily leaving a house and crossing the village square jumped upon realising Ren's position.

"Many apologies, those unmet, I did not mean to alarm you."

The pair mumbled their replies, and continued on, arm in arm.

ANGELA ARMSTRONG

Ren remained fixed, contemplative.

The Unflinching Ash
Captivates enchants ensnares
Makes gulls of us all

73

ASH

One thing Ash could not long forgo was a good loaf of bread, warm from the oven. Her preferred baker was based on the edge of SeeBurg and must knead Mysteries into his loaves for the fecundity of their flavour. With a purse heavy from her previous night's takings, Ash was bakery-bound.

SeeBurg was a day's walk south of the western hamlet Grete and Wynn called home, although Ash had no such attachment. A permanent residence was a thing a male Mystic would certainly bind his ego up in, but the same was a luxury Ash daren't risk.

Her patronage of this particular SeeBurg bakery was liability enough; but the fragrant call of yeast overrode her careful sensibilities so that her visits almost approached routine.

A good show was often followed by good bread. It felt right.

She'd come early – her preference for *warm* bread demanded it. She was so early she passed a knocker-upper making his rounds – the boy paid to wake others for their day's work. Few beyond the boy and baker were up. It gave Ash a relaxed buoyancy. She even wore her hood on her back instead of shielding her face, allowing the low morning sunlight to dance over her thick hair.

Things were quiet and she'd soon have bread in her belly.

So preoccupied was she, Ash failed to recognise the significance of something she should have known was significant. She saw the thing – the ostentatious beads hanging from the waist of the woman resembling a long-legged water fowl – but she was so enthralled with daybreak and optimism she registered only a devout parishioner to add to her shortlist of early risers.

Ash of the night would have known better, been more careful; embraced suspicion.

Suspicion whispered to Ash too late.

A brief sound of expectoration prefaced a glob of saliva smearing across Ash's cheek and right eye. The spit quickly cooled, but was sizeable enough that it slid fast down her face.

Ash halted, wiping her cheek as she gave the birdlike woman her full attention.

"Witch!" The woman spat her speech too – the word resounding on the quiet street like a fisherman's curse. A second woman hastened from the shadows and caught the arm of the first, hissing correction.

Ash drew herself taller with her inhalation; "You know little of what you speak. Please, step aside."

"I won't. You'll find your breakfast elsewhere, heathen. We don't serve the likes of you in SeeBurg." The tip of the woman's nose moved when she spoke.

The second woman – who had materialised from the eaves – still held to the arm of she who spat. She addressed the spitter; "Sister, you go too far," then to Ash, "Please, forgive Sister Gwen her zeal," then back to Sister Gwen, "Truly Gwen, we are better than this."

Ash was surprised by her decency. "Thank you," Ash said. "Forgiveness comes more readily to a full stomach." Ash appreciated someone speaking up – the hope of wider change it promised. Assaults such as these would soon be a thing of the past. She made to be on her way.

The second woman nodded as she spoke, "A fair point made. Will you fill your belly after casting a line, then?"

Ash was fairly certain the woman knew where she intended to fill her belly. Had she not defended her right to do so moments ago?

"Not this morn. A morn as glorious as this, calls for glorious bread – something your town does so well."

"Sister Gwen overstepped." The woman shot a glance to her companion before offering Ash an expression tightened by some semblance of sympathy. "But the warning remains. I hate to be the one to deliver such news, but I will, if it saves another sister the disgrace of being turned away." The woman leaned closer, and added softly, "You won't break your fast here, unmet. I seek only to warn you."

Ash took in the thread of the stitch edging the second woman's mantle, the curl in her front-locks and her shoes' lack of wear. Ash had made a gross oversight – the tells were all there.

"Then let us be met, *sister*." Ash offered her hand. "I am Ash. And you are...?"

The front-locks gave the slightest shake. The chin lifted from its former position of confidence. No hand was proffered, though the woman's reply came: "Mistress Odell Gregory."

Eugh, Ash knew that name. This woman was surely the wife of SeeBurg's bishop.

The first woman's lips curled inward, regaled at the delivery of her companion's punchline.

Ash withdrew the hand she'd offered and considered her reply for the span of two knife-throws before delivering it. "It appears you care little for sisterhood after all. Gregory, you say? Not a name I'd let bar me from bread."

"Is there any name that would be sufficient?" The first woman, Sister Gwen, interjected. "If I urged you to cease as patron this morn in God's name, would it be enough?"

77

Mistress Gregory twisted her head in disapproval. "Gwen, cease! We cannot force our beliefs on others. Go gently. We seek only to do her a service – which we have done in offering fair warning. Please, Ash, let us not detain you any longer." Though the woman smiled apologetically and her brows were lined in concern, a twitch at the side of her left eye belied satisfaction. She was enjoying this.

So Ash bit. "*God's* name would be enough to stop me."

"Truly?" Mistress Gregory glowed.

"Did you have the name then?" Ash asked.

"She plays dumb now." Gwen shook her head. "She already told you – God's name. You surely must have respect for Him, even if you flout around claiming some measure of His power."

"Ah, yes, I heard you mention God, but I did not hear *a name*. I heard that you think Him male well enough." Ash drew her purse from her waist. "So it seems the answer is *no*, the name of a god won't stop me either, since you don't seem to have it." Ash presented her ear, waiting. "I can wait while you ask God for it, if you wish. Or would you have me stay longer still while you run off to consult your patriarch and bishop – one and the same, if I'm not mistaken – perhaps a man can share with you the name of your man-god?"

Mistress Gregory failed to hide her vexation now, but her words remained calm. "I am humble enough to know better than to claim access to Him."

The smell of loaves beckoned. "I see," Ash looked to the baker's. "And I am hopeful enough to know better than to claim you can't." Ash offered a pained frown. "So I will give to the count of five for you to commune with your god. I'll not rule out a Mystery's-bled intervention." Ash clasped her hands in front of her, tipped her head at 45 degrees, and drew infinity with her irises. "Five. Neither of us appears to have had word from God, so I'm forced to conclude He or She is allowing free will to reign – a gift, wouldn't you agree? I see well enough my visit vexes *you*, and I've no desire to rile the people of SeeBurg, so I'll be quick about it." Ash threw her coin once in the air and caught it with a downwards swipe. "I merely want bread, m'am, I've a stomach like everyone else." Ash stepped around the women, taking care not to touch them.

The bird who had spat, unable to help herself, called with her neck outstretched: "But you won't, *witch*, you'll see. Nicholas Baker knows full well should he serve a woman of your kind he'll not have orders from thirty households close by."

A clench of Mistress Gregory's teeth sent lines up her jaw. "I did try to spare you this embarrassment."

Ash stood steadfast, the words falling down her back. She gave no answer.

"Stubborn witch," the second hissed.

Mistress Gregory chided, "Enough, Gwen! Some subtlety! Some compassion! You're embarrassing yourself. One can't help how one has been raised..."

Ash's wont for even-handedness compelled her to answer the women in kind while her ambition to see things through to Queen's Day stilled her tongue. She did not need a trial led by a band of zealots. But she wanted bread. She deserved bread.

She chose restraint, and left the ambush behind. Mistress Gregory's words fell at her heels, "He'll tell you nothing we haven't already. Remember well, I tried to spare you the shame about to befall you."

It was clear Ash would be unable to return for bread from this bakery, so if today was to be her last chance to enjoy it, by All Untold, she was going to get her last loaf while it was warm. When she entered the "fair establishment," she knew from one look at Nicholas Baker she would not be having that last loaf. She'd sadly eaten that already without having known it. "It's true then?" She lifted her chin, resolved not to be affected by further slight.

"Miss, I'm sorry. A baker's nothing without his orders. Nothing but an empty oven and empty bellies upstairs." Apron-clad Nicholas Baker motioned above him with a thumb. "I am truly sorry."

"I understand. Here," Ash counted out the cost of a loaf and laid it on the table before Mister Baker. "You'll not count the loss of the sale I would have

Ash stroked a scar on the shell of her ear where she'd once been nicked. It had been her own fault, but her mother had never forgiven herself. *How Ash missed her.*

It was while Ash paused, recalling her Mapa's worried frown, callused hands and husky laugh, that Mrs Odell Gregory's voice came to her from outside the sanctuary. "You will do well. The archbishop knows the value of our support. You will impress upon him the need to keep the foundling wheel…and his Grace's respect for you will ensure we save more children from lives away from the light."

Ash tensed. Foundling wheels were installed in each basilica – a giant, circular, stone wheel, mounted like a table behind a door built into the basilica's wall. Desperate parents of little means or little respect placed unwanted babes upon it, turned the wheel, leaving the child within the walls of the sanctuary – away from the harsh elements and witching hours…and away from the more pressing danger they faced for their parentage.

Ash knew a life without parents well, but she'd had Grete, Wynn, and the Mystic circle for allies. Plus fierceness in her belly. She'd had the memories of her childhood and the knowledge she was wanted. Foundlings were not so fortunate, but foundlings of late had surely been many. Ash, caught off guard, wiped at tears with the back of her hand. She understood the necessity of such wheels; preferred them to more frightening alternatives for parents who felt trapped before a noose, but she lamented that a noose loomed – better to cut that at the quick than continue racing to hide all who feared it.

The bishop's voice brought Ash back. "Are you so sure the foundling wheels are the best course? What's to stop the wretched mother from spawning another and another? We're overrun as it is…"

Odell spoke too softly for Ash to catch the start of her answer, but she did hear its end: "You'll see. Tonight will afford opportunity to save the mother as well."

Oh no. The good people of SeeBurg meant to flush out a witch.

Well then, Ash thought, *let's give them two*!

ODELL

Mistress Odell Gregory sat erect upon her pew in SeeBurg's fine basilica. That was the front pew, of course – a show of support. Her husband sat with his aides on the stand, leading a meeting before another meeting. The archbishop himself would attend them in mere hours, and they would be ready.

Odell's attentions drifted. She studied the votive statues, modelling her own posture upon their upright, faithful forms. Taking in the statues' veiled faces, a reminder of their faith in God's will, Odell closed her own eyes. She readied her mind to receive whatever message came from the impending visit. She imagined herself a well, with faith filling and purifying her like water.

She next imagined SeeBurg as a veil, with all its inhabitants adding their own unique fibres to the cloth. Odell was certain her contributions would be constant and visible in the finished working. She imagined them as violet threads running the veil's length. Her husband, a functional administrator, might be seen in the muted browns cross-hatching her own; unremarkable, but without those threads, the veil would be in pieces.

As a man, Bishop Gregory served as a leader in both her church and home. She loved him well enough. But she also knew he was nothing without her, and little compared to her. She did not need a title or position to give her direction. She didn't need a church-given purpose to fortify her standing before God. She daily surrendered her will to Unknown and knew therein lay true power; in surrendering one's will.

She checked the floral arrangements about her, all installed under her commission. They were certainly the finest the archbishop would see on his tour around the Lough, marked by Odell's devotion to every detail. Or not! The stamens on Mistress Brooker's lilies glared at her – a shouting oversight. Odell could see from her seat that pollen speckled the petals of the blooms and the woodwork beneath them. She would quietly correct the error herself, and save Mistress Brooker any embarrassment by discreetly reminding her after the meetings to be more thorough in future.

Calling the woman out in front of others was not Odell's custom.

Just as Sister Gwen's assault in the street had been uncalled for. Though Odell had truly hoped they help the poor girl see – how unseemly her habits were, how risky her occupation. The girl needed help!

The risks she took! She was compromising all of the virtues she should be holding dear as a woman. It was reasonable for most people to look the other way when men chose to dabble in distractions. There was a tired weakness to their responsibility to merely provide physically for their help-meets and children that demanded distraction. But a woman must know she would be challenged, if she sought similar. To seek diversions or create spectacles showed disrespect for the head of a woman's household as well as her attending bishop. Moreover it degraded women – who should be cultivating faith, humility, and modesty – not showiness and daring!

Odell felt some sympathy for the women who fell into the trap of envying and imitating their male counterparts – for they obviously lacked an understanding of their true value and worth. If they really considered the worth of being custodians of the hearth, of being nurturers of young minds, of being the cultivators of beauty and the truly faithful – they wouldn't claw after the positions men held to give them equal purpose to the power women innately possessed.

Gwen's voice had become shrill, drawing Odell from her contemplation to the meeting at hand. "I would take the baby, raise it right."

Bishop Gregory nodded as he replied. "Your willingness is noted, but I think we all know whence this child has sprung, and therein, lies an opportunity."

Odell squinted with suspicion.

"The mother has been moving from house to house, offering unsanctioned blessings over others for months. She knew she couldn't raise the child – that's why we're here – to determine where best to assign this foundling. But...perhaps we rid SeeBurg of this pernicious apostasy that slinks behind closed doors."

Odell straightened and raised her voice. "Are you suggesting we dangle the foundling's fate before Sister Fern like a baited hook?"

"I'm suggesting we might save two souls, God willing," Bishop Gregory replied.

"God willing," all in attendance echoed.

The good bishop had even made it sound like it had been his idea. Good man.

ASH

In SeeBurg, an agitated assembly tremored, an infant
at its centre. The child lay on the basilica's stone
altar, a thin wrap unpeeling in time to the thrashing
of its limbs. A mirrored pair of statues arched
overhead. Even their faces lacked sympathy for the
wailing babe; their stone eyes veiled, heads and
hands directed heavenward in supplication. The
Faithful knew their own helpless sightlessness and
the correct place to look for answers. That, and
SeeBurg had few gulls. Before she was born, Ash's
parents had once been driven from the area. They'd
frequently reminded her as much and avoided it on
their circuit. But Ash loved her bread…and would
be nowhere else, this day.

A rare guest stood before the congregation. He
wore a veil matching those carved onto the effigies
nearby, only his lay at rest over his shoulders. Here
stood the archbishop of Mórlough, the queen's
closest advisor. He was an unexpectedly comely
man, aside from his skin condition. His fair

complexion seemed to be in a constant state of irritation, as though his self-flagellation extended to his morning exfoliation regimen. He raised both of his hands to call for quiet. The eristic crowd hushed. The enraged babe did not.

The archbishop spoke over the child's relentless cries: "In the matter of the foundlings, Her Majesty the Queen has ruled," he paused, "that foundling wheels *will* continue..." The archbishop, Fulton was his chosen name, drank in their disapproval and donned a wan smile. "However," he raised his eyebrows, "in the case of *this* foundling, in light of the Seeker's reports and my own assessment this day, I rule it...possessed."

The basilica housed some sixty rows of filled pews, but an equal body of patrons lined the walls and packed the ingress – over which Ash clung, high above.

And from there, only she caught the whimper that escaped a woman standing below, shawled in threads and shadow. The woman's quiet grief rose above the crowd's surge of satisfaction at Fulton's ruling, wove up into the eaves, and collided with Ash like a physical blow.

The child's mother had dared to come.

And Odell had known she would.

Taking a risk to know what you're up against – Ash understood that well – but a day or two after giving birth? Ash's brow gathered with concern.

The mother should not be here.   Ash wished Odell had been wrong.

Fulton surveyed his audience. "Is there evidence to the contrary? Is this foundling not possessed for having sprung from a mother thrice accused of witchcraft and acts offensive to our God?"

Bishop Gregory looked to Fulton, attempting to communicate something, but Fulton dismissed his expression with a flick of his wrist.

Ash chewed her lip, poised to act – she knew not how – but she knew she must, unless the mother should act first. The baby's cry was growing hoarse. Ash made her calculations. She could disarm at least six of the eight guards who'd accompanied Fulton, sure. She could vanish via one of her four exits, easily. But how would she make flight by way of the altar and through the treetops with a crying child in her grasp? Ash would do the innocent no favours if she were captured alongside it for the morning trial.

Though that would still be better than nothing; the child shouldn't be alone. But what of the mother, then? She would figure that part out later; one rescue at a time.

Ash was decided; a reactive racket should muffle their getaway. She'd tie the babe to her chest to free up her hands for climbing.

Her, she'd tie *her* to her chest. Ash could see now the child was a girl, for the child had freed herself from her meagre covering when Fulton made his condemning pronouncement.

Ash was just bracing herself against a soffit and beginning to slink into a new position when a disruption below made her pause. *Please not the mother. Please not the mother.*

Not the mother. *She* remained shrouded, though a subtle shudder in her shoulders told Ash she wept. The disorder sprung from a central pew, where a man stood with one arm raised in interjection.

When he spoke, Ash knew his voice.

"I claim the child. She is no daughter of a witch. I will see her safely from this place and find her a good nurse far away from SeeBurg." Ash knew those shoulders. She knew that stillness – a stillness that was constant even now, as an uproar ruptured around it – sober, at balance and somehow courteous in its determination.

Archbishop Fulton subdued the crowd's protests with a twirl of his wrists, as though conducting minstrels, "And you are?"

Don't say your real name.

"Ren, Lord."

He said his real name. *What is he doing here?* There'd be time to examine that later.

"If I may, Lord." A new voice, but another voice known. Ash's lip curled. Mistress Odell Gregory spoke from the front row, allowed by a nod from Fulton. "What place does an unmet have in SeeBurg affairs? We all know who the mother was – we saw her swell up with the poor child," she pointed towards the girl-child, "and we all heard its cries as she brought it into this world. Not a full day passed before the foundling wheel was turned! Please, dear Sister, if you are here, come forward, so we can help you, and perhaps thereby help your child. You need help."

More like an ambush. Ash knew what kind of "help" the basilica had to offer. That poor mother. Ash counted her exits. She made a quick study of the wheel Odell spoke of, carved into the basilica's wall, now stationary and empty, since the child had been shifted to the altar. It would not serve as an exit for her this night.

Ash added Ren to her plans. Could he take out a share of the guards while she rescued the baby? His sleight of hand was good, but she knew little of how he fared in disarmament or combat.

Her gut told her his shoulders were serviceable.

Alright, the two of them together then. She'd get the baby.

Ash removed her blade from its place beneath her girdle, at her back, then halted. The mother had moved closer to the front and now raised her chin so it protruded through her shawl. Her eyes were rimmed red, her face drawn in anguish and rage.

Don't speak.

She spoke. *Curses to All Unknown.* "The man speaks true. The child is his to claim. I did give birth – I won't deny it – but I gave my boy to his father who promised me he'd see him to a good home. That's not my child, Lord. I bore a son." The mother trembled.

Ash knew the lie for what it was, but admired the woman's effort.

"Lord, allow me to remove this foundling as a concern to you." Ren added to the woman's appeal. "She is innocent." His voice broke and Ash felt her last lonely thread of resistance to liking him break with it.

Fulton wore an expression of mock sympathy. He made a grand sweep outwards with both arms, covered his eyes with his veil and tied it with a bow behind his head – the signal he intended to commune with the Mysteries on behalf of the people. Murmurs dulled in reverence and anticipation – even the baby, who had cried herself into a shivering sleep – lay quiet.

New plan. Ash sheathed her blade and changed her course through the dark eaves, working her way to an empty vestry that lay beyond the mother – a smaller wing with a lowered ceiling at right-angles to the main chapel that gave no view of the proceedings.

The quiet anticipation below required greater stealth. Ash found her footholds with all possible care, blowing air gently from her mouth. *By All Unknown, do not let my toes liberate a mischief of rats from their nest this night.*

Ash froze. Fulton had raised his hands to make a pronouncement. Still blindfolded, he declared: "The

Mysteries and our God who reigns over them have spoken."

Ash noted Odell leaned forward, unable to hide her eagerness. Playing the kinder accuser in the street with a young woman was one thing, but Ash could not comprehend how she could prey upon an infant and her aching mother this way.

The archbishop continued, "Mister Ren may take the child, now soothed, far from SeeBurg." A trifling of surprised whispers. "Mistress Gregory, you may enquire after the offspring of the Thrice Accused." What was that? Odell's face pinched in relief. Did Odell care for the woman? Or was she part of this "help farce." Ash was sure the woman had come for blood. "And guards, secure the Thrice Accused for a Trial by Ordeal on the morrow."

Ah, and there it was. A translation from the good leadership of the church – "help" equated to "Trial by Ordeal." Or as it might better be known, "torture until a confession of guilt is obtained and evil is purged." *Help.* Ash suppressed a scoff.

That would not be happening.

Ash swung, soundless, from a woodwork support and dropped into the vestry.

The two guards closest to the mother began weaving towards their target, who stood in hunched surrender.

Ren approached the child.

There was no time for a choke-hold. Ash recalled the exact hoick of Gwen's spit as she brought the hilt of her blade down on the vestry guard's head. He'd likely live. She thought of the bread she'd not been permitted as she shoved through the press of bodies eager to see the mother seized. She moved to the corner furthest from the veil-candles and dropped, landing, undetected, in a feline crouch. She would have to tell Grete about that landing later, because it was flawless. While Ren and the guards drew focus, Ash darted, low, through the forest of legs. It was likely she had caused a subtle trail of shifting movement, so she must be fast. She barrelled on until she came to a woman with blood on her shoes. Ash seized her by the wrist and drew the woman down to the ground.

The heads of the advancing guards spun in confusion. One called for a third with a better view, to guide them through the crowd.

Odell's skirts swished through the din as she made her own advance.

On the ground, a command was issued.

Most people were engrossed, weighing in on the proceedings behind hands and into ears.

The third guard pointed towards the mother, who was visible again, close to where she'd last been seen. The two guards resumed their course, rougher in parting their paths. The mother appeared to come to herself and make a late move to run. A few brave attendees nudged her back toward her aggressors. She writhed against their elbows and shoulders. The guards reached her. Their grip was not kind. A small cry of protest issued from the mother, then silent defeat. She hung her head, resigned, as the guards hauled her towards Fulton for further instruction.

Odell craned over the crowd. Seeing the guards and mother approach, she squinted with suspicion. "Wait!" she called.

The guards continued towards Fulton, duty-bound – respecters of rank.

Odell leaned across a bickering married couple, her fingers clawing and desperate. She managed to grasp near the ear of the mother's shawl and tear it down, frenzied.

And found...Ash – her smile blazing like an imp's.

Odell recoiled and dipped her chin in confusion.

Ash knew then that toning down her swagger had not been enough. Having never stood next to the mother, she'd failed to correctly ascertain her height. Thinking back to her observations from above, she now realised the mother was considerably shorter than she. She should have stooped to evade detection a little longer.

Odell's eyes searched Ash's as she called to the archbishop. He could not hear her in the confusion. Ash could not resist shrugging and biting her bottom lip.

Odell's unkind grip on the shawl loosened with uncertainty.

Ash twisted, dropped, and took the second exit.

The guards bellowed. They shoved through the crowd, checking each face.

Odell shrieked "Everyone, please! Help us find Sister Fern!"

But all they found was a pile of bloodied rags on the floor.

ASH

Ash sang a coronach from the treetops. The witching hour was on her side. The guards made cursory surveillance of the basilica's surrounds, but dared not venture into the wood. Emboldened by their fear, Ash sang louder.

Odell appeared at the vestry's door, a restless silhouette framed by light from the sconces within. Ash held up her finger and thumb, viewing Odell between them – *an impetuous woodlouse, at this distance.* Odell's frame heaved with ragged breaths. Faithful Statuaries mocked her overhead, their veiled eyes offering no aid in finding the fugitives. Ash brought her fingers together; *crush.* She drew them apart again. The officious woman remained, vulturine.

Ash watched for the baby's mother, but saw no mark of her passing.

Good for her.

Ash sang until she grew tired, then dozed against the trunk. She missed her cloak in the cold.

When she woke and deemed the church dark and still, she made a cautious descent.

It was time to leave behind her burned bridges in SeeBurg. Ash made her way north.

She reached the wharf closest to Bess's Fry at dawn and helped pull in the kiddles in return for a cut of eel. She was clearing the place where she'd eaten in the kitchens when a new cook approached her. "You Ash?"

"I know her."

"Oh. A man left a note here for someone called Ash." The cook pointed with a pestle to a folded piece of paper, pinned by a cleaver to a hanging wooden board. Bess came in from cleaning out the weirs and gave Ash a knowing look.

"I can get the message to Ash," Ash said. Bess shook her head but remained silent.

The cook turned from the garlic he was mashing to pass the note to Ash but found the note and the cleaver gone. He spun to comment on how swiftly she'd taken them but could not see Ash anywhere in the kitchen. Turning back to the garlic, he rubbed his nose with the back of his hand.

Thunk.

The cleaver shook in the board, a handspan from the new cook's cap. He lowered his arm from his nose-swipe, looking in alarm to Bess for an explanation.

Bess shrugged in answer, but silently hoped she would not need another new cook so soon.

This was folly.

Ash reread the note. Rather, she reviewed its drawings. The paper she had collected at Bess's resembled a pictogram, consisting of three quick sketches; a pistol, a fence, and hands either clasped together or clapping. It was this medley of imagery that had brought her here – to the only place she could conclude the trio of images meant to convey – to the fencepost where Ren had applauded her roulette act. *And where she had blushed.*

What had brought Ren to SeeBurg? And how had he come to father a child in this town if he had arrived so recently?

Ash climbed onto the fence, near the post, and folded the note along its creases.

She felt exposed here. No hood, no structures, no flora concealing her from view. And yet, this same openness afforded her a clear shot of many exit-routes, along with a low risk of ambush. Well chosen, Ren. That is, if he *had* chosen this place. Ash had yet to confirm she'd correctly deciphered the pictorial riddle.

Free from the night's crowds, the pasture was an excellent meeting point for wary Mystics.

If Ren had chosen it.

REN

Ren stood near the place where he had first been given reason to hope – that he might have a chance with Ash – the place where he had seen her blush. He was almost certain she had blushed.

He stood near the spot, but not too near. He wanted to watch Ash arrive, after all.

As Ren sensed Ash's approach, he steadied his breaths, though his lungs begged to choke out a laugh of triumph. Ash had succeeded in decoding the pictograms he had left her. This confirmed she felt the place was significant too. Which made sense – blushers being aware of their blushes, as they are. It happened.

Ren warmed just remembering it. How it had given her elegant features a tinge of vulnerability. He compared the Ash of that night to the Ash he saw now. She carried herself with confidence, but it was clear she was keenly tuned to all around her. Gone was the openness she had allowed to temporarily steal over her performance mask. Here was a regal athlete, assessing and reviewing everything.

Almost everything. She had not detected him yet, though she could not be blamed for that. Stealth was one of Ren's finest skills.

He gripped what he had brought with him in one hand, smiling, and took one step out of the shade and into the light. He now stood three stage-spans away from The Spot.

Ash did not miss his deliberate entrance. She met his eyes but moved no closer.

Holding her gaze, Ren walked another ten paces before he spoke. "You got my clues," he called.

"How did you know I'd go to Bess's?"

"I imagine the Fry holds a special place in your heart now, since it is where we *properly* met." Ren emphasised properly, as the first encounter in the inn with the chairs and his disappearing act could hardly be counted. It was only when Ash had sat to face him at Bess's Fry – and they had truly seen each other – that Ren considered them truly met.

He drew close enough that Ash could see what he was carrying. She smiled – without the dimple – so it was less intoxicating than her usual display, but it still triggered an intermingling of hope and fire inside him.

"You left notes in inns all over the Western Tract, didn't you?"

"I did." Ren leaned against a fence post, reducing the space between them to a wagon's width. "With

good reason. I thought you might be missing this."
This was Ash's cloak, which Ren held out to her.

"How'd you know it was mine?"

Ren tipped his head, closed his eyes, and crumpled his lips and eyebrows.

"You helped Fern get away safely then?" Ash cocked an eyebrow.

"It wasn't hard…" Ren shrugged.

"No, I suppose not." Ash did a poor imitation of boredom. Ren knew he had her attention; she gave it all away when she added, "And to you Fern is…"

"Are you asking what relationship I have with Miss Fern?"

"Only because your story's not adding up. Babies tend to take some time to reach maturity, you know. I thought you were new around here, yet you claimed…"

Ren stopped her there. "I had not met the mother before that night." Did he see relief briefly lift her cheeks? Had she truly thought him to be the father? The child did not bear the distinctive shape of his eyes, nor his complexion, one whit. *But oh! This was good. Ash cared!* Ren suppressed the urge to celebrate. "It was a good lie, I believe." Something Ren believed in, but his former kinsman had not. "I could not stand for what was happening. And apparently, neither could you."

Ash pursed her lips, eyes alight. All Ren's thoughts of his former life fled. This. This was honour. This was kinship. "I could not." she said. "A good lie. I like that."

Ren imagined Ash tasting the expression – rolling it around on her tongue, drawing out its savour. She drew on the cloak he had reclaimed with a snap, untucking her hair from its collar. Even off-stage, her execution of every movement was precise and refined. "But won't the mother be cold now?" She drew her hood up against the wind.

"I think not." Ren spoke with conviction because he *knew* she was not cold. He had seen to that. Then he saw Ash chew on her cheek. She appeared...mildly riled. So quick to forget the phrase she'd just relished. Ren restrained his consternation; "I only did for her what you would have done, had you come upon her first."

Ash's face sparked with surprise. Had he guessed a measure of her thoughts, then? It was clear Ash had also wished to help the woman – she had given the mother her own mantle, after all. But that was not all. It was Ren who had spoken for her – and more. Ren presumed this was something Ash could not risk doing. She confirmed his thinking, saying, "Indeed. How fine it must be to be seen. To act in the light."

The mother's face, stricken and desperate, flashed in Ren's memory. He wondered if it haunted Ash still too. He'd learned from the mother, from Fern, that Ash had – after wrapping Fern in her own cloak – told her to crawl out of the basilica to safety. He chuckled recalling how Fern had described her saviour. It had taken Fern a moment to realise Ash was an ally, as she had come across...somewhat menacing, in the woman's retelling of it.

"Does it amuse you? That I thought you a father, then?"

"Yes, but that is not what I was thinking on. I was recalling Fern's telling of how she came by such an excellent cloak from 'a very headstrong woman?'" He nodded towards Ash, his voice ascending on the last as though asking a question. "Apparently you can be quite persuasive."

"Please, she was in shock! I doubt I could have overdone my communicating the urgency for her need to get moving!"

"Perhaps not. You succeeded."

"*We* succeeded." Ash gave a small nod and a reluctant, fuller smile. Her eyebrows seemed to offer both apology and thanks.

"I said from the start we would make a fine team." Ren pulled himself up to sit on the fence.

Ash rolled her eyes. "She got away because she was lucky. Or because the Mysteries favoured her – she's still not truly free. A thrice-accused is still a branded enemy to the basilica and throne...an uprising to stamp out. It isn't finished." Ash jumped up onto the railing beside him. If Ren stretched his arm to its full, he could touch her.

"It can be nice to count small wins though, no?" Ren looked to her, tracing her profile with his mind's pencil, inscribing it into his memory. "For one, you seemed, relieved earlier.   That I am…without attachments?"

"Oh, did I?"   Ash gave Ren a side eye, her tone refuting.

"You did."

They were quiet for the length of a card act. Ren assumed Ash was also attuned to a bee's nest nearby, the wind, and little else. Unless she was also very aware of her heartbeat.

She startled him a measure when she spoke, but he sent the energy of it to his toes and allowed no disruption of   his calm to show."Will *Fern* be…unattached? And the child? You spoke of a wet nurse you knew – was that farce too?"

"It was Fern's will the baby go to the nurse. I met the other woman on my way to Mórlough. She lost her own, in birth…"

Ash's countenance fell. "How awful."

"I am sure.   Though the Mysteries have now brought these three together – I merely introduced them. I hope Fern may visit and know her daughter, even if she does not wish to keep her…"

"…while she's on the run?" Ash finished. "Sorry, it's not your fault she has to run – you're trying to be party to change – I just…" she released a sound of exasperation. "Slow change is hard." Ash turned to him.

Ren placed his hand on his chest.   "I cannot imagine how hard." His head fell with his hand. He watched the ground, waiting.

Ash tracked his gaze, until it appeared as though they both examined the truth in the grass. Good, he would not presume to know things he could not. It was enough. Ash dragged her head upwards, willing Ren's to follow. "Well, at least last night's solution came together neatly. You seem to have everything summed and sorted."

"Not even close." Ren did look up. He studied her face, unabashed if his unguarded stare told Ash exactly what he yet hoped to sum and sort. It took some effort for Ren to pull his eyes away. He looked skyward. "One thing I do not understand," he murmured, "is why the man Fulton flipped so quickly from calling the child possessed to allowing me to take the infant. I was readying for a skirmish, I had not foreseen it could be so easy…"

Ash leaned back, considering Ren. "Fulton set out from the palace to deliver Valencia's ruling on the Foundling Wheels. The debate over the baby's origin was a complication. Local leadership had suggested the chance to entice a witch to make herself known, and he took it."

"You mean he never intended to harm the child?"

"Oh, I'm sure he'd see it through if it met his ends, but even the most sanctimonious of the Faithful horde blanch at Trials for infants." Ren's eyebrows gathered as he listened. "Fulton played the people, like he always does – he perceived who the people deemed the real villain to be, and did his best to appease the masses." Ash unfolded then refolded the pictogram along its creases. Ren felt a surge of affection that she had kept it. "A dash of mercy," she alighted from the fencepost, "and a dose of justice. Fulton's not too fussed on hapless infants and they're a drain on communities, but he despises witchcraft and their challenge to his authority."

Ash brushed off the seat of her cloak and eyed the direction Ren assumed she intended to travel. She gazed back up at him, no doubt feeling his eyes upon her again. "May the Mysteries untold share your will," she said in farewell.

"Mysteries willing," Ren whispered at Ash's cloak, which was already flapping in the wind as she cut a path through the field.

ASH

Their next meeting would be a *planned* encounter.
An encounter of *Ash's* planning.

The next day, Ash heard tell that one "Besuto
Ren" would be appearing in the Western Tract that
very night. Ash guessed *besuto* meant best –
affording Ren a stage name befitting a peregrine
stranger, if ever Ash heard one.

She wondered what Ren would do between now
and his showing that evening. Dusk was
approaching, and the gulls enjoyed Mystics best after
nightfall. Did Ren rehearse? Was he retrieving his
unclaimed notes from west-side inns?

The better question was, what Ash would do until
his show.

A nagging, raw disquiet answered from within.
Ash tugged out a clutch of her hair, fiddling a braid
into being. She needed to see Grete; needed sister-
time.

Ash adjusted her course, hugging the lake's edge
working her way across a meadow and through a

cemetery to the southern boundary of the Appleby orchard, but still away from the road. Scooping a fresh-fallen quince with a deft toe, she caught it without slowing her stride, checking for ants before taking a bite.

Quinces always reminded Ash of her day of naming…and her parents. She best remembered two expressions upon their faces: the first was pride, the second was resolve – that things must change. Ash had chosen the Mystic life…which meant performance, prowess…and danger.

Not all of Mórlough had proven as hostile as SeeBurg, but something about Odell's fervour coupled with the basilica crowd's passion combined to leave Ash shaken. The woman – or her friend – had rallied a slew of households to join her protest preceding Ash's own street-side assault; she'd known Ash might be coming – the morning after a show. That premeditation, added to the fact Ash had been caught off-guard might have been enough for Ash to come unstrung, but Ash's surreptitious attendance to the SeeBurg meeting had sharpened all the edges of the first encounter. She could dismiss being shamed by a pair of fanatics in the streets, but not Odell's active pursuit of another accused so soon after.

Still, hostility was nothing new – why was she more shaken than usual?

She blamed Ren for some of it. Twice she had been caught off-guard in his company and once in its afterglow. Thankfully she'd kept her wits at the church.

Ash knew she could only truly blame herself for slipping. She had to do better. The Seal was not yet won and Queen's Day was only five nights away. Ash gave a tight smirk as she spat the quince seeds out (she'd eaten the bitter fruit core and all). Only five more days that Ash had to endure the Odells and Gwens of Mórlough and all their ilk.

Five days for her to be on-guard in spite of *Besuto Ren*.

ASH

Ash came to Wynn and Grete Appleby's back door. She heard their voices inside, and paused, unsettled by an unusual quality to their tone.

Wynn's voice came to her first; "I was thinking we should do something for her birthday." Ash stood, quince-pilfering and alert at the door at seventeen years-of-age, but three more nights and she'd be eighteen – just old enough to perform, come Queen's Day.

"You don't think allowing this whole obsession with Queen's Day is gift enough?" Grete retorted. Ash winced.

"Come blossom, her plans are not new. There's no stopping her." It warmed Ash to hear Wynn defend her, but she understood Grete's reluctance to follow suit. Grete knew loss well. She didn't want to risk any more.

"But what of us? What of *our* plans?" Ash had to lean closer to the door to catch Grete's lowered voice.

"Our plans are ours, and hers are hers, Grete." Wynn answered quietly. "We all grieve in our own way."

"But what about where those plans meet, Wynn? That place in the middle where a brazen girl incites whispers of sedition that spill over to affect those she loves. What happens when a midwife refuses us because she's learned I'm the sister of a witch?"

Ash's shoulders crumpled. She never wanted the cloud of prejudice that followed her to rain down on Wynn and Grete...and the baby, not yet showing.

"She's no witch."

"*I* know that. *You* know that. *They* don't know that." Ash recognised the tell of tears in her elder sister's voice – the slight elevation in timbre, the hoarseness unveiled. "And what *they believe* is as good as what *is*. I won't have this baby born without the help she deserves because my younger sister is determined to prove a point!"

Wynn made soothing sounds before replying. "The baby will have everything she deserves and more, I promise you that, blossom. But shouldn't she have an aunt too, and a fierce one at that? Because it sounds like you're suggesting we distance ourselves..."

"No, you're right. We can't do that. I'm just...afraid, Wynn. And what with the archbishop passing through for SeeBurg..."

"I know."

"I can't bear to lose her."

"Ash, or the baby?"

"Either!"

The hushing returned, and Ash felt she'd greatly trespassed for having overheard this exchange...but she felt grateful too, for being reminded of the ripples her choices made for those she loved.

Wynn spoke again, more jovially: "So you think we've a girl in there then?"

"Well, yes, I do." Grete hiccupped a laugh.

"Then all the more reason we need an Aunt like the one she's got – fighting for a better Mórlough for her to grow up strong in."

"Stop it, you. She'll be an Appleby, and that'll mean she won't need a place in Mystic circles."

"She'll be an Appleby yes, but better an Appleby in Ash's Mórlough than in the Mórlough we have now – then she'll have a place anywhere."

"Listen to you. You sound just like her. Maybe you'd have been better off yoking your wagon..."

"Now *you* stop it. There's only ever been one woman I've wanted to make an Appleby, and I'm holding her."

Ash smiled to hear Wynn pay this devotion. She crept back three paces and made a new, louder approach, followed by a quiet rap on the door.

She heard some movement inside and then saw Grete's face at a window further along the wall. Grete gave Wynn a nod and an only-slightly-strained smile, to which he opened the back door.

"Ash!"

"My favourite Applebys! Am I intruding upon lovers in-thrall?"

"Actually, yes!" Wynn grabbed Grete at the waist and pulled her in for a loud kiss on the cheek. "But we'll continue it properly later." He gave Grete a wink, which she returned with laughter in her eyes.

"Very good, very good. Well, I don't want to stay long – I'm wary of you decent folk being seen with the likes of me..." Ash trailed off, her heightened sensitivity to the truth of her words lent them a raw sincerity.

"You do draw stares." Grete gave Ash a pointed glance. Ash looked down at her fitted attire peeking out beneath her cloak and knew exactly what Grete meant. "But I'll always take you as you are, Ash. Always."

Ash wondered if Grete suspected she'd overheard more and was launching a counter-offensive, but then she took in the set of her sister's shoulders – relaxed and loving – and decided *no*. "I appreciate it. Both of you. I know it isn't easy to...be my people – I know that my path affects yours – and I'm sorry for it. But soon there'll be a birthday and a Queen's Day and I imagine arduous-but-magical true *birth*-day, and hopefully the other kind of stares will be long behind us."

"Hopefully indeed," Grete spoke through a welcoming hug.

"Speaking of the babe," Ash took a seat and nodded at Grete's still-small middle, "I'm quite certain there's a girl in there."

"Is that right?" Grete shot Wynn a beaming *I-told-you-so* look.

"Mysteries willing! Mórlough needs more women of good stock." Ash thought of Odell and the spitter, as she spoke.

"You mean women like you?" Grete arched a brow.

"Hmm. In time I hope there will be scores of women like me, but no, dear Grete, if she's like you she'll be very fine stock indeed."

Grete smiled and rolled her eyes. She squeezed Ash's shoulder then lifted a spoon and stirred. "Are you staying for dinner?"

"No. But thank you." She wanted to, but after overhearing her sister and brother-in-law, knew it wasn't the time. She would've stayed late. They would've laughed and thrown dice. They wouldn't have talked about the emotional burden she was. Ash knew her sister. Grete needed three things when she felt anxious – quiet time, talk-time, and then an activity to ease her stress. Given that Ash was the cause of that stress and *the way* Ash knew Grete enjoyed easing her stress, Wynn was the person she needed this night. "I just stopped on my way to see Besuto Ren. He's showing tonight, is the word."

Wynn's eyebrows lifted with interest.

"Is this the man I've heard has finally stolen your heart?" Grete kicked the back of Ash's chair.

"Is that what you've heard?"   Ash sent a menacing corrective glare Wynn's way.

"But he is, isn't he?" Grete insisted.   "The one from the other night? Then Bess's Fry? The slippery one. That one's name is Ren…"

"The very same," Ash said, though she did not mention that he was now also the man of SeeBurg basilica, or the man of The Fence-line. Or that he was the man who retrieved cloaks from mothers fleeing Mórlough's unkindness.

"Wynn, you should go with her." Grete held up a hand to signal Wynn should not interrupt her, "Tell me all about it. Especially the parts where she swoons." Seeing her husband deflate she added, "But get back quickly…you've a promise to honour." Grete's eyebrow arched again.

Ash gave a brief cough, but smiled. This would give Grete her quiet time before talking and…stress-easing. "If you're sure, Grete. But there'll be no swooning, just clear-headed assessment of the competition."

"Riiight." Grete said.

Ash knew Grete didn't like her little sister scouting shows on her own, or how much time Ash spent unchaperoned by day. But her eagerness tonight to support her stepping out with Wynn had little to do with adding security at a Mystic's showing and everything to do with *which* Mystic was showing. Because Ash knew that for Grete this Mystic represented hope. Hope Ash might settle down…be safer. Grete wanted Ash to explore the option of safety and settling.

Ash felt a twisting, not entirely unpleasant truth making its home in her chest; a truth her elder sister had already discerned.

There may be little chance of Ash "settling down," but that did not rule out the possibility of swooning.

Ash's last thought as she left was, All Untold, deal me sobriety of thought!

ASH

A sponsoring lord had allowed the night's rabble to muster on his land. There was always one of those around who couldn't resist a good night's show, nor the coin their farmers reported came into the farm-gate stalls for the swell in traffic.

Hood up, Ash wove amongst the crowd. Wynn was two steps behind. A minstrel to their right enjoyed a small audience – mostly couples with linked arms. Ash caught herself smelling her own cloak inside its hood to see if its scent was changed for having been on loan. No, it still smelled like her – beds in underbrush, morning lake swims, and faint kitchen-smoke.

Ash and Wynn approached a pair of acrobats performing atop a main-stage of hay, a position that drew more of the gulls.

Besuto Ren would surely appear on that same stage. Wynn's report of Ren's mounting reputation suggested he'd show nowhere else.

So Ash canvassed vantage points surrounding the hay-stage, peripherally taking in the acrobats' performance. They weren't bad, this pair.

But she wasn't here for acrobats.

She assessed a small opening in the crowd by a nearby fence – removed, in shadow, and backed by a stand of trees. A few gulls sat on the fence's top railing, but they were sparse and would only provide better cover. Fence-lines held a new appeal, too. Ash smiled to herself, remembering Ren's position at her own show and their reunion thereafter.

She counted the escapes from her nominated point. It would do nicely. Ash led Wynn on and took up a pose of practised nonchalance. She wasn't sure even *she* bought it. After all, Ren had eluded her twice and surprised her once. And his vest and stance and eyes and *compassion* all added up to… something. Something that had her attention.

"So we're weighing the competition?" Wynn asked.

"That's right."

"Not swooning."

"Precisely."

"Grete sounded less sure on the second count…"

"Hush now."

Wrought-iron lanterns dotted the grounds in generous numbers. Ash had always liked that about this lord – he made a show of his wealth which, in turn, made a better show for her; Ash's acts did not rely on smoke and shadows to conceal anything;

light was her friend. The haybale-stage's proximity to the lanterns' flames seemed a touch hairy, but then so did fire near almost anything around Mórlough – so many dwellings resembled tinder to a critical eye. Ren surely wouldn't work in fire. His pick-pocketing to date strongly hinted at transposition, with a heavy reliance on diversions and sleight of hand. This type of illusion held scant appeal for Ash in the past, but recent exchanges considered, transposition was swiftly gaining traction.

If you were picking through specifics in the Mystic tongue, Ash was a Mentalist who mostly worked in prediction. In gull terms, she was a Psychic known for mind-reading and stunts of bravery. All it took to produce awe from the average audience member was naming an unmet's profession – so oblivious were they to any number of clues that announced as much for them.

"I hope he's next. I'm hungry," Wynn whispered. He'd left with a serving spoon of the stew Grete had stirred and a kiss of promise. Ash knew it wasn't only his stomach's appetite that made him time-conscious.

"He'll be next." Ash had overheard at least four hushed whispers that corroborated this notion, and her own intuition echoed it. The timing was right for a Mystic to take the stage. The atmosphere would certainly have invited her to the stage, if she were here to perform rather than spectate.

Her intuition proved correct. She had not been long clapping the acrobats' finish when Besuto Ren was announced and forthright appeared. Curiously, his show attire was the same winged vest she associated with him wearing day to day; different, distinctive and...simple. Then she noted he was just as at ease upon the stage as he had been the first time she'd seen him inside the tavern. A lure of stillness, a pole for the night's calm.

Ash saw several women in the crowd exchange glances. Though they all hung from a man's arm, their eyes said what their voices could not about the performer who'd taken the stage. So Ash wasn't the only one who found Ren attractive. She steadied her gaze. *Weigh.* She was here to weigh the competition.

Ren began, "My name is Ren."

Calls came from the crowd, "Besuto Ren! Besuto!"

"You may call me Besuto Ren," Ren announced, dipping his chin and allowing his fists to bloom acquiescent near his shoulders as he added: "If you insist upon such a name." He then stood with one palm to his chest. "I bring to Mórlough a simple show, and ask only that you watch very closely, so that your eyes are not deceived." His precision of language and slight accent were somehow even more appealing on the stage.

Ren produced a deck of picture cards. Ash had seen a set once in Adhmad Thoir, at the Eastern side of the Lough, but she knew little of how such a prop would be met here.

Ash recounted her exits, for this show had just become of great interest to any covert watcher in their midst. She gauged the crowd for its reaction but found them curious rather than horrified by what the zealots described as a "vain thing which enticeth man to sin." Ash didn't understand how something unfamiliar and enticing could produce repugnance...she'd quite like to get her hands on a set. She tempered her enthusiasm, else she risked prematurely declaring her Mystic affiliation; she could not afford to make too plain that the unknown didn't lead her to dismiss or denounce, it enlivened her, called to her.

Satisfied with her exit-count, Ash looked back to Ren, who held his cards aloft and said, "I invite anyone here who wishes to do so – to select a card, and mark it – right across its picture." Ren repeated his instructions a second time, slower, scanning the crowd. Ash could not resist selecting her own Top Three Marks from the cluster; a furrier adorned in his wares, a stable-hand she'd smelled as they'd passed him, and a wet-nurse who'd padded her chest against leakage whilst away from the job. Three varied marks, three Ash could point out were screaming their thoughts, if anyone asked (throat-clearing, finger-stretching and forearm-scratching, respectively).

But no one was asking.

Ren took instead…a volunteer.

Ash recognised the cordwainer he'd chosen – one of the few faces here tonight she knew as he made good shoes. His name was Eude Corwin, for the leathers he used for his craft.

Eude did as Ren bid – he selected a card and marked it while Ren looked on some four paces away. The mark inked upon the chosen card appeared to be a crude outline of a lady's boot. Eude made to return the card and pen to Ren.

"Please, before you do, Mister Corwin, examine the cards and confirm for everyone here that all of the cards are different on one side, but no other card bears any such mark as the one you have made." Ash craned to see all of Ren, watching even his legs for movement. "Is this so, Mister Corwin?"

"Yessir," Eude replied. "Just the one…card." He waved his marked card again towards Ren first, then the audience.

"Thank you. Well, you have ruined my card, but I asked you to, so there is no animosity between us." A few laughs came from the crowd. "Please witness also that when overturned, all of the cards are identical in their design."

Eude said, "Yessir, on this side they all look to be the same."

"Please stand here with me, Mister Corwin." Ren motioned he should come closer, which Eude did. "Now I will shuffle – which is to say I will mix your card in with all of these other pictures, so that it is difficult to know when looking at them like so," he fanned the cards to display their matching backs, "which is your card."

Ash watched Ren closely, but his movements were so fast and fluid she could scarcely take them in. The cards were split in half in a single hand and pivoted and replaced. The cards rifled and restacked at blurring speed – two stacks into one like a waterfall down his arm – then finally Ren pulled smaller stacks from the top of one stack over and over like steps into his other hand. Eude was hunched over in amazement. There were whispers in the audience – perhaps some growing apprehension at the unfamiliar. Ash couldn't fully measure the extent of this without taking her eyes from Ren, and her eyes were assuredly fixed on Ren.

"Tell me when to stop, Mister Corwin?"

"Stop?" Eude's obedient reply came as a question, but Ren obliged.

"Now, I will find your card." Ren threw the stack of cards in the air so that they sprayed and formed a fluttering shower of colour *at the same time* as drawing a blade from his back. The blade had been entirely undetectable to Ash until the moment it left Ren's hand. It sang through the air as it flashed through the card flurry and struck a fencepost three posts north of where Ash now stood.

Ash resisted the urge to gasp. What was Ren about? Had he been aiming at her? It seemed an extravagant ruse if this had all been about ending her. He'd had earlier and easier opportunities.

Unless he'd been toying with her.

Then Ash pulled herself together and reminded herself her hood was up, she was simply someone passing through, and this show most certainly was not about her.

"M'lady?" Ren called from the stage. "You – the one who did not flinch."

Oh no he didn't.

"You, with the elegant bearing beneath that hood. Would you be so kind as to retrieve my tanto? That is, my blade."

Ash gritted her teeth and made for the fencepost. It was then she saw what was pinned beneath the weapon. A picture card, with a woman's boot clearly inked across it.

How?

And curses to All Unknown that she'd been so obvious – selecting a position that might be deemed "their spot." She'd been predictable...and she'd even revealed sentimentality.

Ash pulled the blade from the wood with some effort and remained hooded for her walk through the parting crowd to the stage.

"Mister Corwin, is that your card?" Ren pointed to the blade in Ash's hand, Eude's card skewered at its end.

Eude was shaking his head, stunned. He came forward and examined the card and its picture of a boot, then slid it from the blade and held it in the air. "It is! His blade found my card in all of those!" He was looking about him, at the hay littered with fallen cards.

"Thank you for your assistance this night, Mister Corwin. You may keep the card, if you wish. Though drawn on and sliced through...it's of little use." Ren's words this time seduced laughter and giggles both, from the crowd.

"Oh, I mustn't. The missus would never allow it to be found in her house by daylight. But thank *you*, thank you Besuto Ren. It was an honour." Ash waited while Eude clasped hands with Ren before she made to return Ren's tanto. She thrust it towards him and dared only a moment's eye contact – her cheeks aflame she was sure – in which time he gripped her shoulder and whispered, "Thank you, too." Her cheeks burned brighter. She had to get out of there.

She darted back into the crowd, which pressed towards the stage to ask questions, offer praise, and otherwise (thankfully) detain Ren.

Wynn fell into stride alongside Ash, but remained thoughtfully quiet as they moved away from the stage, back past the minstrel and away from the performers of the night. She could tell Wynn wanted to speak, but was waiting. She knew what he would say, or the general substance of it anyway, "We found him – a Mystic worthy to be named your rival!" or, "Come now, Ash, he *is* good" or perhaps "You can't fault this one, I'd swear it!"

But Wynn said none of those things. What he did say, with some surety, was, "Moon-eyes!"

Now Ash made no habit of striking those she cared for, but after Wynn uttered those words she shoved him fairly solidly to remind him who was in charge of the night's operation. He laughed in reply and at varied volumes, the entire way home to his wife's stew and "dessert." Ash parted from him not long after the shove to slink away to an inn north of the Applebys, the whole way replaying what she'd seen in her mind's eye.

She had it.

Ren had never mixed Eude's card back into the deck! He'd known where it was all along. He had to. And she knew his sleight of hand was better than fair – he'd somehow managed to get the card onto the knife before he released it without anyone seeing. But the speed at which he'd drawn his "tanto" – well, that had been unearthly.

Yet for all his skill, foreign terms and sinful props, *he* hadn't had to run after *his* show.

There'd been no mention of devil's whispers coming to this Mystic's aid. She'd soon begin to right the unfairness of it.

Ash kicked at a tie-post in front of the inn before slipping inside. She hadn't been to this inn for a while, but appreciated its discretion.

"A bed." She drew her purse to proffer coin to the man behind the servery, then froze.

No.

Impossible.

While reaching within her bag she found something she had not placed there, and her fingers' study of it conveyed the inconceivable. Drawing out the foreign object, she held it under the light.

The innkeeper interrupted her study. "Coin only, I'll take no trade for a bed."

Ash gave him a brief look of bewilderment before returning her eyes to the thing she now held.

It was a simple thing – a boot, inked across a picture card – with a neat cut through its centre.

Oh, he was good. He was very good.

Mysteries, have mercy.

ODELL

Long before attending to bishops, basilica canticles, flower arrangements, and pitiless examinations of naked girls thrice accused, Odell had been gladdened by the arrival of Mystics.

Odell had seen seventeen summers and no naked girls or boys when she'd first seen the Mystic wagons gather. Seen them erect bunting-strings and pennants, and unroll rugs. They'd formed a circle, and nodded with smiles to all who passed by on their way to the *marketplatz*. Odell, being accompanied by Mapa, had the decency not to engage, nay even allow an eye to stray in their direction...but from the borders of her vision, Odell had observed and taken painstaking note. With mimping lips and sporadic sounds of expectoration, Mapa made her aversion to the onset of this people-plague known. That only made Odell want to go closer. But they had gone home.

Then, while her agelast father and servile mother reviewed scripture by candle-light in their loft bed,

Odell parted the curtain to the downward passage leading to their animals' accommodations, and crept through the dark. She nudged her way through the stock, chiding a goat that presumed an extra meal was on offer. Once past the animals, Odell found her way out into the night.

She smelled the Mystic band before seeing it. Notes of rosemary and lavender assailed her before she rounded the bend in the road. Then she saw – lights somehow strung up in lines, other lights in orbs hung upon poles – a glowing corona over the circle of colourful carts. Alongside the curious light-strings and bunting, she saw bushels of the fragrant herbs that had beckoned her on, moments earlier.

Odell's gut was wrenched low by a sudden sense of alarm. She was alone. The witching hours were ripe and she was solitary and reckless for the plucking.

And yet...

She was free.

Odell noted others making their way toward the circle – a couple sharing a shawl, whispering and tittering, an older gentleman aided by a walking stick, a triumph of bold older girls, arms linked. Odell's recently ascended freedom relinquished its impulsive claim on her throne to a more familiar ruler, loneliness.

Loneliness seeped from its presiding position in Odell's chest to trickle in icy rivulets down her limbs, filling her belly with a cold and palpable weight.

Odell hastened on – desperate to feel but a fraction of the liberating deliverance she had briefly tasted instead. She drifted into place behind the chain of girls, drawing her mantle tighter around her, doing her best to appear as though she had snuck away to explore the Mysteries many nights agone. As they entered under the aromatic threshold, all awareness of any warring emotions within her abated. Her senses overloaded.

Odell was birthed into a mass of milling patrons of the night – bodies occasionally pressed in on her as the assemblage collected in pockets around each spectacle. A pair of Mystics in matching citrine moved in unearthly synchronicity here. There, a woman with hair in tight, gold-banded coils, doubled back so her body formed a perfect circle from head to hip. A male minstrel with skin of warm umber kissed an enchanting euphony from panpipes – his eyes closed without creasing – white moths dancing to his tune in the string-lights above him.

The press of each appreciative encircling crowd felt comforting, not inappropriate.

Odell marvelled. Mapa had made such places sound like harems, overrun with debauchery and bodies writhing in fornication. Odell found nothing of the like. And what she saw? Well. If this – all this! – was infidelity to God and the basilica, Odell was not sure she wanted to be faithful.

As Odell moved deeper, the dancers, the woman emulating a bread ring, and the insect inveigler dissolved around the wagon circle's heart. Additional light hit a staged area in stripes from multiple sides. The presence of the pair upon that stage demanded Odell make this act a singular sharpened point of focus. It was clearly evident, of all the Mystics, this couple attracted the largest crowd. The man was throwing three blades up in the airspace before him, talking too, while catching each by the hilt on its descent before sending it immediately up again and catching the next. A woman was sharpening another blade. No – she held a blade no longer! Where was it? Odell craned to see. She found it. The male Mystic now kept four blades aloft.

Odell had to get *closer.*

She wove through mantled people of the night, offering whispers of apology. As she wove, she could not take her eyes off of the pair – leading her to knock into more than one patron in her path. She stopped when she could hear what the male mystic was saying – now close enough to see the shapeliness of the woman's eyebrows and the flex of the man's jaw.

The male mystic seemed to speak as though he were sharing a secret with only Odell, in tones one might speak in the basilica transept...yet she could hear him plainly over the significant sound of the many blooming circles of attraction within the greater circle. Even the way the male Mystic's voice carried through the din was of the Unknown; "Though my timing is fine and fair, Pabla is the one to watch."

Despite the man's directive, Odell had missed something – for something had changed, though she could not discern what. The woman's arm had flashed out. It was all so fast.

In time with a mutual rumble of realisation rippling out from the stage-crowd's heart, Odell knew too; the man had only three blades once more. Where was the fourth blade? The woman, Pabla, held none. Odell scanned around, rising on the toes of her night slippers in an attempt to better see. Then, she allowed a gasp to escape. She'd located the missing blade. It protruded from a tree trunk beside the stage. This was not all. Skewered beneath it, an apple hung suspended against the tree's bark.

How was it possible?

Even as Odell made a study of the tree – searching for devices or concealed apparatus aiding the performance, a second blade appeared beside the first, spearing a second apple, which had appeared from the Unknown.

What kind of communion with the Mysteries?

Odell honed in on the two blades remaining in the air, whistling in harmony and faultless formation. Pabla – with the swiftness of a whip – struck out – her dark eyes on the crowd, then released both intercepted blades to land in the trunk, thunk thunk.

Again, each held an apple in place. The final two blades arrived in precise symmetry to the former two, so that the four blades formed a square. The man, his hands free, spread his arms wide, as though he would embrace all watching.

If he tried, Odell would let him.

She was clapping before she realised she'd decided to.

Pabla took one side-step nearer to the man, and he did something which astounded Odell more than any part of the couple's stunt with the blades. He drew the woman to himself with a hooked arm at her waist, pressing his lips to her temple with a tenderness that made Time stop and take note of its significance. Odell's heart hammered in her chest like the blades that struck the tree, thunk thunk. Thunk thunk. Like her applause, Odell realised late her breath had caught in wonder at the intimacy of it.

Odell had seen measures of affection before. Rare times, between couples thinking she wasn't watching. Odell would catch a leg-squeeze or whisper between companions – those whose relationships were known to all or, even more rarely, between those who loved in secret. But none compared to the intensity and heat of what she witnessed between the Mystics that night. It was not merely that they flaunted common convention to keep such demonstrations private – though this would have been astonishing enough – it was that passion rippled from them, thriving beneath public gaze.

Odell's attentions fixed on Pabla. She glowed. Her teeth bright, locks dark, and confidence confounding. Her countenance radiated the way Odell formerly imagined an angel's might, yet seeing Pabla, Odell's imaginings altered for the better. An angelic face with a smile capable of mischief evoked a superior beauty Odell had failed to fathom until faced with it on this forbidden excursion during forbidden hours.

Pabla covered the man's hand at her waist, their fingers sliding into a familiar interlocking grip. They bowed in unison – no curtsy from Pabla – and rose on the wave of answering whistles from the audience.

That's when the screaming began.

A horn of alarm briefly sounded but was cut short.

The circles within circles disbanded, running. The Mystics seemed to evaporate into the darkness.

A wagon toppled.

Fire erupted.

A baby cried.

Odell's father materialised, his hand bruising on her arm, pulling her from the ground. How had she gotten there? She didn't remember falling.

When she tried to go to the baby crying within a burning wagon, Papal had dragged her the rest of the way by her hair.

THE UNFLINCHING ASH

In the days that followed, Papal had instructed Odell by her sickbed. She was so confined, deemed "unwell," unfit for going outdoors. She received a daily homily about the fleeting Mystic life, with its habitual and eventual destruction. She was exhorted to seek duty, careful gentleness, companionship and loyalty that she could count on; an unchanging basilica of stone, not a wagon circle of wood that died back like summer leaves only to resprout and require further pruning. She was to find a man, acquit herself of her childishness, and secure her power of being a carrier and attendant of life. Be provided for, not scrounged for. Be proud and dignified in who she was instead of consigned to the shadows. And while her father spoke, each day, he held her hand. He had never done that before. And as he held her hand, she felt safe. He was right. The wagon circle was an illusion of happiness. The couple was enjoying a fleeting joy. How readily it had been dashed.

So why, having done all her father had asked, did being provided for and being dignified chafe so?

Why did she see Pabla's face in her dreams – when Odell managed to sleep – not dead in the water, but merely sleeping?

138

ASH

Ash approached the Applebys' via the orchard. She found Grete out back, sorting through buckets of quinces – plucking leaves, dunking muddied fruit in a neighbouring tub of water, checking for rot or blemishes. Grete partnered Wynn in his inherited family business, though many wives would disapprove of how equally they shared this responsibility. Although a wife might influence her husband behind closed doors, most believed it wasn't becoming for a woman to be anything but subservient. But a woman could learn the orchard trade if she tried and Grete knew nesh from scroggling as well as any man.

Ash took up a position beside her older sister and mirrored her labours.

"I hear this Ren of yours is good," Grete said.

"Oh, so you two managed to get some talking in last night then?" Ash bumped her sister facetiously. "And Ren *of mine*? What are you about? I've only seen the man a few times."

Grete continued as though Ash had made no retort, "I also hear there was definite swooning."

Ash groaned in defeat.

"He should come here for dinner."

"That's hardly my style."

"That's hardly *been* your style, but that's not to say it cannot be…"

"Ever the optimist, my Grete." Ash gave her sister an overly tight smile.

"Fine, don't give your word, but don't rule it out. The Mysteries have presented a true enigma of a man at the very time one might argue one was needed…"

"Hey!" Ash slapped a splash of grey-water in Grete's direction. "I do not *need* any such thing."

Grete flinched but carried on with her work. "So you deny the swooning?"

Ash stilled her hands and turned to face her sister. "I don't. There, are you pleased? But just as you know this one's got my attention, you *know* that me sitting down and playing house at some *dinner* is…an unlikely scheme."

"That I do." Grete smiled into her bucket. "But I'll always be here to whisper reason. Someone has to."

Ash looked into her bucket too. "He *is* good."

Grete hummed two M's playfully. "He'd have to be! I've scarce sensed real attraction from you towards anyone, let alone respect!" Grete had always read Ash's tells well.

"Maybe after Queen's Day…"

"Yeeeees....?"

"...I'll explore what non-dinner-type arrangements one might make with a true enigma of a man who also happens to be good." Ash's shoulders and eyebrows crumpled in unison. "He really is uncannily good, Grete – I've seen no one like him." Ash considered the card in her purse – ruined, yes – but she'd kept the token from him all the same.

"What makes you think he'll wait that long?" Grete presented one cheek with this question.

"Any man who cares to see me will learn quickly that it's my terms or none at all." Five days until Queen's Day. Then she could attend to the tremulous cool that each inhale brought whenever that breath accompanied thoughts of Ren.

In this moment, she needed to be with Grete though. Her sister tugged a small lock of Ash's hair free from the mass and began plaiting, repeating a conspiratorial teasing hum of "mmhmm" as she wove. Ash leaned back into her sister, pausing in her work to relish the moment. She was recommitting Grete's smell to memory –fruit from her skin, hazel carried on her breath, and lime from her hair – when she realised Grete's breathing hitched and she was no longer braiding. She was crying.

Ash turned to take her in. "Grete?"

"Five more days, right?" Grete's eyes shone.

"Ya, only five more days." Ash took Grete's hands in her own. "We're not talking about Ren anymore, are we?"

"We're not."

"I'll get it."

"You better." Grete turned Ash back around and commenced a new braid. "Ash?"

"Ya?"

"You can always withdraw, you know." Grete stilled Ash, who tried to turn to retort. Ash relented, resumed washing fruit, letting Grete finish and speak into her little sister's hair. "I know you enjoy the risk...the thrill...and I love you as you are. But if ever a performance gets away from you, *you can always withdraw.*" Grete stroked the scar on Ash's ear. "Remember that for me, will you?"

"I'll remember." Ash meant it. "I love you, Gree."

"And I you." Grete dropped the braid and hugged Ash close, resting her chin on Ash's shoulder so their cheeks touched. "More than anything."

And then Ash said something she hadn't said since the girls were small. Something she had said every time Grete said she loved Ash *more than anything*. Ash had been unable to resist singsonging this thing playfully each time, back then, but since, it had felt too raw to continue the habit. Today, she said it. "More than Mapa and Papal!?"

Grete choked out one sob, hearing the old refrain. She rejoined their old script: "More than any*thing*, dear sister, more than any*thing*." Then she added. "They would be right proud."

Ash held onto Grete's arms around her imagining Grete was her Mapa and Grete in one. Grete's arms always felt right – like a place where she belonged.

What Ash risked beyond her life alone had never felt more real.

Dusk was falling.

Ash was just leaving the Applebys', an empty discomfort around her shoulders where her sister's arms had been. She hoped Grete spoke true, that their parents would be proud.

She left via the opposite side of the orchard from the cemetery – being more conscious of the vulnerability of invariability.

It should have been enough.

It wasn't.

She saw the bloodied horse first. She made to turn but it was too late.

Astride the grotesquely-painted animal sat a man who resembled a noble in bearing and clothing. Embellished in silver and gold, his back was knife-straight. A beard rimmed his mouth only, as though he'd kissed a sooty plate. His eyes steeled for seeing her.

The rider spoke: "Ash, daughter of Mystics Pabla and Alex?"

Ash made no answer, though their names were too good for his filthy mouth.

The man continued his declaration: "You have been twice accused of heresy and acts offensive to our God. We have come to secure you for a warning council on the morrow, as soon as SeeBurg's Bishop may attend."

Ash reached for her blade. It was the best bet for self-defence. Guns so often misfired and took a comparative age to load.

"I wouldn't." These two words of discouragement came only a single count before a rope was slung around her and drawn tight. No sooner had her upper arms been bound than she felt hands upon her as two of the men accompanying the rider tightened the cords and added further bindings.

"You've not even confirmed I am the person you're looking for."

"The morning's council will confirm all we need know."

"What is *your* name?" Ash raised her chin, indignant.

The rider looked as though he'd been struck in the throat, so affronted was he by this question. Of course she knew *what* he was. All knew the bloodied horse of the one who came for those accused; the Seeker. But the Seeker's name... ? Ash thought it fair to ask. The Seeker's retort came in a huff. "*I* am not on trial here."

"I will call you... Arsebeard."

Arsebeard's eyes were mostly white. "The accused is giving us trouble; subdue her."

She'd known the insult would cost her, but it had also allowed her to read the Seeker's response – she'd learned he was prone to anger over fear, but that he entertained measures of both.

The clout for her trouble came from her right side. Her head rung immediately.

Skull pounding, fists still clenched in rage, Ash was slung across the back of a second mount. She could see little of her captor's accomplices, but all of Arsebeard's horse's rump if she twisted to her left. Mostly, she watched the road, staring down. Her position was inglorious and the situation looked poorly, yet all she desperately hoped was that neither Grete nor Wynn should pass by at this moment and be drawn into the mess.

Whispers, closing doors and the occasional missile soon enveloped their passage. She knew where they were headed and was already making calculations. Through her head's throbbing she replayed what she had learned of Arsebeard through their exchange. He was slightly afraid of her, although more pronounced was his anger at her audacity. He thought her rude but only mildly threatening, and easily subdued. Let him think that. Let them all think she was nothing to worry about.

They came to a stop. With a twist of her head, Ash confirmed their destination in the darkening evening. The ribbed vaulting was unmistakable.

They'd reached the largest Western basilica – the nearest suitable venue for a morning trial. No one was coming or going for worship, but instead all hastened through dimpse-time for home. Except for those hastily securing the Twice Accused in the twilight.

Ash was unceremoniously removed from the horse and tied by three men to a thick-trunked tree. The darkness revealed little of their faces, but two stank of sweat and the third of something fouler.

"I'm glad you've found some control over yourself. You'll need it." Arsebeard remained atop his blood-soaked charger. It would be lamb's blood, Ash knew – considered a ward against evil by extremists.

One of the unwashed brutes approached with a device. It resembled an unusual fork at the first, but Ash soon felt its divergence from something so benign. The brute secured the device around Ash's neck by a belt. He then attached it to a metal piece with two opposed bi-pronged forks. Ash could feel them both if she moved, for they bit into the flesh beneath her chin and sternum.

"This is but a preliminary trial." Arsebeard informed her. "Come the morn, if you confess you are a witch to the presiding bishop, the trial may end. If not, your protection through the witching hours alongside your silence will result in a third accusal, upon which, we will proceed to the second trial."

Anger and excitement roiled within Ash. They meant for her to plead her guilt before them bleary-eyed and sleep-deprived come dawn. *Really? She had until morning.* Ash heard only a challenge. "Come the morn?"

"Unless you wish to confess now, before these witnesses?"

Ha! They'd issued a challenge *and* they'd failed to take her weapon. Fools. They thought sleep deprivation was security enough. She was growing cockier. "Ah, the witching hour is upon us, won't you come closer? Or are you afraid to come down from that horse and speak to me on my level, Arsebeard?" She hoped she'd read him right. There was pride and anger in that man, but she'd seen fear there too.

"Gag her," he answered.

The foulest smelling of the lackey trio complied with Arsebeard's order. In gagging her, he caused Ash's chin to jerk into the double-pronged device, drawing blood.

"Until morning." Arsebeard nodded in parting. The man who had gagged her made a swift grab of her breast before leaving, to which Ash responded by crushing her heel into his right foot. A correcting backward glance from Arsebeard saw him limp away without further harassment, but Ash marked his gait and scent.

They were going to leave her here rather than spend the night near one who might call down any number of curses or plagues upon them and their houses. She'd hoped for this; the man who'd hit her had worried at a hangnail at the mention of the witching hour. Add to that Arsebeard's thinly-veiled apprehension, and Ash was confident these men had agreed to secure her and leave her until dawn, and that they all agreed this was the best course, given the inherent "risks." The lecherous groper had even made the sign of the basilica across his eyes as he'd limped away, incensed.

Something akin to fear snuck inside Ash's chest as she weighed the time her escape would take against the possibility of the reeky man's vengeful return. She'd favour being snappy over precision, in case, which equated to the realisation: there'd be some blood.

Ash began with the cords at her wrists (she'd obviously tensed and rotated one wrist at their tying so she might now twist them straight to give the binding slack). There wasn't much, but working her wrists against each other, she made progress. Blood ran hot into her décolletage. The night fell darker still. A copse of trees bordering the basilica obscured residences from view, but Ash remembered well from the ride how very close the whispers and closed doors had been. Twice Accused, he'd said, and yet her accusers appeared now to cower from the consequences of their pointing fingers. Cowered from the hours they believed belonged to her and her kind.

And what of her captors? Did they really think her so frail and helpless that darkness, some rope, and a perversion of blacksmithery would be sufficient to hold the daughter of Pabla la Presica and Alexact? Whatever the grounds, Ash was grateful for their underestimation, superstition and greed, which surely played a part in calling them away. She imagined the four of them boasting of their success – the promise of bounty paid, an appalling wage earned. Mapa and Papal's show-knots had been thrice as tight – for the gulls who tested them – and she'd been blindfolded. Ash managed to free one hand and, giving preference to speed, manoeuvred within the ropes around her torso and ankles with some force, causing the device to cut sharp and deep. Howls from the woodland at her back made her smile. She wouldn't be here when nocturnal hunters came scouting.

Bleeding, head a-riot, and a touch light-headed, Ash freed herself from the ropes. She then began work on untying the insidious collar. Once free of its grip, she flung it to the ground.

She looked at the bindings they'd attempted to hold her with – cut and heaped about the earth. There was still a possibility one or more of the ruffians would return sooner than the morn for a confession. Or worse. So she *should* put distance between herself and this Mysteries-forsaken site; she knew they wouldn't leave her unguarded a second time. Besides, staying after a show was hardly her way. But Ash couldn't resist sparing a moment to make neat of the ropes, lying so jumbled in her wake. She had to make a few more cuts with her blade, which she held in her teeth between each edit, completing a hasty arrangement. Then, dusting herself off and sheathing her blade beneath her girdle, Ash appraised her work.

It would do. Clearly legible, the ropes now spelled a single word.

"Arsebeard."

Well, she *had* asked the gull his name.

With one last look in the direction she'd seen her assailants depart, she took off contrary, into the pitch-shadows of the forest canopy.

ODELL

The Bishop snored. Odell had loved him once, but such sentiments were faded and offered little room in her crowded mind.

Rather, she was consumed by images and sounds from the past few days, rising and setting over and over again in her mind like a harried sun. A Thrice Accused's naked form under scrutiny in search of a mark at her first trial. The Thrice Accused's choking horror, at her second, when her hand had plunged into a boiling pot to grasp a stone. The guttural moans as she'd gripped the stone firm. The agony of her sobs as she cradled her hand upon releasing it. Days later, the pus oozing from the girl's angry palm when it was exposed for the council to bear witness of her failure.

The way the woman's feet never stilled when she hanged. Odell's hand instinctively went to her own throat.

The lamb had not confessed, changed, and returned before being sent into God's Unknown. The girl could have ended things sooner, if she had but confessed.

Odell drew down her prayer veil from the bed canopy's frame, fastening it about her eyes. She recited the prayer for humility and peace. A flashing image of the pus' hue and viscosity invaded her invocation. Next, though no such prayer had been approved by the archbishop, Odell added her own entreaty: that all those Twice Accused upon the basilica's records would feel urged by God to amend their ways and save the Western Tract any further Trials by Ordeal. *Please God, help them change. Make them know their wrongs. Make them seek instead a good life, free from pursuing Mysteries that are Thine alone, free from claiming unsanctioned access to Thy ways without ritual, without submission, without worshipping Thee. Guide them back to Thee and away from their sin. Bring them to salvation.* But she knew, some would resist saving.

This vexed her greatly.

Knowing this to be an unholy emotion, Odell left the veil on, hoping that even in sleep it might instil further virtue. The memories were not kept without the veil, nor did it keep out the dark imaginings that assailed her. She could not shake the notion that should she dare cross her threshold and out into the witching dark, she'd make out in the Mysteries-light across the square, the girl's feet still swaying.

The girl's death had been swift. There was compassion in that. But it did not bring the satisfaction of saving that Odell so craved.

These widespread sins should not be left unchecked – of that there was no doubt – but why was this cross hers to bear? She would prefer to welcome the rescued lambs home, help them change, and leave the Trials to others. But the witch insurgence was so much bigger than she; Odell was but one good woman, after all, charged with saving so many.

They were but one basilica with such a charge, rather, she corrected herself.

Odell recalled the way the heretic had dared her to supply God's name – had challenged her, right on the street. That one was beyond saving.

She knew then what she must do. She rose from the bed.

SeeBurg was but one town in a larger district-full of problems needing redress. She needed to go higher. Odell snatched up a pen and ink and took her place at the writing desk. If higher authority was called upon, perhaps then they could stay the tide. She began her missive to the archbishop, feverish with thrill. Archbishop Fulton was clearly in need of more information.

> *Many of the sinners spreading their way of thinking are transient, nomadic folk. The problem is greater than SeeBurg and therefore requires your attention...*

Writing a letter felt good, like a contribution Odell was called to make – she was helping the cause, and perhaps inviting a better sleep, while still ensuring justice was served.

> *One particularly obstinate Accused is one Ash the Unflinching...*

Archbishop Fulton would take care of her.

Odell sat back, swelling in the warmth of purpose. The missive had been inspired, she knew.

Sometimes these things needed to be helped along, and one could work wiser to share that burden. It felt good to be a powerful instrument in God's hands. The kind of woman her father would approve of.

She'd signed it from her husband, naturally.

ASH

Ash took in a yawning breath and dove back beneath the surface. She'd run for most of the night, alternating between stretches of swimming in the lake and running on land, hoping to make tracking her more difficult. She had taken a short rest in a boat moored near the Northern settlement border and then slept in a tree beyond the first Northern township. There'd been no sign of pursuit.

She rose again for air. Now daybreak, she pulled herself through the water again. It was cold, yes, but it kept her awake. As always, she felt connected to an energy beyond people and prejudice and pain. The lake was constant. The lake was home.

After a few breaststrokes, she returned beneath the surface, timing her submersion. Upon reaching a count of 180, she came up for air. It was hard in her waterlogged clothing, but she pushed beyond the tearing in her muscles and the dizziness of her head's ache. She had to ensure the water remained hers.

Approaching a lively dock of fisherman, Ash moved into the reeds and shallows to rest. She startled some fowl, but this did not appear to draw any attention from the nearby docks. She settled into reeds that held her dry above water close to the birds' nest. She lay on her back, closing her eyes. After restoring a normal rhythm to her breath and dismissing some of the limpness in her limbs, Ash rolled over and parted the reeds, looking for cress. All Untold had mercy, for after a few minutes she found some growing near where her feet had been. She lay on her back looking up at the brightening sky as she chewed on her peppery breakfast.

She smiled at the thought of the message daybreak was bringing to those back at the Western basilica.

Her expression turned grave. Three days remained until Queen's Day. To perform there, Ash first needed to receive a commendation from a lord or lady. Her recent escape and flagrant departing message had likely earned her a place on the Thrice Accused record already. So Ash simply had to draw attention and lay low at once – simple. Fortunately for Ash, the open-minded residents of Mórlough tended to assemble away from those who would judge their proclivities and attentions.

Ash flicked the muddy root of a reed-stalk into the lake and commenced chewing a new stalk while she plotted. She would have to perform again for an assemblage, but also in front of someone who could get her that commendation. If she moved far enough north she might stay ahead of the Seeker. Once she performed for the Queen, she could stop running. The Seal would see to that. They couldn't touch her then.

But could she get through three more days without a second assault?

She'd endured three years waiting for her eighteenth birthday – what were three more days? Well, they were three days more days with a festering sore called hysteria threatening to kill her, she supposed.

Thinking then of her literal wounds, Ash checked her neck and her sternum. The fork's cuts weren't scabbing, but the bleeding had ebbed in the lake's cold. She smelled of wet leathers, though her outer layer was now dry on her front. She rolled onto her stomach to allow her back to be warmed. *Ugh*. Ash's face soured. There was only so much cress a Mystic on the run could ingest. She reckoned the length of a short doze would see her dry enough, then she would haggle for fish.

ASH

Ash woke stiff and shivering. Her crude nest was now in the shade. She scooted sideways and into the sun, rubbing at her limbs. Sitting up, she could see through the reeds she must be further north than her first estimation. The docks she'd spied earlier were only the edge of what she could now see formed a waterfront maze with cruck housing beyond. The line that pulled her onward suddenly felt taut and insistent with realisation. She must be at the southernmost quay of the Queen's City! Sure enough, as she turned, she saw bright colours trailing from ramparts beyond the outer circle.

Wait… three days before Queen's Day meant… oh blinded foolishness! With everything going on, Ash had completely forgotten what three days before Queen's Day meant. Three days before Queen's Day was Dawn's Veil. At Dawn's Veil, pious men and maidens arose early, toting their veils. They tied one at their threshold, one at their place of business, and one over their own eyes as they stood somewhere picturesque – often hand-in-hand with a loved one – to entirely miss the visual splendour of sunrise.

Ash didn't begrudge them their religion. She even found some charm in the Dawn's Veil tradition. More than once she had closed her eyes against the sun to better enjoy its warmth on her eyelids. But that had been without incantation, without the costly veils – needlessly replaced to follow each year's fashion – without the ritual that declared utter ignorance and dependence upon the basilica and its "visionaries."

Today she'd slept in reeds through the prayer intoned across the land;

> *Still my inner voices*
> *so I hear only thine*
> *and that of our Queen*
> *Long may she guide us*
> *Through the Mysteries*
> *governed*
> *by thee*

She wasn't sorry for having slept through it. By now worshippers would be spending coin, breaking bread, exchanging gifts to mark the occasion, meeting with others to discuss where they had *not*-seen in the dawn that day.

Lovers would be parting to speak of a kiss they'd shared at dawn, veiled – a symbolic submission of their romance to God and His will.

Ash weighed the insistence of her appetite against the risk of showing herself in a day crowd. The fishermen would have gone out for their catch. The excitement of Dawn's Veil should busy the gossips, hopefully leaving little space in conversation for talk of an interrupted "preliminary" trial of a witch further south. That left a small group for whom business reigned paramount. And Dawn's Veil brought great business, signalling a succession of days good for business, with Queen's Day coming so soon after. Big sellers would be searching for word of what buyers for the royal residence predicted was needed for Queen Valencia's celebration. Small sellers would be readying stock for local celebrations. That meant everyone was busy. Hunger or discretion?

Ash's stomach won. She eyed the lakeline and noted some shrubbery, although she'd have to track back a distance to reach it. Navigating on her forearms through the dry beds within the reeds, Ash came up behind the shrubs. A muddied knee resulting from solid ground misjudgement was her only mishap (along with sacrificing a morsel of pride). After crawling beyond the shrubs and into the trees, Ash stood and prepared to subject herself to closer scrutiny. Her injuries from the device were probably the worst detraction. Her damp undergarments chafed uncomfortably. Her hair was a tangled mess. She worked her hands through her mane and tucked it tightly behind her ears. It would have to do.

Thank goodness for fishermen caring more for the moods of the lake than the affairs of the land. Within minutes of walking amongst the docks' crowd, Ash could see most worshippers had returned in-land, leaving those usually at the docks to their docks. If anyone was bothered by her appearance, they didn't show it. Within half an hour she'd given coin and eaten a fried grayling. She wouldn't tell Bess so, but it was surely the finest fish she'd ever tasted.

Ash let gratitude for a hot meal settle over her a moment before she faced moving on. It stung to think of Grete and Wynn, whom she could see no time soon and who would have received word of a heretic fugitive. They would be worried.

Though late to the day's ritual, Ash closed her eyes and allowed the sun to soothe her by way of warming her eyelids as she took deep, meditative breaths. Her own meditation, her own primal song inside;

Almost there. Queen's day approaches. Three nights remain. The Seal is yours.

Ash heard someone come down beside her, she presumed to eat a lush flaky grayling, as she had. She salivated at the memory a moment before opening her eyes. A superficial glance towards her new neighbour revealed impressive thigh musculature and boots that resembled slippers in their cut. Curious.

She all-out twisted her head to see her neighbour's face and found he was indeed enjoying fish from the same vendor. Also, he was Ren.

For reasons she could not entirely understand, her chest lurched with emotion. He was not Grete or Wynn, but he was familiar. And he was here. After the night's ordeal she felt an unprovoked urge to hug him.

"You are a hard woman to track down," Ren said. He still looked out across the lake as he ate his grayling.

"Is that so?"

"It was like you knew I was trying to find you, and you made it as difficult as you possibly could." Now he turned to her, shading his eyes from the sun with his hand. There was warmth in his expression as he squinted while looking at her, then concern blossomed: "What... what happened to you?"

Did she look *that* bad? No one else at the docks had paled and wilted in concern as Ren did now. She felt a flush creep up her neck at the same time as the returning urge to hold onto him... someone... anyone who wouldn't hurt her.

"Your neck...." He set down his plate of fish and waved a finger over her injuries.

"Oh that. Well, I met with a small brangle last night. You should see the state of my adversary." She smirked at the thought. Although she'd exacted no physical injury, she imagined the state of the Seeker's face. Beet-red, perhaps? At least she hoped that was his response to her message left in ropes. Ren needn't know that.

"Are you hurt anywhere else?" Deep lines of concern ploughed Ren's brow.

"I'm fine. I have to be. There are three days left."

"Until Queen's Day?"

"Of course I mean until Queen's Day."

"But you are still not on the list."

"You sure know how to make a woman feel special… "

"Let me start over. This is why I came. I received my commendation from a lord not far from here – Hughes is his name – he has commended my name for the list. I wanted to find you and offer once more – we could join acts, and you could be seen on Queen's Day, at my side. I have already secured a spot."

"My answer hasn't changed."

"But how will you get in? I can see it is important to you, but I can also tell that it is not easy for… a woman. Is it worth the risk of performing again without the Seal's protection? Does it matter how you get before the queen so long as you *do* get there?"

"It matters." Ash went quiet. The pan hissed behind them and the trade-calls of the docks resounded around them.

"Do you think we could walk? It is easier to think when one may... " Ren struggled for the words, "forest-bathe."

Ash laughed silently and answered, "Sure."

They both returned their plates and headed inland. Ren made to walk the road, through flapping veils and groups of laughter, but Ash redirected him by crossing to the forest beyond. Ren adjusted his course and followed. Finding some quiet beneath the trees' canopy, Ash sat and leaned against a tree. She drew her knees up to rest her arms on them. Ren did the same, facing her.

He spoke first, "I presume you got my card?"

Ash couldn't help smiling. "Yes." It was a soggy mess in her coin purse, complete with its piercing from his act, but she'd kept it, and carried it still. It had been years since a knife had been thrown so close to her. She'd missed it. Ash arched an eyebrow at him. "You are very good, you know."

"So they tell me." Ren spread his hands in confession.

"What does 'Besuto' mean?"

"Best."

"HA! I thought so."

They smiled at each other. "I did not choose it."

"So our first meeting, it was about joining shows. The second meeting was to warn me about Collier?"

"I also wished to compliment you... and just see you... "

Ash continued, but only just, wavering at his directness, "You followed me this time to ensure I got the commendation?"

"Yes. I want to help – one way or another. You deserve to be seen." He tipped his head and she caught his eyes on her wounds again. "And not just by me, although I am enjoying it immensely, even if seeing you this way... hurt, is unpleasant. I would spare you this... " he gestured loosely towards her. She fought the urge to blush again. "If you will not join me, will you at least allow me to help guard you against this brutality?"

"No." Ash's head shake was terse. "You don't understand."

"*Help me* understand."

Ash's hair fell forward on one side. She left it, and looked beyond, to Ren's earnest face. Caution had long been Grete's mistress, but Ash felt its pull now as this man begged confidence. "You first. Where do you keep that blade you threw the other night?"

"Here." Ren raised a bent arm, deliberately slowing his actions for Ash's benefit. His hand withdrew a blade from within a seam hugging the contour of his right rhomboid muscle. Ash leaned forward to better see how the weapon was concealed, although she was somewhat distracted by the profile of Ren's arms.

"That *is* impressive. There are few that can say they get a weapon by me."

"*A* weapon?" Ren produced a merger of both pout and smile. "I have six blades with me now."

Ash's eyes widened. She smiled with teeth and an open mouth. "Show me." Ren stood. He retrieved each blade from its place – one lining each forearm, another at his mirrored rhomboid, one at his thigh, and one at his calf. Ash shook her head in wonder. The blades were all relatively short, but extremely well-cared for.

Ren was effectively disarmed before her. He sat again, laying his blades out between them. "What else do you seek to understand?"

Ash concentrated her thoughts on Ren, although the events of the night before coloured her line of questioning. "What are you running from?"

"Is it that obvious?"

Ash had been part-guessing but didn't reveal her self-satisfaction for being correct. "You said you came to the Lough for the Seal, but there's more to it than that."

"That is true. Where I am from, what I do… there is little respect for it. It is not a discipline of value in my… circles."

"You mean in your family?"

"In anyone's family."

"So you left?"

"Yes."

"Sounds lonely."

"So was living without respect."

Ash hummed a single note. "Well, my parents died doing what I do – or near enough. Without the Seal, I can't make peace with that. I can't safely do what I enjoy most *or* feel satisfied my parents' deaths meant something. The Seal is the only thing I've really ever wanted, and the only thing I've been able to fix on for as long as I can remember." *The only thing that'll come anywhere near soothing the hurt of them not being here*, she thought.

Ren shuffled slightly closer and asked quietly, "Is it my turn? Would you help me understand... your parents?"

Ash considered the man before her, and everything her gut was telling her about him. Her own sister's usual caution had been countered by enthusiasm for him, and Ash – well, she could use someone to talk to. Having given Wynn and Grete the distance they deserved, and smarting from an attempted trial, was it so wrong to seek a listener and some understanding?

And so she told him what happened that day.

ASH

Ash had been fifteen. She had been small, flexible, and ever-determined to be central to her family's act.

That day she'd sat curled in a ball, concealed within a box. The lines on the box's exterior suggested to the audience it was smaller than it was in truth. It was because of this deception that the audience gasped as her mother – then blooming in her Pabla la Precisa persona – inserted blade after blade into the box. The swords' wide handles contributed to the illusion too, making the blades appear larger and impossible to avoid. Inside the box, Ash contorted into the shrinking space with exactness until the next stage, when she released a door beneath the entire box and moved into the box's base. This was not a comfortable position, and she could not hold it for long before her muscles would seize, but she need only remain in the restricted space so long as the box's front door above her stood open to reveal the array of criss-crossing blades, winking menacingly. That part always induced a mass exclamation from the gulls. It came to her muffled. After the door closed, Ash could return into the space between the blades, a space that grew as each was withdrawn. Her muscles would scream in relief as she unfurled within the greater space until finally – finally – she could re-emerge unscathed and join her mother for their final bows.

But that day, the swords remained in place. The front door stood open too long – displaying a skewered box without any girl. The girl lay curled in mounting agony beneath it. Waiting. Nearly passing-out.

She heard screams. She could not move – the door was jammed.

It was not until Grete came and hastily withdrew the swords, unjammed the door at the box's base, and held her like a babe – in spasms and harrowed breaths beside her – that Ash learned what had happened.

Accusers had come. And they had taken her parents.

The trial for them had been swift, at least. Or so Grete had said. Grete explained her mother's insistence that her daughter had vanished. To the mob's perfunctory inspection, her words appeared true. This protected Ash from trial, and served as Pabla's confession. She had conspired with All Unknown to commandeer powers reserved only for God, to make such things be.

Alexact – poor Papal – was given the opportunity to denounce his wife, to claim she was the only one so possessed and over-reaching; an opportunity to neatly stand apart from this witch. But he stood at her side, her hand gripped in his, avowing her innocence and her right to perform alongside him with equal deference. This was received hungrily by the mob, voracious in their drive for holy justice.

So it was that Pabla and Alex were dragged to the lake, stripped to their undergarments, bound, and thrown into its depths. Grete had remained hidden – Ash learned her mother had made Grete promise she would, that she would stay safe to be there for Ash – though Grete said she could barely see or breathe through her weeping. She heard her parents' accusers and executioners – for they were one and the same – pronouncing the state of affairs. They asserted that their unclean bodies would be rejected by the lake, showing God was unwilling to allow their immersion and baptism. Should they bob on the surface, they would be pulled back in by a rope to be hanged. If innocent, they would be received by the waters, and sink. Best efforts would be made to pull them back in by the ropes tied about them, but accidents could not be helped.

Grete choked through the visage of her parents' deaths. It was all over in minutes.

She'd pulled the horse and wagon into a position that obscured the deserted stage from the dissolving mob's view, then had seen to liberating Ash.

And there they'd clung to each other until forced by the band and Grete's urging to move on. They'd come in disguise to their own parents' burial. The Mystics understood. No one questioned why. But it had hurt not to speak over their graves.

REN

"He went willingly? He... orphaned you both?" Ren asked. He could feel he was crying, though he didn't remember starting. He didn't wipe the tears away. Instead he looked to Ash, who still looked somewhere over his shoulder, as she had throughout the retelling.

"I have never felt anger for that. He loved her. He loved us. Grete told me they had made it very clear to her, before that day, should the day ever come – where they..." Ash paused to swallow before continuing, "She was to stay, to not leave me alone. Papal knew if he were to stay... he wouldn't be here, not really. And he wasn't sure we could ever forgive him for cowardice... for leaving her to them, all alone." Ash looked at Ren now. "His choice only made my path clearer. Papal believed he deserved the same as his wife; that a woman deserves the same as a man." Ash straightened. "I fight for that now."

Ash waited. Did she want him to move closer? To hold her? He wanted to cup her head in his hands and press his lips to her forehead, gently. He wanted to guide her head to his shoulder, and hold it there, applying pressure that was light, but constant. Ren did none of those things because he did not want her to feel he had taken advantage of her vulnerability.

He said, "You must perform. Hughes is hosting a final, pre-Queen's Day showing on his holding this night, you must get that commendation. You, not with me, not with any man, but you alone. I am sorry now I ever suggested anything else."

"Performing is becoming increasingly challenging. The people that took my parents? It was people like them that took me yesterday."

"I suspected." Ren winced.

"They won't have given up looking for me."

"I know. Is accepting my service as your guard still out of the question… ?"

"Yes. Don't ask again." Ash knew he was concerned for her safety, but she was concerned with the message she sent. She had to achieve this without a man as a shield. "Now to performing – I'll only have one shot. I won't get away with a second. I'll have to make it count."

"You will," Ren said.

Then he reached and squeezed her ankle. Nothing more. A firm squeeze. She frowned.

"Your hair is awfully clean and shiny," she said. "Almost to the point of being rude, considering."

Ren bit his lip. "Thank you… and I am sorry?"

Ash raised her chin as though bestowing a royal edict. "I'll allow it."

"If you win that Seal, it will go a long way toward seeing that you are treated... better."

"*If?*" Ash kicked at him and barked disbelief.

"Well, I *am* still entering... " Ash continued laughing. "If you think telling me this sad story means I will throw this thing, well... " And then Ren laughed. It was sweet and genuine, like a healing balm.

Ash scooted closer to him. "Ren?"

"Yes?"

"Thank you." Ash tucked her hair behind her ear and leaned slowly closer. Ren concentrated on the pulse of the lake inside him, steadied his breaths. She froze, and clarified, "I'm going to hug you now. Don't get your hopes up."

Ren opened his arms to receive her and enfolded her into his chest, where he held her firmly. He concentrated on pouring all of his concern, admiration and hopefulness into that embrace. Each time desire interrupted, he sent it scurrying to the wings and reinstated the former three, centre stage. He wanted Ash to feel what he meant in this hug.

Still in his arms, Ash whispered near his ear. "There will be no throwing of contests."

"I know."

She smiled, he could feel her cheeks lift. Ash seemed to collect herself, conscious of how long they'd been so seated, and made to pull away. Ren immediately released her.

"You asked if you could help?" she said.

"Tell me what I can do that will not detract from your... solo woman's quest."

"Would you deliver a message?"

"To the clumsy one?"

"Yes," she laughed. "And his wife. She is my sister."

"Ah. It makes sense – she is also... " he drew a circle over his whole face, "you know... "

Ash raised an eyebrow and waited.

"You know exactly what you both are."

"I'd like to hear you say it." Ash tilted her head.

"Breath-stealing."

Ash only lost direction for the span of one shot before shaking her head sharply and asking, "Do you have paper hidden in that thing somewhere?" She looked over his vest.

"I have something better."

He presented a playing card, and thereon Ash inked a message to her loved ones. She pressed it into Ren's grip, then squeezed his hand.

"I thank the Mysteries you came this day," she said, her eyes looking into his own. "A messenger and a friend when both were sorely needed."

Ren swallowed the title without complaint. He would give her time.

"So, where is this Lord Hughes' holding?"

Ren was about to answer when an eruption of cries from the north called them both to attention.

"Do you know what that is about?"

Ash's expression soured. "Dawn's Veil gaiety continuing on well past dawn, no doubt." Her sarcasm was thick.

"I did not see you amongst those celebrating. You do not enjoy... Dawn's Veil?"

"There are aspects I enjoy." Ash half- concealed a smile.

"But there are aspects you do not." Ren dipped his head, studying Ash's face.

"Well put." She smiled. "From the volume of those cries... I'd say there's a champion's fight happening inside the city wall."

"There is much day left between now and the showing at Hughes' holding." Friend or not, Ren wanted more time.

"I am meant to be lying low."

"Is that not what this is for?" Holding her gaze, Ren reached out cautiously – as though any rapid moves might startle her – then drew up Ash's hood.

Ash appeared to hold her breath. Interesting.

Ren lowered his hand. "There. Are we not ready to go make the most of this day. Shall we go see a champion?"

Ash shook her head, looked down, and laughed quietly.

Ren added, "I'm sure we can find a fence-line to lurk about."

Ash lifted her eyes to Ren's and it now was his turn to hold his breath. "Sold," she said. "To the man who's not half-bad at throwing a knife."

But the champion's fight was nothing like what Ren hoped it would be. Ash saw his disappointment drag all of his features low. The champion – nominated by the archbishop, it appeared – was a beast. His opponent, a man clearly beaten before combat had begun, was attempting to rise from the ground.

The archbishop, pasty and scoured, was in attendance himself. He sat on a raised dais, a be-ringed hand raised as though conducting the engagement before him.

Ren and Ash watched from a flat-stone roof-top amongst a constellation of mostly cruck housing. The pair lay so still and so low that a multitude of birds needling and scratching in the neighbouring straw thatching continued about their business, undisturbed.

The cries from the mung, pressing in and chanting, drew a signal from the archbishop. He called: "If God shares your will, He will intervene and save you." He addressed the man, crumpled on the earth once more, the church-head's champion towering over him. Spittle bubbled from the mouth of the underdog and mixed with the dirt beneath him. He raised himself to one elbow briefly, then onto both, then worked to stand.

The champion turned slowly, then laughed to see the smaller man's feeble attempts at a return to the fight.

Ren whispered, "How might God intervene?" Both of his eyebrows were raised. His eyes searched Ash's, earnest.

Ash loved Ren's sincerity, laid bare. She tore her gaze away, scanning the scene. Ren did the same.

Ash settled upon one piece of the puzzle, near her third exit. "Are you thinking what I'm thinking?" Ash waited for Ren to catch on, then generously used her head to point towards a clue.

Ren's widest smile bloomed. "I think I am *now.*"

And so it was that a Dawn's Veil attraction turned from appalling disadvantage to mung. Ash and Ren aimed in unison. Their missiles found their marks with precision. An answering murmuration appeared, frightened from their concentrated scratching. Birds in their thousands took flight over the scene, cawing and wheeling over the combatants – a cloud of wings, from the heavens it seemed – suddenly and inexplicably fraught with confusion.

The archbishop's guards raised their shields and escorted their high and mighty guest cowering beneath them to his transport.

Someone dear to the almost-defeated dove beneath the ring's railing and bore the man away.

No one fleeing the scene observed the two Mystics, grinning, elbow-deep in the thatch above.

REN

"So this is not... unusual for you?" Ren asked.

"Not really." Ash plucked a cluster of drupelets from the Elderberry tree where she and Ren perched.

"So you often court suitors in the trees?"

Ash coughed. "I meant it's not unusual for me to have lunch in a tree." She shrugged, "It's easier to be still and wait out passers-by if you're already hidden."

She lobbed another berry across the bough to Ren's perch. He caught it in his mouth, barely. "You can't move!"

"I thought that was going wide... "

"It wasn't."

"I know that *now*."

"I'll explain again. The aim is not that you catch scattershot nesh. The aim is that I meet my target, and that my target not move."

"Got it." The crease that formed as his smile tugged upward made her smile. A compliant target is a good target. Ren parted his mouth, but not wide. His eyes confirmed this was calculated.

"You're finally beginning to understand!" Ash squinted one eye, then threw. Ren held still. Then Ren chewed the berry that had landed on his tongue.

"Do I get a turn?"

"Every throw it's your turn – to be the target."

"You know what I meant."

"Fine." Ash thought of the blade in the card at the fenceline. She opened her mouth... slightly.

Ren aimed, and pitched his juicy missile.

It met Ash's lips at their corner then fell down to the forest litter below.

"You did not catch it."

Ash opened her eyes wide and tipped her head.

"The rules, I remember." Ren ate a berry from the cluster dangling from his hand. "Sorry then. I am at fault."

The juice itched where Ren had left his mark. Ash wanted to lick it away... but Ren was watching her. And she was watching him. And licking anything when your eyes are locked with someone you are attracted to shouted a great deal more than Ash was ready to say.

Ash swiped the mark clean with her thumb as neutrally as she could. But engaged in the persistence of seeing one another, looking... she messed up the speed of it. It was all wrong – the wipe was slow. Her body betrayed her by producing an equally sultry call of attention to her lips. She was so, so glad that two limbs and a bough lay between them then.

She blurted, "I need to go."

"U-huh." It was the first incoherent words Ash had ever heard Ren utter.

"See you tonight." She called up from below, having already dropped from the tree.

"Ya... I will... get that message to your kin."

She was already gone.

REN

Ren knocked. And knocked again. After the second effort rendered no response, he took a step back, searching for signs anyone was in. Whistling came from beyond the house. Though it lacked propriety, he moved side-long toward the wall in an attempt to view behind the dwelling. He'd not alternated between running on foot and lurching along in the back of an offal cart without sleep to simply turn around and repeat the same journey *and* report failure. To Ash.

Ash. She'd asked for his help.

A table sat beside the house. Upon it, a stack of upturned crates and signs lay face-down. Ren rapped upon the table. The whistling stopped. A woman, like but unlike Ash, stepped into view. Her clumsy husband appeared like an inflated, comical shadow leaning at precisely the same angle as his wife. Ren concealed his amusement.

Wynn called, "Apologies, unmet – sold out – all that's ripe, anyway. Y've got to be in early for Queen's Day."

"Nay, not unmet. It is Ren. I was sent... " Ren paused, not wanting even to say her name.

"Ren!" Wynn wiped his hands upon his thighs, then beckoned. "Come! Come!"

Ren made his way to the back door and followed the couple inside. They three sat around a circular table in the Appleby kitchen.

Now introduced, Ren numbered Grete's willingness to make an unabashed study of him amongst the like traits between the sisters. Grete knew Ren could see her looking, and she made no apology for it. She took in his garments, his hair, his posture, and his face. Closely. Her hesitancy to give away anything about herself made her examination of Ren all the more bold.

Wynn was watching his wife, shaking his head with his arms crossed. "Are you finished?" he asked.

Grete ignored the question. "So this is the one."

"The one?" Ren quirked one brow.

"How does she fare and why should we believe you?"

Ren added suspicion to his like-traits count. He thought better of explaining; he should move to the prestige instead. And so he produced the card and message Ash had sent for her kin.

Grete's resolute carriage crumpled as she took it up in her hands, read it, re-read it, and held it to her breast.

"I'll read it later then," said Wynn.

"Sorry, my love." Grete pressed the card into Wynn's hands and squeezed them. She turned back to Ren while Wynn read the message. "Ren. Thank you for bringing us word. We'd heard of her Accusation and her holding... and escape... and twice they've come looking for her here." Wynn reached over and gripped her knee at that. "We weren't sure what to think."

"She fares well." Ren offered a weak smile. "Though I worry, naturally." Ren shrugged.

"Oh you do, do you?" Grete said with a smile. Ren numbered a further match. That smile – now granted reign upon her features, had the effect of stunning the people who bore its intensity front-on.

"To know her is to fear for her," Ren answered.

Wynn frowned. "Y'mean to know her is to fear *her*." Wynn choked out a laugh. "She's no small power to be reckoned with."

Grete elbowed Wynn. A fourth similarity.

"I agree." Ren nodded. "One cannot spend long with Ash without deeming her unstoppable."

"You are proving a disappointment." Grete acted as though one of her hangnails required her urgent attention.

"Forgive me... ? Have I offended thee?" Ren leaned forward, his hand on his chest.

"I liked you better speaking reason. We should all fear for her. She's not unassailable!"

Wynn said, "Pay no heed to Grete, she hoped you'd distract Ash from her 'purpose' – or find her a new one – not seek to propel her or cheer her onward to… "

"Peril? Danger? Ruin? Calamity? Tragedy? Please Wynn, how *would* you finish that sentence?" Grete's eyebrows were high.

"The Seal. I was going to say the Seal," Wynn finished.

"I think there is little chance of anyone dissuading Ash from something she has set her sights upon," Ren said.

Grete's expression changed. She squinted, and studied Ren anew. "Well, stay for supper and get back to her. Failing a diversion," she shook her head, "I'd have her accompanied by an ally."

Grete stood and moved to the kitchen. Wynn raised the card Ren had delivered. "Our thanks, for this." He looked down at the message. "You didn't bear insult by it, I hope?"

Ren tipped his head sideways, not understanding.

Wynn waved the card. "The message. You didn't bear any insult by her message… " Wynn's eyes opened wide. "You didn't read it!"

Grete turned from the kitchen.

Ren looked between them, confused.

"You brought this some distance – we assume, as Ash would not bring danger anywhere near us by staying close by – and you never thought to read what you were going to such lengths to deliver?" asked Grete.

"The message was not intended for me." Ren was at a loss.

"Give it to him." Grete urged Wynn at his shoulder with a tap from the back of her hand.

Wynn slid the card across the table, message-side up.

> *You can trust him,*
> *even though his speech and dress are odd.*
> *I am close yet far.*
> *To It and to you.*
> *I'm sorry.*

Then smaller, crammed in at the bottom:

> *Call her Pabla, won't you?*

Ren looked up, sunny.

"So not offended then... " Wynn led.

He knew, by her entrusting him with visiting those she loved, that he had earned some measure of Ash's trust, but to read her endorsement in her hasty hand somehow sharpened the outlines of the shape of what was between them. Trust, for a beginning.

"I thought because she calls your clothes and talk odd maybe... "

Ren ignored Wynn's sympathies, asking instead, "Call whom, Pabla?"

Grete and Wynn looked at each other.

"Pabla was our mother," Grete answered, then rested her hand on her abdomen. "Ash is suggesting I name the baby after our mother."

Ren bowed in his seat. "I did not know. May the Mysteries untold share your will."

Wynn nodded in thanks.

Grete continued. "Ash always worshipped our mapa. Everyone did. But Ash – she was more blind to danger and more reckless than Mapa ever was. Mapa and Papal devoted hefty amounts of coin to fine mail underclothing, avoided the places in a person where blood flows like a river instead of a stream," Grete gripped her own neck, then looked down at her thigh. "They embedded magnets to draw the knives in their back boards, and even within a few trees around the Lough," Grete paused to laugh here, looking up at the memory, "That way they could agree to a spontaneous showing of 'unrigged' skill, without a stage – or so it seemed. There were always safeties in their acts. They were smart. They prized each other above all else."

"I wish I had met them." Ren spoke sincerely.

Grete nodded.

"Ash always pushed the boundaries. And after they were gone... it only got worse. Her risks are some twisted mix of punishing herself... and helping herself feel alive."

"And of brilliance?" Ren added.

Grete laughed, though tears reflected the setting sun's light from outside. "And brilliance, yes. She was… is… brilliant. I've never been able to develop a taste for a war of admiration and terror in my belly." Grete lifted her chin. Ren understood then why Wynn attended Ash's shows, and Grete did not. He imagined it also served as a way Grete could send an ally in her own absence… as she intended to allow with him. "She's chosen her path, and I've accepted it. I simply cannot watch."

Ren took a deep breath in understanding. "My father always told me that not hindering those who seek change is still being party to the change. He meant it as a threat, at the time, but in your case, I believe it is a tribute."

Grete tilted her head. Ren did not so much as twitch under her appraisal.

"And my mother told me, the most powerful messages are inscribed in fire upon one's soul." Grete responded. "I hold the fire, but temper it. Because I must."

"Ash does not."

"She does not." Grete's cheeks lifted and went tight as she smiled and shrugged.

Ren marvelled. Ash did not tackle life's challenges as her family would, but they respected that. Nay, even loved Ash for it. Even if that divergence in their ways meant a sleepless night here and there. Even if it meant only morsels of news carried to them by way of male Mystic-messenger. He was honoured to serve such a family.

ASH

It was clear this man Hughes was a luminary – even the children in the streets had been whispering his name that day. Hughes had built an outdoor amphitheatre on his holding, modelled after something the lord had seen on a far southern coast, according to a free-speaking veneur close by. Instead of elevating performers above the gulls, Hughes had built a grand, cone-shaped gallery for the gulls to fill the hills surrounding the stage. It was a far cry from the hay Ash had last seen Ren atop, although he'd been magnificent to behold on that hay.

Lord Hughes himself sat in prime position, on an upholstered chair brought out from the manor. Ash was familiar with the lavish proclivities of the north. She was returning to the place where she and her parents had performed most, after all.

Before.

Her hood was up. She had everything she needed to perform when the opportunity came – herself –

and yet, as she took personal inventory each time she came up short. Ash attended shows alone much more often than Grete approved of, but Wynn's persistent vacancy left her side cold. She needed no man, she knew, but she needed a friend. She needed family. What was victory without them?

This led her to thinking of Ren – who'd magnanimously agreed to take a message to her kin earlier that day. Whose lips she'd watched as she'd stroked her own clean.

She didn't *need* him here either.

But she hoped he would return from the errand in time. She'd cleaned herself up in the hopes he would. But if he didn't, no matter – there'd be plenty of time for sweet-smelling reunions *after* Queen's Day. In fact, they'd be better then. Safer.

The night was crisp, the stars sharp and approving.

A red-headed minnesinger from the eastern side of the Lough had serenaded Lady Hughes and – with the lord's approval – the poet had stood and bowed before the Lord and Lady, and even taken the latter's hand to his lips. Ash was glad she'd washed, abruptly conscious of her own skin. Although she felt no attraction for the Lord, his confidence aroused some sentiment in her. The Lord himself appeared jovial and easily given to laughter, and completely unthreatened by others' charms. She suspected he'd commended many jesters to the queen's court. But he'd also commended Ren.

After the ballad and subsequent amorous display, a troubadour took the stage. He cast his voice up and into the stand, setting a narrative scene of chivalry and adventure. Lady Hughes was captivated, and her lord squeezed her hand affectionately. Ash smiled at this display. Perhaps Lord Hughes was a kind man, although Ash realised she cared more that he be an astute and fair one.

Some of the gulls held sticks with knotted ribbons overhead. These bore colours from the Hughes' coat of arms. Ash had declined purchasing her own on her way onto the estate, though she appreciated the festivity they lent the occasion and how they marked the Hughes' support. There was no forgetting whose generosity afforded this night, but neither was there room to resent them for it – they seemed... sweet. Ash was smiling still at the marital fondness and fluttering ribbons when Ren appeared at the side of her least favoured exit (of five avenues worth counting).

"You took your time," Ash spoke through her smile.

"I gave my time. It is different." Ren followed Ash's gaze, his voice low.

Ash dropped her shield of indifference. "They are well?"

"They are well. Although they worry still." Ren looked to her.

She looked back, offering a grim smile. "I believe that." Though chary to touch Ren again so soon, she dismissed her hesitation and squeezed Ren's shoulder. "But I'll not let them take me again." She turned her eyes back to the troubadour. "And if they do, I'll be ready." She counted her exits again, then ran her finger over a fishhook sewn into the hem of her undergarment sleeve. After Ren had left on her errand – for which a shoulder-squeeze was hardly enough thanks, she knew – Ash had returned to the docks. Ren's revelatory demonstration under the tree canopy that morning had given her an idea – six blades, concealed well.

Ash knew three changes her captors would make should they succeed in taking her again: they would not leave her unguarded, they would disarm her, and her trial would be forthwith, and more severe.

And so she planned to carry her blade still, ripe for the plucking. The fish hook newly-obtained – and the sharpest she could find – was invisible to the untrained eye and within easy grasp inside the sleeve finishing at her forearm. Beyond that, she'd work with whatever she could lay her hands upon to help her.

The better plan was not being caught.

Ash noted one of her exit routes was now obscured by a couple who stood in the aisle, giving coin for a stick and ribbon. She saw Ren smile with understanding.

"They will sit soon enough, the way is still good."

Ash smiled, incredulous. She was glad Ren had come. And just in time, for the chivalrous knight of the troubadour's tale had vanquished a sea serpent spewed from the Unknown and returned with a necklace of scales for his lady waiting on distant shores. Typical. But on with it, for Collier had been announced next by a guildsman acting as master of the night's ceremony. The couple sat again, suitably armed with sticks and ribbons, which Ren confirmed with a nudge and a nod.

"I saw, I saw." Then Ash clenched her jaw. She'd just seen Hallam and Peony in the audience near the now-seated couple, and further along, two men who'd twice let her hitch a ride on their wagon to SeeBurg when they'd made their delivery of swede. She scanned further, both happy and sorry to see Mave too – the candlemaker who'd checked the chambers of Ash's gun at her last showing. The woman had called her "Miss" and claimed Ash had made her suffer with worry for Ash's safety. Mave waved a ribbon on a stick. The northern migration for Queen's Day had begun. It meant fewer unmets to win over, but more gulls who'd know her well enough to alert the basilica of her reappearance. She'd have to trust the witching hour was enough to deter any true zealots from attending such a showing. She'd be making a fast exit at her show's end, she knew that much.

Ash drew her hood further forward. "Where's this Collier?"

She quietly fingered the hook in her hem once more, then chided herself and shifted to smoothing her cloak along its embroidered hem. She wished she were next and not after this newcomer. She knew little of him. He'd come from abroad – by sea, it was told – and brought with him unseen Mysteries. She was yet to verify that rumour. Ren had said he was good, though he leaned towards excess. Ash thought of Banyan and his ridiculous gun. She missed hers, even if it was of little use with an assailing mob.

Collier was announced again. Ash stood taller.

Collier took the stage with a retinue: a man a head smaller than him, and a boy. The boy carried two tables on to the stage, one at a time. Collier stood centre-stage, his arms spread wide, his sleeves fluted and billowing with his movements. He spun slowly, as though drawing in energy from the crowd. His eyes were unusually light like his fair hair and brows. His jaw was square, but very close-shaven – Ash could detect no shadow. It bespoke wealth.

"My friends, of the North!" Ribbons danced in reply. "This night I invite All Untold to attend us, and allow you the privilege of seeing Mysteries' hand." He had an accent. *Friends.* Ha! Misguided and presumptuous if ever she'd heard a crowd wooed.

Ash looked to Ren, who, feeling her eyes on him, rolled his own and blew out some air. She responded with silent laughter, her pursed lips the only clue, the shudder of her stomach concealed by her beloved cloak.

"First, my friends, I invite you to examine this table. Come – see it is ordinary in every way." Collier looked over the audience, and beckoned to Lady Hughes. The lady checked with her husband and, gaining his approval, was led on the arm of Collier's assistant to the stage. There she walked around the table, even ducking to look beneath it.

"What do you see, m'lady?" Collier loudly asked Lady Hughes. His sleeves gaped deep and dark as he motioned towards the table.

"But only a table, sir." Lady Hughes clutched some sort of fan to her chest.

"Thank you, Lady Hughes. You may return to the good Lord."

Ash wanted to gag. The man's fawning over the gulls knew no bounds. "Come now, man, win them with your talent, not your words." she whispered. He'd made his pledge well – yes, all can see the ordinary thing (that probably isn't ordinary) – what magic will you work?

Ren gave her a gentle nudge, but he was smiling.

Collier drew a long black square of cloth from one of his generous sleeves and flicked it through the air with a snap. He then stretched and waved it until it fell neatly over the table. Looking sideways at the table, he snapped his fingers as though a thought had just occurred to him. His assistant instantly appeared with a vase, which he placed on the table. Collier then flashed his voluminous sleeve before the vase to reveal the vase suddenly filled with flowers. He stood back, appearing more satisfied with the table so adorned. He received only quiet applause, which was fair, for it had been mere sleight of hand.

Ash readied herself for the turn; Collier now would do what all Illusionists did – take the ordinary thing and make it do something extraordinary. Well, make it *seem* to at least.

And so he did. With sleeves that almost reached the ground themselves, Collier bent down and gently lifted the cloth by its corners. He raised the tips of the fabric to show the audience empty space beneath the table and emphasise its ordinary appearance. "Now friends, I invite All Untold to attend." And while Collier still held the corners of the black cloth in a soft cradle between his fingers and the table-top, the table rose. It appeared to float at Collier's knees. He dipped one toe then the other beneath it, to show no apparatus held it aloft.

Gasps came from the audience. The sign of the basilica was drawn across more than one pair of eyes. Ash modified her exits accordingly – she'd not leave past one of *those*. The table levitated higher still, and then, it was as if it danced, and Collier merely held it by its skirt. It moved left and right. The odd delighted clap or cheer came from the audience, but most craned necks and clasped hands in silent fascination. He had them. She could see he had them. But! He had yet to deliver the third act of this table trick; the prestige. The table dance was one thing, but now – even though the gulls wanted to believe it was not – Collier had to prove it was still an ordinary table beneath that black cloth.

And so he did. With another flaunt-filled motion, the covering was torn away – the vase along with it – and the vase and cloth vanished to reveal that a table remained; an ordinary table, motionless and at rest on Hughes' stage.

Lofty whistles and hoots harmonised with the rumbling applause that followed. Collier bowed deeply. Lady Hughes alternated between genteel clapping and waving her fan towards Collier.

"My friends, I seem to have misplaced my tablecloth!" Collier called over the gulls. He levelled a hand over his eyes as though scanning them. "Have you seen it?"

No, he didn't.

He did!

A hiccup of surprise came from Lady Hughes, who stood up and turned to check in her seat. There, beneath her, lay fabric black and neatly folded. She made an exclamation before drawing it up. "It is here, Sir Collier, it is here!" She waved it above her.

"M'lady, I thank you! You don't also have my flowers, perchance?"

Then Lord Hughes rose – having also made a discovery. He pulled a bouquet of flowers (greatly *resembling* those just seen on the stage) from the back of his seat.

"They are yours, m'lady, care of Lord Hughes," Collier called to his hostess.

With a small bow, Lord Hughes presented his wife with the flowers. She clutched them with her fan as she took her seat.

Transportation. He'd followed levitation with transportation.

Collier sure knew how to work a crowd.

Ash could see from Lord Hughes' expression that Collier also knew how to work a lord. He would be leaving with a commendation, assuredly.

It appeared Collier would not even have to wait until night's end – Hughes raised a hand to signal the guildsman who'd been announcing each act. Hughes spoke into the guildsman's ear, who drew up and gave a curt nod. He returned to the stage and held his arm towards Collier while addressing the audience.

"And what think ye of The Luminous Collier?" The guildsman held both hands cupped to his ears. The crowd answered with a cheer and a flurry of waved ribbons. "The Lord Hughes agrees! The Luminous Collier is thus awarded a commendation to perform for the queen, may it be recorded and sent forthwith."

It was that simple. Collier had taken to the stage – with a modified table, ridiculous sleeves and the help of a cunning pawn in his employ (who'd placed the identical cloth and flowers behind their marks) – wooed them, and left having confirmed a commendation was received.

He'd made it look simple.

Ash whispered to Ren, "If Hughes likes *him,* I'm not so sure he'll like *me.*"

Ren squeezed her shoulder much like she had his earlier. "He will. He will see you and that you are without these... trappings and tricks... that you are Ash the Unflinching – without illusion, but Mystical no less."

Ren seemed certain, and Ash liked that very much. Enough that she almost lost track of her modified exits. She turned back to them, checking them each in turn.

"If you're wrong, I'll find a way to make this your fault," she replied.

"I am not wrong." He tightened his grip on her shoulder before releasing it, then looked back to the guildsman, who was readying to make an announcement – his arms calling for the crowd to quieten.

"Ash?"

"Ya?"

"In case I do not see you after... "

"What do you mean?"

"You know exactly what I mean," he said. She smiled. *"Because I will not see you after*, I will ask now. Will you meet me three jetties north of Hughes' own, tomorrow, at sunset?" Ren was right, he would *not* see Ash after – no one would. She wouldn't stay to confirm the commendation personally. She knew, if it was given, it would be sent "forthwith" anyway. It did not depend on her hearing it – and now – her swallow moved scabs at her throat – was no time to start dallying after showings. It had never been her way. It came as a fine windfall that she'd confirmed there were familiars present who would likely explain exactly that upon her departure: *That is always how a showing by Ash the Unflinching ends, Lord – with vanishing!*

The guildsman was announcing The Unflinching Ash.

He was announcing *her*.

Ash turned to the man beside her, Besuto Ren to all of them; *Ren*, to her. A man who had delivered a message for her to Grete and Wynn. A man who'd told her of this opportunity. A man who even now caused no small degree of swooning. He was asking her to commit to a meeting place when she was making no small amount of a point to be scarce. A meeting that could well be a trap, if she had read him wrong.

But the message delivery. The ankle squeeze in the woods. The sincerity.

She had not misread him.

And what cause would he have to endanger her?

Ash trusted her instincts, and they spoke well of Ren.

Ren frowned intently, and repeated. "Will you?"

"I will."

"May the Mysteries untold share your will."

She smiled in answer, then left for the stage.

The guildsman had to repeat his announcement. This time Ash paid less attention to Ren and more to her audience, and so heard the crowd's answer: they cheered.

The gulls were cheering for The Unflinching Ash to perform. Someone near the front must've noticed her approach and drawn attention to it, since the audience began to turn towards her as she made her way to the stage. She lowered her hood to reveal her face, her hair hanging loose and unfettered. She drank in the wave of hushed conjecture and awe.

I am her.

Hallam, Peony and Mave waved at her – each in ways suited to their sensibilities, but each waving just the same. Ash nodded in acknowledgement after she ascended the stairs.

Ash the Unflinching removed her cloak, balled it, and threw it to the side of the stage. She received a few chuckles for that. Although she'd slept in them, time in the lake meant her grey-blue dress and leather girdle were clean at the least. Some in the audience were obviously new to her shows, for sounds of shock echoed all around. Her clothing hugged her frame some, it was true. Ash gave their judgement little thought. It was an important element of her performance; she wasn't hiding anything up her sleeves – which as always, finished mid-forearm. Several women in the crowd covered their husband's eyes, while they meanwhile continued ogling Ash themselves. Ash *was* glorious. And she owned that stage – every stage – without assistance, without carried-on furniture, alone.

She tucked her hair behind her ears and began as she always did: "Welcome, discerning defendants of the Mysteries that be. Before we begin, let's get to know some of *you* better – after all, without you we would be without a show this night."

She counted her exits. She took in the tells. She confirmed her chief mark. She'd seen enough of Lady Hughes already to know she reached for her husband's hand when worried, and that she waved her fan when she felt some guilt. Lady Hughes did neither now, so at ease was she, in her prime position with Collier's bouquet in her lap.

"Tell me, who here works the farms for the good Lord Hughes?" Ash raised her dark eyebrows. She smiled with her mouth slightly parted, inviting, anticipating raised hands. Her teeth gleamed. Hands raised throughout the crowd – more than she'd expected – suggesting he was a good lord indeed for allowing so many of his workers time off-duty. Ash committed three of these workers to memory – a burly man, a man hunched over, and a woman close beside the second. Ash had seen the freshly-mowed lawns on her approach to Hughes' showing. There was at least one scythe on this holding, and her coin was on these three for knowing where it lay.

"For my show this night, I require a tool both sharp and long – the sharper the better – and I believe I know who can supply it. And better still, the supplier will confirm the tool is not my own and has never before been seen by me."

There. The burly man shifted his weight and the woman nudged her husband with her knee. Ash was right about those three. She jumped from the stage and landed with casual finesse in a crouch. In a few strides she drew near the workers she'd marked.

"You two – you know of just the tool," Ash pointed to Burly and Hunched. Both men's eyes went wide; the wife folded her arms. "You know best though, don't you?" Ash tipped her head to the wife.

She received some cheers and the odd clap from the crowd looking on. "I do, for he asked me to sharpen it!" The woman elbowed her husband in the ribs. He doubled over with a smile and a wince, then squeezed his wife around the shoulders.

"That I did, just for today m'Lord, my back ached at day's end!" The hunched-over husband called apologetically towards Hughes, who waved dismissively in reply. Ash was grateful she hadn't gotten her marks in trouble. "And I love her for helping me," Hunch added, then squeezed his wife into his side before nodding towards Burly. "Tolm, you fetch it."

Tolm glanced briefly to receive Lord Hughes' approval, then took off at a jog.

"Thank you, Tolm." Ash called. She continued to speak as she walked backwards, towards her place centre stage, a place that was hers to claim. "Now,

I'm in need of dark fabric. Fabric you all trust I have not tampered with in any way. Where might I find... ?" Ash tapped her lips with a single finger in jest.

Lady Hughes chirped in answer, holding the black tablecloth from Collier's earlier act aloft. "Will this do?"

"Yes, Lady Hughes, it will. If you don't mind what becomes of it?"

"No, please take it!"

Ash did not wait for the guildsman or any waitstaff from the Hughes household to serve her. She again alighted from the stage, ascended to Lady Hughes and accepted the black fabric with a masculine bow. Ash returned to the stage in a few bounds, her breath unchanged for it. She turned the fabric this way and that – allowing the audience to observe it was simply black cloth, still. Her pledge was genuine, for the cloth truly was an ordinary thing, and not even *her* thing.

Ash told herself to forget Ren was there, though she wanted to look to him. She would love to see his smile. Now, anytime, or always – she couldn't decide which. But more than that wanting, she wanted to make clear she was doing all of this alone. So she did not look.

Ash drew out her knife and poked a small hole near the edge of the black cloth. Then she tore, hard, rending it in a long straight line until she had two pieces of cloth. The fabric gave way freely – a wonderful gratuity. She repeated the process twice more, until she had four black squares, which she held up for the audience's inspection.

It was then that Tolm returned from his errand, *his* breath changed for it, carrying a scythe.

Excellent.

He brought it to the edge of the stage, which came to his chest. "Will this do?" he asked, holding it up for Ash's scrutiny.

"Is this the scythe you sharpened?" Ash called back to the wife.

"The very same! It's sharper than a knight's blade, that."

"And I've not spoken with you before this night?"

"I've not met you before. It's my first show!" the woman called back, loose grey hairs beside her face swinging with her enthusiasm.

"Then yes, Tolm, this will do. Thank you, again."

Tolm nodded and returned to his place near the older couple.

Ash was especially pleased that this scythe blade was near dead-straight and was attached by a metal cuff to its wooden handle, the cuff secured by a bolt. She still held her blade in one hand, and four squares of black in the other. She placed the squares over her shoulder like a mother might lay a burp-cloth. She gathered up the scythe, positioning the long wooden handle between her knees so that the blade was out in front of her. She then pulled forward a lock of her hair and cut it near its base with her knife. A few ladies gasped – which made Ash smile – they'd seen nothing yet. Ash sheathed her blade, raised the lock of dark, lush hair with two hands, stretching it between her fingers to form a line at parallel to the stage.

"I don't doubt your word, but for the audience…" Ash then released her hair from high above the blade, so that the hair came down at right angles with some speed across the scythe's sharpened edge.

The lock of hair fell either side of the tool, severed soundlessly into two lifeless clumps on the stage.

"Your name?" Ash called to the wife.

"Eilsa!" she called back.

"Defendants of the Mysteries, please, give Eilsa a round of applause – her work is *very good*." Ash led by example, her hands aloft. She permitted herself a glance at Ren. He was clapping, and his handsome smile was a fan to the determined fire inside her.

"Let us not forget Eilsa's husband, who was truly wise to enlist the help of one whose work is very good!" The crowd laughed and jostled each other, including Lord Hughes. Ash took it all in, studying Tolm, Eilsa and Lady Hughes foremost.

"Now, I won't require all of… this," Ash waved her hand along the length of the scythe's handle. She pulled the blade closer, drew out her knife, and used it sideways to loosen the bolt securing the metal blade at its head to the wooden handle. Expertly, she slid the entire attachment from its lever and placed the blade alone upon the stage.

"We'll come to that later. Now, who here will bestow upon me the generous gift of a stick and ribbon?" Ash's mouth parted slightly again as she scanned the crowd. "I need only three." She winked and held up three fingers. At least thirty sticks and ribbons waved in offering. "You'll not get them back, I warn you." A few offering arms were lowered, but most remained. And two more were raised, apparently more interested now they knew the stakes.

Ash descended and collected three sticks and ribbons in donation.

"Now we have the makings for a show!" Ash's teeth, her skin, her well-proportioned cheekbones, the sparkles within her eyes – clean, hiding nothing, and lovely. Ash looked back to the burly retriever. "If you will, Tolm, I ask for your help?"

He stepped forward, chest to stage's edge.

"I suspect... " Ash began, then crouched to the stage, "it is possible we might... " Ash stuck a stick and ribbon in a gap between the stage boards so that it stood like a small flagpole. She gave it a light tap so that it wedged firmly into place. "Yes, we can!" Ash stood and made a flourish above the stick and ribbon. "Isn't it lovely?" The crowd laughed mildly, some still unsure. "You're right, that's hardly impressive." Ash pulled a square of black fabric from her shoulder and draped it over the stick, forming a small, tented dark mass. "Better?" Ash called up into the stands. More uncertain laughter. "I'll get to the point."

Lord Hughes leaned forward, squinting. She still deemed him kind – and *curious,* which was even better.

"Tolm, would you balance this scythe-blade on its end?" Ash carefully retrieved the metal attachment removed from its handle and gave it to Tolm. He did as he was instructed, so the scythe sat facing sharp end up, beside the tented stick. Ash adjusted the height of the stick beside it so that it matched the height of the scythe's blade more closely. Then Ash took another piece of black fabric, and slowly, gently lowered it over the scythe – it was only in the precise positioning of the blade and the slow covering of its sharp point that the fabric might resemble the tented stick, and not cut through. She stood.

"Now, we all know which is which... " Ash motioned towards the two concealed objects. "But do they look the same?" Ash raised her eyebrows and spread her arms out as if to embrace the gulls. She closed her hands as though catching the nods offered in answer. "Agreed." Ash swiftly removed the fabric from the stick and ribbon to reveal... the same stick and ribbon.

Many in the audience had leaned forward in anticipation, only to melt back into their seats in disappointment. Ash laughed, "Oh no, they're still where we left them. But we're not through." Ash stood, pulled the remaining two squares of fabric from her shoulder, and handed them to Tolm. Then she handed him the remaining three sticks with ribbons. "Tolm, please arrange these sticks and this scythe beneath these pieces of cloth, all in a row, while my back is turned. Tell me when you are done."

Tolm shifted his weight on his feet before taking the items.

Ash moved to the back of the stage. She spread her legs in a strong pose, folded her arms, then motioned a "go ahead" with one hand above her head.

Tolm went ahead.

The crowd waited, many murmuring, all looking on. Ash heard Tolm's feet shuffle the length of the stage, but saw nothing as Tolm adjusted the heights of the sticks.

Without turning, Ash called back, "Lady Hughes, are you satisfied I have not seen where the scythe is hidden?"

"Yes!" Lady Hughes called back, somewhat discomfited by raising her voice, but her cadence suggested some part of her thrilled to be included in the show.

"And Lady Hughes, are you satisfied the sticks and scythe look the same beneath the fabric you so kindly gave me?"

"Yes again!" Lady Hughes was growing bolder.

"They're ready Tolm?" Ash asked.

"Ya." Tolm answered.

Ash turned. Tolm had done well.

Four small black tents lay in a straight line across the front of the stage. It was impossible to tell from looking at them which lay concealed a sharpened blade and which housed mere twigs.

"Excellent arrangement, Tolm. It seems I can't stop thanking you." Ash gave a small curtsy, sending a blush fierce and bright to Tolm's cheeks. Bless him.

"I ask all of you now: would it be worse for a Mystic to lose a hand, or a foot?" Ash asked the crowd.

Cries came for both, but more called "hand!"

"What is the verdict, Lord Hughes? Which has the vote of your guests?"

"A hand" he called. "To lose a hand would be worse."

"My hand it is. On the count of three, I will smash three of the little tents Tolm has kindly made, and smash them as level to the stage as I can, with all the strength that I have. With my precious, Mystical hand." Ash raised a hand high, wiggled her fingers, and beamed.

Lady Hughes reached for Lord Hughes' hand.

Eilsa, eyes wide, shook her head slowly.

Tolm wrung his own hands.

Ash approached the suddenly chilling array and crouched to stage left. Stage left was the side closest to where Tolm and his fellow workers stood. It was the least likely place for the scythe. Gulls rarely chose the edges, always favouring the middle as more "hidden." Ash raised her hand above the tent at the end, looked into the eyes of many in the front row, catching a small exhale from Lady Hughes – who now clasped both her hands in her lap.

Ash slammed her hand down on the concealed object beneath.

It hurt, for sure, but beneath the fabric a stick snapped, and a crumpled heap of matter no taller than a coin purse remained.

"Thank you, Tolm, for not placing the scythe there." Ash nodded, but resisted a wink in light of the man's recent blush.

Ash rubbed at her palm, where a red welt now lay. It was nothing to whine about.

"Is it… ?" Ash hovered her hand atop the remaining three tents in turn, watching her marks, three. They were fighting their tells, not wanting to give her fodder, but failing. For Ash saw it well enough – Lady Hughes' clasped hands fluttered as Ash hovered over the third in the row – she didn't give in to reaching again for her husband, but she'd fought the urge to do so… and on the third item. As Ash drew back across the suspected scythe, Eilsa gave an almost imperceptible nod, and Tolm rubbed his fingers against his palms, as though sweaty. That was enough for Ash. Ash drew back her hand. The scythe was in the middle of the three objects still standing, she'd stake her hand on it. Literally.

"Tolm!" Ash called to him. "One last thing?" She went to the stage's edge and drew up her balled cape. She put it on, came to the very edge of the stage, and spread her arms wide, allowing her cape to form a wall obscuring the object line-up from view. "Switch them, will you, Tolm? So *only* you know where the scythe rests." Lady Hughes gave in to the urge and reached for Lord Hughes' hand.

"Please, will you all make some noise?" Ash called up to the stands. The crowd answered with hoots, whistles and applause. Some stamped, others beat on their laps like drums. As a group, they easily obscured the sounds of Tolm behind her.

With her arms still outstretched and holding fast to her cloak as a barrier, Ash opened one hand as though it said "ho!" – calling for quiet. The cacophony subsided.

"Tolm? Are you ready?" she asked.

"I am."

Ash lowered her cloak. She stepped to the side to reveal the three tents. They appeared much the same. But Ash doubted that. Tolm's need for Lord Hughes' approval earlier and swiftness to follow Hunch's order – all without complaint – pointed towards compliance, and she found nothing to suggest him devious, from his visage.

He'd moved the scythe, which meant it was no longer in third position from her starting place (which would make it the middle of the three that remained). It now stood at either end, she was *almost* certain.

She only had one mark to rely upon to ascertain *which* end.

She was not afraid.

"Alright, shall we try this again?" Ash reproduced the exact same posture – her hand hovered above the object now concealed closest to Tolm and the workers (again the least likely position, for most gulls, without centre as an option, instinctively placed weapons and danger further from themselves).

Ash feigned interest only in Lady Hughes, but she watched Tolm at her left. Tolm gave the smallest, infinitesimal smile – barely a smile, unless you were looking for it – his cast serious.

But Ash saw.

The crowd was leaning towards her – she had them. Lady Hughes, Ash couldn't help but observe, was a wreck. She clutched her chest and husband's hand both. Lord Hughes gripped her hand back.

Ash slammed her hand down towards the stage.

The stick and ribbon cracked beneath the cloth. Her hand smarted and bled readily, but was not pierced-through by the show-toy beneath.

Ash was met with loud applause. Lord Hughes even stood.

Ash had not flinched. Not even infinitesimally.

"We're not done yet!" Ash called. Lord Hughes slowly sat, his own hand stretched behind him to guide him into his chair so he needn't turn away from the performance.

Ash brought her hand to what had been the middle of the three hidden objects. She held it there, flat and still. She watched Lord Hughes this time, or seemed to, but instead took in all of Tolm, stage left. He was perfectly still. Perfectly. She moved her hand up and down slightly, hoping for his micro-smile to return. It didn't come. Neither did his shifting of weight. Interesting. Ash reconsidered her confidence he *had* moved the scythe from its original position and added it to her certainty that his weight shift was his truest tell. Without further thought, and with the collective drawn-breath of a Lord's holding-full of guests, Ash sent her palm smashing down on the second-to-last little tent.

Crack.

Wood.

Ribbon.

Victory.

The crowd gave their applause. A whistle through fingers from Ren. But she knew a further surge in appreciation was still to come. Ash moved her hand – swiping it once across her side to remove the blood – then over to the final tent. The laughter and applause ceased. Ash lowered her hand closer, then gently pulled – much like Collier had – on the very edge of the black cloth covering the final object. She pulled downwards just enough that the scythe cut cleanly through to reveal itself, glistening by torchlight. A torn quarter of Collier's black fabric fell like a funeral shroud to pool around the tool.

"Your handiwork, Eilsa." Ash framed the scythe-head with her two hands. Applause for Eilsa. Then Ash stood and held her hands out in front of her as though in offering to the crowd. "And here mine," Ash looked to her two hands, one red, weeping and hot, but without permanent impairment.

Applause for her.

She jumped once more from the stage, made a bow towards the Lord and Lady of the estate, and then with a raised hood and a gull's blink... she was gone.

Tolm, Eilsa and husband, guildsman, and two household staff were asked to find her – Lord Hughes instructed them to bring her back to the stage so he could be sure she would hear his verdict.

But The Unflinching Ash could not be found anywhere among the sticks and ribbons. Whispers spread news of her absence, then remarks of wonder for it.

Well, most whispered.

From a peregrine stranger on the fringe, stage-right, came a quiet but deep and affectionate laugh.

ODELL

Odell had sent the letter to Archbishop Fulton. Yet reports continued of the brazen girl. Nicholas Baker had even posted a sign upon his door: "All served within." Well, everyone knew what that meant, and many patrons frequented the bakery nonetheless. Forscamien!

There were whispers too, amongst the Seeker's informers, that the girl had even received a commendation – a Lord and Lady had actually recommended the girl appear before the queen – for being unapologetically in opposition with faith in the church and its sovereign. If Odell's father were alive, he would be appalled.

And while she waited for action, Odell's hallucinations only grew more vivid, more insistent.

She would have to rally the people of SeeBurg then.

The girl had left her no choice.

REN

Ren's body ran; his soul lingered.

It was as though the very forest had shed its sedate green dress and donned instead a daring gown of blazing reds with flavescent lace. Ren mused Earth Mother knew it was time to be bold and festive. She would soon abide by a shroud of necessary brown, but until then... until then, even the leaves celebrated.

The carriage-way bustled with an ever-streaming Northbound current of revellers, so Ren made his way through the trees by the wayside. He needed to make good time, but was torn with the desire to linger, and revel some himself – not in anticipating Queen's Day – but in the forest's adornments.

As he bolted through a copse of maples with his precious consignment, he allowed himself to remember autumns in another home. Leaf-hunting. As he wove through trunks and serotinal debris he remembered his father beside him in a similar grove, but moving at a very different pace. They sought a clearing, the water's edge or an elevated position so they might best admire the changing leaves. This was their custom every year.

Ren's father was like the broad-leaved deciduous trees, Ren's father had his seasons. When they were alone, he was gentle and imaginative – cultivating the same in Ren with tender, patient care. With others, he assumed a severe manner that left Ren lost and confused in his younger years. Until Ren learned. There was a dignity he must mimic in society, a sense of priorities. His playfulness and flair for performing should be neatly stowed away for private occasions, for these were frivolous affectations that did little to help a country repeatedly torn by civil war. Or so most thought. *Ren* believed a time marked by warlords and *Daimyo* fighting for prominence was the *best* time for a little frivolity. That distraction and levity were not desertion, but a valid contribution to the war effort. That perhaps the central government would do better to unify the people with a little laughter. Few shared Ren's beliefs.

But among the beeches and maidenhair trees, Ren had been permitted the delight of pulling those pleasures from their hiding place; fanning leaves in his hands, burrowing where they collected, pitching them skyward to create a slow rain to spin beneath.

Ren leapt over a fallen tree without breaking stride. This discipline, he knew, came from his mother. In his short time in Mórlough, Ren had observed that the good basilica instructed women to be fair, gentle and compassionate. All traits Ren's own mother despised. If his father was a maple, his mother was an evergreen. While some occasions allowed Ren to enjoy an unguarded and bright version of his *Otousan*, Ren's *Haha* was constant in her rigour for decorum. Constant in her disappointment with her son.

Ren brushed away a thicket of low branches to clear the path from his face with a deft hand as he continued at speed. The trees readied for winter by stilling the water supply to their leaves which, in answer, lost their pigment and eventually fell to be crushed underfoot.

Ren had been a fallen leaf underfoot. Away from his family for a season, he felt here his own changing and finding of himself was celebrated instead of trampled. Here, he saw many of the same pressures and expectations, yes, but a monarch thirsty for art and culture had sanctioned a society that could thirst too. By day the thirst might be denied and reluctant, but by night – by night! – Ren smiled to think of the enthusiasm he had met at his shows.

Perhaps someday Ren's own parents would see comparable changes stirring. But for now they were grey, life-worn, and reasonably preoccupied with unrest. Ren needed to be part of another kind of change sooner, and that had meant taking time away during a window of peace in his homeland, to be part of change where it was already happening. Ren wanted children to be free to revel in the leaves anytime, not only in secret. He wanted it to be acceptable if a boy chose to perform instead of fight. He needed to feel he need not hide who he was.

Here, to Ren, the crush of dry leaves beneath his feet voiced the shape of things around the Lough itself. Arid. Waiting. There would be a hard winter ahead, but new life would come. Soon.

And Ash? She rode a waterhorse upon the cresting wave of change with the reins in her teeth.

ASH

Ash slept beneath an upturned *ḍieṁgī*, certain the boat had been assigned its name – Immortal Pathfinder – as a good omen. It smelled mostly of spice, a more auspicious soporific than fish, which was the usual aroma boasted by boats.

She'd dreamt of her parents – of them residing deep in the lake, living but voiceless, mouthing unintelligible words to her, their faces framed in lakeweed. It had brought both chill and comfort, though the former weighed more heavily throughout the day. Ash had thrown her knife in the morning (over and over at a trunk), gone swimming for lunch, working up to a count of over 200 while immersed and holding her breath, and then parted with the last of her coin for a dinner (of eggs and cabbage).

For Mysteries-forsaken foolishness, she'd been chewing parsley ever since. She didn't want to have eggs on her breath when she saw Ren. There it was. She wasn't sure Ren would have opportunity to know her breath's quality... *and yet...* since her lacklustre meal she'd been through an entire bushel of the herb. It had gone some way in helping satiate her returning hunger as well, but she'd have to snare a rabbit tomorrow. The eggs and cabbage wouldn't do 'til Queen's day.

Ash now approached the jetty Ren had shrewdly named *before* her show on Hughes' holding. The jetty three north of the lord's own.

It was nigh unto sunset – the witching hours hastening in – yet Ren had named dimpse-time fitting to meet. Ren's dissimilarity to all the men Ash had ever known piqued a desire in her – to know more, yes, but also simply... desire. It unsettled her. Enough men – and women – had shown her favour in recent years, her beauty proving more enticing than their fear of her. But none had earned her respect, and none deemed her suitable for more than a single night's dalliance. If they were to bear the risk of association with a woman so whispered-about, it was only one night they were after. She was yet to meet a man who was brave enough to ally himself to someone possessing Ash's ferocity and passion for the Mysteries. Even Wynn – whom Ash was fond of – had never seen her as someone to settle down with, nor had she ever been tempted by him.

Ash had never thought she would find anyone she'd want to settle down with. In truth, she still was not convinced of that particular. What intrigued her now was a novel possibility, winking at her mind's horizon. Could she *not* settle down with someone, but still have someone – and him have her – for much more than the type of dalliance she'd many times declined?

She tore off another spray of parsley and popped it in her mouth. It was Mysteries-forsaken foolishness, this wondering.

Ash surveyed the jetty's surrounds. She approved of Ren's choice. He'd paid some scrutiny to their rendezvous location before suggesting it. Clear line-of-sight from the jetty measured the length of a ship's keel. That made an ambush difficult. Although it was growing dark, she was confident she'd arrived first. No one yet waited at the jetty. She moved closer still, taking careful and quiet steps out of habit, preventing twigs and other autumn litter from alerting rousing nocturnal animals of her approach.

Then she saw the line. It was strung between trees surrounding the jetty and barely detectable. It was fisherman's line – near-transparent as they could craft, to disguise its attachment to their lures. Amused, she crouched. She followed the line a distance until she could confirm what this was. And confirm she did. Secured to the line – behind a tree should you approach from the land – were coins. Coins like none she'd seen. Each circular disk bore intricate characters she could not begin to decipher, and at each coin's centre, a square-shaped hole. The line ran through these holes creating an anklet for the trees. She was pleased with herself for having detected the trap before setting it off, but disappointed with a resulting realisation; she had been mistaken in something else.

She had *not* arrived first.

She drew a slow breath as she crouched, closed her eyes, and considered the scene. All indications suggested this was Ren's work – he knew she was coming and the coins were as Other as he was. All indications also suggested Ren was friend not foe, and so it followed this trap was not for her. He'd set an alarm about the perimeter. *For* her.

If it wasn't the most romantic thing she'd ever seen…

Ash opened her eyes but remained in her crouch. "I'm over here. But you probably know that already."

Ren materialised from the dark. He leaned against a tree closer to the lake's edge – though no trees were too close at this site – and he became visible for moving (something he didn't always do, she'd noted). He waved. It was an almost bashful gesture. She took in his form, leaning there – strong, patient, and ready; his wave – unsure, self-conscious and kind.

Her lungs tugged in reply to her observations.

She was glad she'd chewed parsley.

She rose from her crouch and took an exaggerated, high-knee step over the line. Ren shrugged off the tree and made his approach when she finished crossing it. As he came closer, Ash could make out more than his silhouette; the distinctive shape of his eyes, the lines that pulled on his cheeks, and the dark vest he wore like a uniform as an outer garment. He carried a veil loosely in his left hand and not for one moment did she fear he had any ill intentions toward her. Grete would be disappointed.

Ren looked up briefly. Ash smiled and inclined her head at the tell, regally, awaiting his impending speech. He began, "I hope anyone else who might approach us this night will be less astute than you." Ren nodded towards his trap. "It is something. The leaves may serve as the first defence. Maybe this will serve as the second… to allow you to be… a little at ease? But I will listen always, as a supporting watch to your first, for any sign of danger. You may decline, but if I may – that is, if you trust me – I would ask that you wear this, over your eyes. I take you to be one who… peeks." Ren offered her the veil in his hand.

Ash pouted as she considered. Her thoughts went briefly to the gag, and her fingers twitched instinctively to check the wounds at her throat.

Ren added, "I would not tie it. You do that – tie it loose, so you may remove it easily."

"I trust you." As she said it, she knew it was true.

Her chest teemed with warmth as she wore the truth of it. It was unusual. Her thoughts were bright with promise and excitement at what giving someone new trust meant. She knew too she would withdraw it in an instant, given the slightest cause. But she trusted there wouldn't be one.

She reached for the veil and drew it from Ren's hand. Rather than releasing it to her readily, he allowed it to feed through his fingers like the eye of a needle as she drew it into her own. There was an intimacy in his gentle hold and in the susurrus of silk as it left his loose grip.

Ash gulped.

She raised her arms and tied the veil over her eyes. The motions came readily to her muscles' memory, this act reminiscent of the preface to so many family shows.

Ren came closer, then asked, "May I?"

Not knowing what he was asking permission to do, Ash hesitated, her mouth open but unspeaking, her heart hammering at the realisation she wanted to say "yes" no matter what the question. "May you…?"

"Straighten the veil?"

"You may." Ash frowned in amusement.

Ren's hands came to her face and he unfolded a crease in the veil, pulling it lower on her cheek. The dorsal of his hand grazed her cheek after doing so and Ash feared her resulting swallow would set off the string of alarm.

"Better," Ren said. "May I hold your hand?"

"You may."

Ren's fingers came smoothly into Ash's right hand – she was sure he'd left her the favoured hand in defence on purpose. His hands were warm, his grip firm. The warmth eddied around Ash's own hand and swelled beyond her wrist before raging in a torrential line up her arm to her chest. Ren squeezed where their hands met, twice. Then he gently pulled at their grip, towards the jetty.

But the wooden boards of the structure did not come beneath her feet. Instead, Ren whispered directions, carefully guiding her across the clearing and down a bank. Once he placed his hand at her waist when she slipped – causing a pleasant alarm all of her own to sound within.

They crossed lakestones a short distance before coming to a halt.

"You can remove the blindfold." Ren said, releasing her hand. It felt cold instantly.

"You can." Ash smiled in invitation.

She felt his hands at the veil's bow. The veil fell loose around her shoulders. It was then drawn back and away behind her.

Ash opened her eyes. A candle burned in a wooden bowl balanced on an upturned crate. A basket sat close by. Above it all was more string lined with playing cards instead of coins. Bursts of colour and monochromatic patterns hung suspended like Queen's Day banners, only these were better suited as a Mystic's bunting, and they were not for a city's merriment or even an encampment's small festivities. They were only for her.

"Your sister told me that today is your birthday. Although she understood why, she was very sorry she would not see you... and that you might be alone for this day."

Ash felt tears budding in her lashes. She examined what Ren had done and she recognised the eye-stitched fabric in the basket – it had been her mother's. Grete had filled that basket.

Could she smell... ? No. It could not be.

Ren still stood close. Close enough that Ash retook his hand in hers and squeezed it, twice. Then she turned to look at him and let a tear fall. "Thank you." She said it as earnestly as she could.

"You waited a long time for this birthday?" Ren asked.

"Years. Ever since... "

"... they were taken from you." Ren finished.

"Yes." With that answer came a deluge of memories. Mapa tying a veil over Ash's eyes in rehearsal, hugging her from behind once it was on tight. Papal juggling fruit from Wynn's family orchard while Grete stirred dinner behind him on the stove and rolled her eyes. Mapa and Papal secreting themselves to embrace in the lake, thinking Grete and Ash none the wiser in their straw ticks back in the wagon. Mapa making an announcement of which new act Ash would be permitted to join – a declaration she reserved for Ash's birthday each year. While the city was diverted by carousing and impending celebrations… their family had turned inward, and rehearsed.

But Ash's birthday and the Queen's had always been interconnected. For as long as Ash had known of the performers who lit the palace halls, she had set her course to be numbered among them.

Ash turned to Ren; "Did I get the commendation?" For that is what she was eligible to receive, now that she was eighteen summers old. What she hoped she'd received – had put on a good showing she was *sure* she would receive… but feared she fell short, and did not.

"You did not stay and hear for yourself? I assumed… "

"Did I get it?"

"You got it." Ren smiled, seeming stunned to learn Ash had waited this long to confirm as much.

Ash blew out air but said nothing. Quiet grew between them as Ren joined Ash in remembering the parents she had lost and how long she had waited for this birthday, this commendation.

Ren spoke first. "Is it hard to be here? Near the water?"

"No. It's home. And sometimes… I feel them closest when I'm swimming in the lake." She looked out over the inky expanse beside them. Ash knew it might sound strange. She cared not for being thought mad, though she'd made quite a habit of building that exact reputation – persisting with acts deemed blasphemy by a loud few. "I don't blame the lake. The water didn't take them from me. Zealots did."

Then Ash counted her exits. Being under the jetty obstructed her view across the clearing, but it was now true dark. She found Ren's alarm went some ways to reassure her. *She* had detected it in the light; she doubted many Mystics-born would see it now, let alone a band blinded by zeal. Becoming aware once more of Ren's hand in hers she gave it a final squeeze before releasing it and moving towards the basket.

"Is this what I think it is… ?"

"Grete said you were fond of a certain bakery in SeeBurg, so I… "

Ash interrupted him by tugging on his hand and pulling him into a full embrace. "Thank you, Ren. Thank you!" She released him and dove at the basket. "You went to SeeBurg? And you got back here in time to… " her mouth was already full of bread and she stopped to let out a groan, eyes closed. "Ren. Have you had some of this?"

"No. It is not my birthday."

"Sit with me? Please? Have some of this Mysteries-blessed bread!" Ren took a place on the stones beside Ash and carefully broke off a modest piece. He paused a moment, appearing to give some silent thanks, then ate with her. He produced jams and preserves Grete had sent in the basket, laughing at Ash's answering moans of contentment. "Is this still warm? Am I imagining it?" Ash felt delirious.

"I steamed it before you came. It smelled so good warm when I paid for it this morning I felt sure that was how it was best served."

Forget what she'd thought about the perimeter alarm. Traversing lakeside townships to purchase the best bread around the Lough *to then steam it – that* was the most romantic thing Ash ever known.

Or was it?

Ash chewed slower as she considered. Ren had made no indication he felt *romantically* towards her... He'd proposed a business relationship at the first, taken her hand by necessity due to a blindfold, and had only followed her sister's orders in this grand gesture. Was she being presumptuous?

He *had* said she was breath-stealing.

"What is it?" Ren studied her face. She hadn't taken another bite and, given how many and how fast the bites had been until this pause, she could see his cause for concern.

She would be direct. "So you're being nice to me... because... " she paused. "You took that message to my kin because... "

"Because I am... enthralled by you. You are like no woman I have ever met and I cannot believe I will find another half so captivating ever again. Even the forest changes her colours to honour you."

"So... you *like* me?" Ash smiled and took another bite of the bread.

"Very much." Ren also smiled, his gaze unshifting from her eyes.

"You know, I need to get that Seal without any man at my side. I need to be focussed... "

"I know it well."

"But after Queen's Day... " Ash reached for a flask in the basket.

"Yes?" Ren's smile lines were deep when he smiled with his teeth. He'd twisted his head sideways, as though presenting a better ear.

"Well. After Queen's Day we'll see."

Ren relaxed. He'd tensed, poised for her answer. "I can work with 'we'll see.'" He took the flask she'd offered him after taking her share.

"Thank you again." She wiped her lips, suddenly conscious of them. It was the berries and the tree all over again. She kept her eyes on the ground until Ren spoke.

"I know you did not need any of this." He drew a circle in the air and then pointed to the basket. "That is," he looked up, "I am sure you would have fared fine on your own. But it is good sometimes to have things beyond what is needed; to have things we want."

On the word "want" Ash reconsidered her former proviso – apropos things necessarily coming *after* Queen's Day. It seemed so outdated, mere moments later. She knew she *wanted* Ren's hands in her own, she *wanted* to feel his arms encircling her again and *wanted* him to benefit from her foresight with the parsley...

But she knew what she needed first.

Wants could wait.

Not only did she need to make a clear statement when she won the Seal, further attachment was irresponsible. She was willing to die at every show, and she was willing to die because of every show – that was two further obstacles standing between them. Ash already had two people too many that would suffer, should she meet an untimely end...it was better she and Ren remained flirtatious and uncommitted. The risk of accusations and trials would not end until the Seal was won, and Ash's willingness to die was not going to change for any man – it's what gave her her edge. So it was decided. Wants must wait.

Perhaps she could satisfy *some* desire now.

She desired to fill in more of her map of Ren. Ren of preternatural stillness, meticulous planning, swift passage, generous aid and... well, he was also easy on the eyes. But where had he come from?

They kept their voices quiet, alert for the sound of any approach.

"There *is* something I want."

Ren schooled his features, but she saw he clasped his hands together tighter around his knees, which splayed loosely out from his ankles, which met in front of him. "Oh?"

"I told you of my parents. What of yours?"

The brief look up. The answer: "They are alive and well, I assume. And very disappointed. I left my training in Sentakushi Nihon to seek out new places, new things. I had been given no choice of what I wanted. This would have been manageable, if my father and I had... agreed more. My training, my study, and even my marriage were all decided for me."

Ash raised both of her eyebrows in interest, fighting the urge to cough on the bread she'd just swallowed.

"You're married?"

"I was betrothed, as a child. She loved another but was happy with the arrangement for the advancement it offered her household. "

"Oh. Now, back to this place – where is that?"

"Across the desert and the ocean, but more than a world away in custom. Everyone studies such different things here... "

"What was it you studied, exactly?"

"Our history, foreign cultures, poetry, the way of the sword, the way of the warrior, our moral code, meditation... "

"...how to sit so still anyone who saw you would think the Mysteries had taken your soul?"

Ren laughed, as loudly as he dared, given their watchfulness, but louder than he had when watching her gush over the food. Again, it soothed Ash to hear it, as it had the day she'd spoken to him of her own family. Well, the laughter had come after the sombre tale. "Yes, that is part of it. A part I do not mind. But the respect for one's superior, the loyalty one must have for one's master... " the look upwards, "It was unconditional. And now, we are not at war, but all we do is train to fight, seek to advance our station, and blindly obey our master... even if our master has strayed from our code. And even if you feel called to another way of life; imagine a new kind of life." Ren looked down to the stones, toeing them with one foot. Ash could see there was pain in his past too, but of a different kind. He had been let down.

"What parts did you not mind about the teachings in Sentakushi Nihon?" She invited Ren to step away from the pain.

Ren looked at her, smiling that she had remembered his unmet words so well. Ash, meanwhile, felt humbled by her struggle to remember only two, when Ren appeared to have mastered her tongue almost entirely, though he'd never pass as a local. She was eager to hear more of the place where he would be called one. "I was taught not to fear any death that was of my own making," Ren said.

Ash repositioned herself. "What of death that is not of your own making?"

"I will not allow that kind." Ren released a hand from his clasp around his legs and ran it through his black hair. "So ... no fear of death. Like you."

"Like me."

"I am very sorry for what happened to your parents. And for what is happening to you now."

"Those things are not your fault!" Ash laughed as she spoke, although she felt a little anger in the moment – thinking of how unfair things were, how complicated this meeting was, when it shouldn't have to be.

"But those bad things have made you more beautiful. In Sentakushi Nihon, when a piece of pottery is broken; we piece it back together with gold or silver, making no effort to hide that it has come apart and into pieces. We know that such pottery is more beautiful for having been broken." Ren dipped his head and caught Ash's eye. "So it is with you."

Now Ren had stolen her breath. She felt as though she sat upon a precipice launched to fall, not into danger, but into Ren, and that falling was inevitable.

"You are very good with words, for someone from so far away."

"I studied to be, studied harder than most, because I knew I wanted to leave."

"You came for the Seal?"

"I thought that was why I came. I thought maybe if my parents saw that somewhere else, who I was and what I do could have meaning... maybe... "

"I understand." Ash gave Ren a smile laced with sadness. "You say you thought it *was* why you came, as though you since have changed your mind?"

"The Seal was why I came. Then I met you. Now I wonder if the Mysteries knew better."

He meant her. Ren meant he wondered if the Mysteries had brought them together.

Much like her morning dive into the lake, this knowledge immersed Ash in pleasant shock. She felt the realisation all over, all at once. And found she returned his wondering. He'd left no room for doubt of his intentions. Perhaps the Mysteries had a trick yet for them both. Maybe she'd met a man brave enough to stand beside her.

It was a shame she'd have to take that Seal from him.

It was getting late. Insects of the night were singing now and Ash was newly aware of how close Queen's Day and the Seal were – almost close enough to touch, to imagine in her hands as she waved in the face of every spitting bird-woman and every fevered, allied accuser.

After this night, she need only survive its eve, and then... then she would win.

"I must go." She stood, dusting herself off. She offered her hand to him, to pull him up. He looked at it, amused greatly by the gesture, but took it. She pulled him to stand and they faced each other, under the jetty, where a light breeze now caught a string of cards so that they fluttered above them. "But Ren, thank you. Thank you for telling me more about you." Ash offered her arm, and clasped Ren's forearm. Ren's smallest finger slid beneath her sleeve to rest against the delicate flesh beneath her arm, sending light cascading underneath her clothing. She looked into his eyes, knowing she glowed with mischief at his touch.

"See you Queen's Day.   And may the queen award the best Mystic the Seal."

"Mysteries willing," Ren replied.

Ash let go first, grabbed some remaining bread with a flashing smile. She quietly ascended the bank. Feeling warm from the flask and bread, and trusting after Ren's tales, she paused and cast back in a stage-whisper, "I'm growing fond of seeing you, too!" It was safer to say so at this distance.

And before she turned to make for the trees and step over the string hidden there she looked back. Under the jetty and although dark, she thought she could make out something by the flickering candlelight – a gesture resembling jubilant celebration, although quiet: Ren brought both of his hands to his mouth and held them there. To bite at them, inhale them, or whisper a prayer – she did not know – she knew only that Ren had heard her, and Ren was happy she returned some of his affection.

ASH

Ash was eighteen. She'd celebrated her birthday with a man. Alone. In the witching hours.

In an effort to discipline herself against the lingering surrealism of the previous night, she had worked her way northward and found a place to throw her knives. Then she'd practised holding her breath again, retrieving the hook from her hem underwater – dropping it once and losing a good half-hour to its recovery. She'd cursed some, but there was no length she wouldn't go to in preparation for what might await her. She was too close to allow anyone to stop her now.

She'd even taken a hollow reed and cut it short and clean and stowed it in her boot. Chances were if someone came again for her they'd search her well, but a reed might be regarded odd rather than dangerous. Ash had snared a rabbit, cleaned it and eaten it to the bones. She'd moved through the trees, away from the roads. People from all the towns ringing the lake pressed towards the city for Queen's

Day, since it brought the best markets, festivities and gaiety of the year. Ash remembered well from childhood years the merry air the roads had harboured as travel became a social, pleasant thing. All were bound for the Queen's City or some celebration at hand.

She'd been careful. She hadn't been seen.

And she now sat restless.

So much of what she was doing was for her parents. The force of their absence compounded anew in her chest like a vice. It felt wrong that earning the Seal would do nothing to bring them back. Nothing to undo what had been done.

The vice was unrelenting. It demanded she walk.

Eventually, she obeyed its will. Ash started walking further north until she came to a well-worn wagon circle on the edge of the Queen's City. The vice pressed tighter still, colder.

She walked on late into the afternoon, until she came to a cemetery. Many graves were marked by stones, some by plants alone. All appeared quiet. There she stood at its edge, hesitant. She'd not come back here since the day she, Grete and Wynn had attended her parents' funeral in disguise. Their graves were close to where they'd met their deaths, close to where they'd given their last show. Close to where Ash had wept, broken.

Ash skirted the treeline, looking for the tree she and Grete had planted to mark their attendance where their parents' bodies had been laid to rest in a single, hastily dug grave.

There, she saw it. Between the trees, and closer to the grave markers than it had been then, Ash could see a three-year-old sapling surrounded by short grasses and fallen leaves. The other Mystics and performers from their wagon circle had known the place well. They'd tended to the grave, she could see, as it was clean, neat, and undisturbed by later burials.

Ash yearned to go closer, to better see the tree and somehow be close to her parents... although she knew they weren't there. Not really.

The tree was an ash tree.

Grete had suggested it – saying that Ash would always know how to find them. They'd found an old ash tree and carefully removed a small branch sucker from its lower trunk. They'd taken it to the freshly-turned soil of their parents' graves and planted it there. Wynn had added compost from the orchard that day, and Ash suspected, many times since – for Grete. Ash's heart warmed thinking of her sister, but pained with missing her too, and for the worry she was sure she was bringing her sister by staying on the Mystic course. She thought of the left-over bread she'd eaten again for lunch with the rabbit, and reminded herself the Seal was all the more important for it would allow her to see Grete and Wynn and to someday see the child the pair of them had made.

It was with the vice in her chest and the Seal's immunity near her grasp that Ash stepped from the treeline and approached the ash tree.

And it was there they launched their ambush.

There were more of them this time, but Arsebeard was at the front. And that cursed Odell of SeeBurg was among them. There must've been twenty zealots or more, and they descended upon her like wolves. She felt hands at her wrists, back and hair all at once. They took her cloak first. She'd miss it, she loved that cloak. They trampled it, as though knowing. She said not a word. The visit to Pabla and Alex's graves had been unwise. She knew that. But she knew too that no words would save her from the mob's plans.

She'd give the mob their trial, *then* she'd save herself. It wasn't over yet. She'd not allow it.

They searched her, thoroughly, taking her dagger, but leaving her boots on. Ash recognised the groper from the Western basilica, although he no longer limped. Arsebeard remained astride his horse, and there announced the order for her immediate trial, "Direct from Archbishop Fulton himself."

Great. The archbishop had the queen's ear. The queen would've heard of Ash by now, and not in the light she'd been fighting for.

Ash was poked and raked over with angry hands. Women examined her skin as thoroughly as they might their own children for lice.

Odell looked on, growing more and more staunch with every blemish found, each being pronounced a testifying mark of her guilt.

If Ash had ever prayed, she prayed then. She prayed they chose trial by baptism. *Please, choose trial by baptism.*

Be it a god – theirs, hers, or Mysteries unknown – her prayers were heard.

"To the lake! Let God be the judge." The cry went up from more than one, and Ash was dragged by her armpits from the cemetery.

The entire way, Ash fought tears. Not tears of fear, but the dawning of understanding that her parents would have come this way. She was close to crying for *them.* But she rallied within – water was her preference; water she'd prepared for. They'd not been afforded chance to rehearse.

They came to a wharf – a structure hugging the lake's side – long and wide to allow a mob to assemble. Ash almost scoffed. They didn't stop there. They took her to the far end of a pier extending out from the wharf, so that the water would be deep. Good.

She tensed as the knots were tied about her waist and arms, but it was no use, the loop was tighter this time; they'd learned. The loop around her attached to a long rope on the wharf which they would use to draw her back in, should the waters receive her. Arsebeard's words came through a wall of mental insulation, like a distant echo. All sound, scents and sensations were muted as Ash began mentally rehearsing how she would slip from these bindings, how she would escape.

But there were so many.

Should she fail, at least Ren could stop that supercilious Collier from taking the Mystic Seal. It might even do Ren some good with his parents back home – to win the Seal in her place. That gave her consolation. So much so, she smiled. If it would not be hers, then Ren's. She could die knowing that.

A slap came, firm and hard, against her cheek. Her head cracked sideways in answer and the gash at her sternum tore open and wept blood.

"Leave her judgement to God! Unhand her, it is already decided. Leave her!" A woman streamed words of correction – in her defence? Ash guessed from the veins at the woman's neck that it was Mrs Gregory, but it came as a dull background sound barely breaching the place Ash had retreated to inside. She scarcely made out the words directed away from her, to the mob: "God may receive her yet, and then you will be the guilty ones as her accusers!"

"Cast her into the lake!" That was Arsebeard. He continued speaking, but it seemed more distant to Ash, who was being dragged closer to the water. She considered walking, but no, she wanted them to remember what they had done – that they had forced this. There were words about an almighty and ever-living God, and a Son with power to cast out the power of evil, to rescue a man or woman from the kingdom of darkness and communion with the Unknown. Ash heard those last words as though she'd broken the surface, making everything crisp and audible:

"Receive her to thyself by the waters of baptism if she be thy child, or deny her this rite if she be unclean." Ash's back was to the lake. Arsebeard sat atop his bloodied horse, spittle flying from his tut-mouth on the hard consonants of his exhortation. The hairs on his beard shone in the sun and his pulse gleamed visibly under sweat at his temple.

The man was still afraid.

Ash smiled again.

And then she was thrust, ravaged and bleeding, into the waters of the Lough.

ASH

Ash had attended a funeral and two weddings. She'd heard scripture here and there. What came to her mind as she dove deeper into the lake and away from the mob, were the words of a psalm she'd once heard sung by a minstrel:

> *If I to heav'n ascend, thou art there*
> *If I make my bed in hell, thou art there*
> *If I take the wings of the morning*
> *Or dwell in the depths of the sea*
> *Even there wilt thou lead me,*
> *wilt thou hold me*
> *Thou art there*

She allowed herself to drift some then.

She knew if the basilica was singing the psalm they were singing of God or His Son or some other deity she didn't know well. But as the minstrel's words rolled with her through the water, her hair cutting across her face without respite, Ash thought only of her Pabla and Alex – whether they be in heaven or hell, they were there, somewhere.

She was rising to the surface, she could feel it, and so she fought. She was still too close to the wharf. She knew should she float they would pull her in fast, and she'd be hanged by the shore in execution for being found unclean; unworthy of being received in baptism. Sinking was her only hope – for they'd wait then, wait to see if God had claimed her. She brought her legs up and tucked them near her chin, expelled some precious air, and sank. She kicked away from the wharf.

Then she began work for the hook. She twisted and turned, dragging her arms beneath the rope so they were before her. The ropes scratched her raw, they were so tight. She could not get them free. She remembered the faces of her parents in the lake, from her dream. Now she only saw darkness and murk. But the psalm replayed again in her mind and she stopped fighting the ropes. She was not afraid. This could be the end. There was poetry in it, to die this way.

> *If I to heav'n ascend, thou art there*
> *If I make my bed in hell, thou art there*
> *If I take the wings of the morning*
> *Or dwell in the depths of the sea*
> *Even there wilt thou lead me,*
> *wilt thou hold me*
> *Thou art there*

Perhaps the Mysteries had willed it. Perhaps they'd even sent Ren before such an end as a mercy – so she would have that one last night – a birthday to make her smile.

They'd failed at the Western basilica, but today, they'd been many, and maybe they'd won.

The weight of the Lough together with Ash's memory of Grete's words three years earlier came crushing down on her;

"They didn't come back up, Ash; they didn't come back up."

Ash hadn't drawn much breath before they'd pushed her in. She'd also expended much more energy in her struggle than she had during her macabre rehearsals for this day. Her lungs already felt as though being torn, as though they held stones that desperately wanted to break down into her stomach.

She could just let the water in. Let it end.

Thou art there

Mysteries willing.

But what of her will?

No.

She did not will this. None of it.

And she would not allow it.

Something in Ash's arm popped when she pulled it from its binding. She did not allow herself to gasp, though the icy stones within her lungs issued a persuasive invitation. She set to work on the hem of her undergarment. She got the hook free... and instead of working at the knots – fishermen's knots, she could see – she used the hook to pick the rope that led back to shore – the rope they'd pull on to retrieve her corpse.

She was running out of air. Her head ached with it. She thought she'd make it to a count of 150, at best, not 200. There wasn't enough air, she hadn't drawn enough air...

While she worked on the pull-rope, she also pulled on her other arm. It came free more easily. The rope finally frayed, then broke free, but Ash held it fast. Then she dove down and tied it to a hardy weed. Her arm screamed in protest, but she managed the tie. Then she swam – hard and fast, away from the rope stretching back to the pier and the waiting mob. She gave up on using the arm that only sent shots of pain up its length, and relied on strong frog-like kicks from her legs. She had 10 or more counts left. She knew it was all she could give. Her boots made her progress slow, but she was grateful for them, for in them lay her last hope.

Ash reached down, retrieved the hollowed reed and brought it to her lips. She took a last large kick into thickened flora – she'd need the cover – and made for the surface. She allowed only the reed to break the lake's top amongst the weeds, then blew hard into it to clear it. She drew a lurching breath through it. She got some water with it, and coughed into the reed, but propelled herself downwards with a birdlike movement, working with her arm. Her body wanted to rise. It wanted air everywhere, not this meagre sip. The pain in her arm tore through her entire torso, but she was still too close to the pier. She drew as large a gulp as the reed would allow and dove back down, kicking with all she had. She swam away from the pier, away from the mob, and away too from the dream of her parents, waiting in the lake.

Ash would have to come up soon.

She hoped she'd done enough, gone far enough.

REN

Ren was shuffling cards in a tavern corner when he caught word of a Trial by Baptism. A woman at the room's centre bellowed her gossip: "She drowned! My cousin's a timekeeper and waved the final veil by Luca's Docks himself."

Ren's world tilted.

"A witch, was it?" her company pressed.

"Aye, a she-Mystic called Ashleigh or Ashlynn or some other."

Ren did not remember running to the lake, but found himself there. He searched in the weeds surrounding Luca's Docks until his tunic was stiff with sweat and his legs lost feeling. As the witching hours crept in most harried indoors; Ren waded in the murk. At last, he found a trace of what had taken place earlier that day, but not the shred of hope he had been hoping for. A bloodied strip of a blue-grey sleeve was snagged upon the dock's struts. Mosquito larvae danced around it, their siphons trawling the surface while their bodies gyrated in unison.

No. It could not be. This could not be.

Ren could not bring his eyes to focus.

His next memory was waking at the lake's edge to the sound of a trump at dawn. Queen's Day.

Ren disregarded the nightmare of the previous night. Ash must yet live. He would wash himself, attend, and find her laughing in the palace, like she always did after a vanishing. Today would be no different.

REN

The cavernous presence chamber of Queen Valencia's palace was packed. Performers basked in the attentions of encircling admirers, ushered and introduced by their commending Lord and Lady.

One performer stood apart, before the throne.

"I wish to withdraw, your Majesty," Ren announced. His voice carried clearly across the stone floors to the throne. There Queen Valencia sat, back straight, head high, hair coiled.

"Besuto Ren wishes to withdraw, your Majesty," Archbishop Fulton restated. He sat on a demi-throne at the queen's right. It was wooden, high-backed and adorned in a basilica vestment. Fulton sat perched on the seat's edge, his skin its typical veil of inflammation o'er white.

The queen shared a similar pallor (but lacked comparable inflammation). However, her cheeks coloured slightly as she answered her right, "I know who he is." She returned her attention to Ren. "On what grounds? There is simply no precedent; I am curious to know what pressing matter could be of greater import and honour than appearing here." The queen turned out her fingers in a supporting gesture. Although this surely necessitated her arms' movement, her stiff ballooning sleeves concealed it.

Ren knelt on a single knee some distance from the queen on the Presence Chamber floor. He considered stating his motives plainly, but refrained in honour of Ash's wishes. If he revealed his partiality towards her, it would only tarnish the independence of her achievements.

But how partial he was.

And acutely aggrieved. The poem he had penned upon first seeing Ash hammered in his mind, but now with pain instead of intrigue:

> *The Unflinching Ash*
> *After vanishing lingers*
> *Long in a man's mind*

Only Ash had not appeared after this vanishing, as was her usual custom. He had not found her laughing within the palace. Ren feared the worst had become of the best, and he could not perform in such pain.

Ren briefly looked up, then answered, "I pray we may yield the actions of one lowly foreigner as yet another curious mystery on this day filled with the same, your Majesty." And then, though it was an affliction to muster it, Ren did his best to simulate his most engaging smile of entreaty.

Its affecting power was immediate and plainly manifest. Queen Valencia – though her neck was rigidly collared by her ornate lace – appeared slapped by Ren's uncommon allure, even at its reduced capacity. Her simultaneous smile – playful and unguarded – clarified she'd taken no offence at his suggestion she press no further, but rather, was delighted by it. "You wish to withdraw your performance, or *your presence?*" she asked. It was clear the queen was tantalised by the continuance of the latter.

Ren was in the process of formulating an answer when two guards entered via the main doors of the great hall. Titters swelled through the crowd of courtiers lining both sides of the chamber and upper gallery.

The guards lowered their lances in equal time, indicating a report to deliver.

"Guards?" Archbishop Fulton addressed them first.

"Your Grace, your Majesty, there has been a disturbance on the grounds… "

"What kind of disturbance?" the queen asked.

"Well, your Majesty… " the higher-ranking guard stammered, uncertain. "A claim has been made. A Mystic – her name *is* on the List of Commendations… "

The queen pursed her lips, and supposed, "But she is late… "

"And unsuitably presented. And... well... all of it is highly unusual, your Majesty." Both guards remained stooped, awaiting further instruction.

Queen Valencia looked at Ren – still down on one knee – as she said, "Unusual is quite welcome in this court. The question is, whether it is indecent."

"I would not dare to know the mind of the queen, but we found it indecent, your Majesty," said the taller of the two guards.

"I see. The disturbance being... " the queen led.

"Your Majesty, she is insistent she has equal right to be seen this day, though she came out of the very waters of the Lough at the residence boundary. She is... well... hard to argue with."

The queen dipped her chin into her elaborate ruff. "This, I would like to see."

"Your Majesty, I would suggest... "

"Guards, show her in."

Worry lines smeared the expressions of the guards' faces as they backed from the hall.

"Your Majesty, I am not sure it is advisable... " Fulton's hands gripped his armrests as he spoke at the queen's side.

"You could be right, but if there was ever a day to do things ill-advised or on a whim, it is today, is it not, Fulton?" Queen Valencia eyed the archbishop through the corner of her eye, without turning her head. "And you, Besuto Ren, please rise. We will come to you later."

Ren, somewhat stunned, backed into the body of attendants for the Queen's Day celebrations. While people all around him speculated at the latest news, Ren dared to hope the late, commended Mystic was The Mystic he cared so deeply for.

The same pair of guards returned, this time with a third party in tow.

One of Ren's knees gave out at the sight.

Ash. Beautiful, erect and proud. Also: dripping in undergarments only partly obscured by a guard's cloak.

"I see!" The queen's cheeks lifted with amusement. She raised both eyebrows at Archbishop Fulton with a slight twist of her head then turned frontwards once more. "You must be The Unflinching Ash. How fitting."

Ash gave a moment's hesitation, Ren saw, but she dropped to one knee before making her address. "Your Majesty, I offer my sincerest apologies for my late arrival this day. It was never my intention to tender such a slight – nay, I have been counting down to this day with eagerness I imagine is second only to your own. I assume I *was* expected… "

Fulton interrupted. "Your Majesty, I know this subject and I wish to speak with you."

The queen sharply turned at the waist towards Fulton. "You have not been addressed." She faced forward again, speaking to the guards. "You did not confirm for her she was on the List of Commendations?"

"We were unsure if it was best, your Majesty, to entertain false hopes given the state of the Mystic's... undress... "

"Ash. You were expected. You *are* late. And your current state is... unacceptable."

"Your Majesty, if I may?" Ash called from her knee.

The queen nodded minutely and gesticulated Ash might rise.

Ash rose and explained, "I am honoured to be expected, your Majesty." Ren saw relief briefly flash across Ash's face too, but he doubted anyone else caught it. "I am late due to a case of mistaken identity, entirely outside of my control. I believe his Grace was about to apologise for as much, when he misspoke." Ash shifted her gaze momentarily to Fulton, whose face soured. "Similarly, my improper state is a result of the same error, and is not of my choosing, although I am as ready now as always to perform at the pleasure of the queen." Ash gave a small bow. Her bow seemed to underscore every word. Ren tried not to laugh his disbelief.

"Mistaken identity? Do you know something of this maid's inconvenience, Fulton?"

"I do believe this maid, but yester-morn, was subject to an inquisition, your Majesty." the archbishop answered.

"I should say her standing here serves our verdict," the queen looked over Ash, appraisingly. Fulton made no answer. "Well, our Mystics have made quite a display already, and the day's barely begun! Let us adjourn for intermediary refreshment while they regroup themselves, and Kynaston? A masque thereafter?"

"Yes, Your Majesty," answered the Master of Revels. He was tall, moderately handsome – as were most men Queen Valencia chose to keep close – but unequivocally sure of his place beneath the queen in the Mysteries' Chain of Being.

The queen and an orbiting body of guards led out. The court retinue followed thereafter, with the gallery emptying to match. The hall quickly became near-empty, excepting stationed sentries, a queen's attendant, the two men guarding Ash (still dripping onto the marble floor), and Ren – lingering in a stupor. The departing mass had given Ash a wide berth, most with indifference, a few with raised noses, and one baron with open fascination.

The queen's attendant approached, her face pinched with etiquette but her eyes kind. "Her Majesty offers rooms to all Queen's Day players, should they have need of laving or retirement. I can show you the way and I am certain we should also be able to find you... suitable attire for your return to the court."

Ren moved closer, but waited.

"At the pleasure of the queen." Ash dipped her head respectfully. It was when she raised her head that she saw Ren. He leaned on a column in the side chamber of the main hall. He smiled as Ash continued to the attendant, "May I take a moment to gather myself?"

"Of course. I will wait at this door." The attendant indicated a side exit. She next addressed the guards who'd escorted Ash within the royal residence. They shifted uncomfortably beside her. "You may return to your posts."

The pair, appearing grateful, turned about. The shorter of the two paused and whispered something to Ash.

Ash offered a side-smile but spoke so Ren could hear. "I take back what I said about your posterity. Things got rather heated out there, and a lass'll say what she must to gain an audience."

"Aye to that," the guard said. "M'lady." He dipped his head, bashfully, but also in wonderment. Ash had that effect on most Mysteries-fearing men and women alike.

The pair left Ash to stand a moment in the hall. She wasn't as alone as Ren wished he could find her, with sentries generously flanking the chamber, but it was quiet.

First, Ren took all of her in – the small dimple nestled into one side of her smile, the freckles sprayed across her face when you came close enough to see, the warmth in her dark eyes. Ren made his approach, soft in step and then in speech. "I thought… "

"I know."

"I was a wreck."

"Truly?"

"I withdrew."

"You *what*?" Ash gaped at him.

Ren spoke fast. "I feared they had taken you from this world. For a morning, I thought they had won. And I could not bear to be a part of some... *celebration*... in light of such rumour." He had grown fractionally louder, and collected himself. "Not only could nothing distract me from... despairing over... *the world's* loss, I could not support any monarchy that allowed such a light to go out." He was breathless with exasperation.

Ash smiled, but feigned shock. "You thought they'd beaten me!" It was not a question.

"I feared it. I feared it like I have feared nothing before." Ren's eyes searched Ash for some acknowledgement that she returned what he was clearly proclaiming in his anguish.

"You're forgiven. For a moment I feared they had beaten me too. But don't doubt me again. We've used up that allowance, and there won't be any more of it." She dusted her hands against each other. "I have some scrubbing up to do, and *you* need to see to the business of appealing your return to the day's programme." Ash drew the guard's cape tighter over her transparent underclothes to muster some decorum. "Oh, and Ren?"

"Ya?"

"I won't be beaten."

"So it seems." He chewed on his words briefly. "Looking as you do... " he gestured from the scratches on her cheek to the puddle at her feet, "you are only more of a breath-stealing force to be reckoned with."

"Enough of that. Do me a real favour and pop my arm back in its socket, would you?"

Ren laughed then. She was alive. She was like no one he had ever met. And he believed she would win a Seal to ensure she stayed around for him to be surprised by her again and again, if she would indulge him.

So Ren offered a deck of cards for Ash to bite down on. "Itch onwy partial, itch shouldn't take much... "

Ash hiss-moaned with surprised pain and pleasure – with precision like nothing she'd ever seen, Ren had already performed the task. His efficacy had all at once drawn from her agony and relief, and a surge in attraction for him. Ash wiped a tear from Ren's cheek, letting the heel of her hand linger, tempted. She shook her head briskly. "Appeal! Make your appeal!" Ash shooed him off, feeling a blush rising.

Ren backed away, smiling, his eyes not finished with their reunion.

She lived.

ODELL

There'd been no body.

Odell wouldn't let it sour her mood. It was Queen's Day, after all.

She supped in the open air, a pew's distance from the city wall. Upturned barrels and crates served as auxiliary furnishings for the influx of revellers spilling out of taverns, inns and public houses. Odell shared her table with her husband, other bishops and their wives, from all around the Lough. All wore polite smiles as thin shrouds over unmistakable disapproval. The day was altogether too boisterous to be proper, and yet here they were – in the world, but not of it. It was good to show their people they knew how to have a good time and support the queen.

Little girls and boys wore crowns braided from scarves worn days earlier at Dawn's Veil, whirling revels of small royals. They spun in circles, hand-in-hand, chanting until they turned their circle inside out;

Queen's Day, Queen's Day
Eyes are all turned in
Our day, our day,
She'll never see our sin.

Two of the wives tut-tutted the children. Odell –
determined to enjoy herself – could not help but feel
sickened by the triviality of it. So what? A few
children felt devilish and hadn't brushed their hair.
They'd likely had far less guidance in their
upbringing than the bishops' wives had had, who
were they to judge? Where was their compassion?

There were graver things to worry about.

Children's rhymes – ha! Odell had scarcely slept
since the most recent trial.

The irresolution of it had left her… turning.

The children released each other's hands and each
spun in place with their hands over their eyes,
laughing until they bumped into someone.

A band had begun playing though it was still day.
Odell winced.

A shameless *ong*-tongue two barrels away,
blustered a report. "I was there – when she magicked
away that whore back home in SeeBurg. I was there
the morning they discovered she had been spirited
away from her trial by ordeal and I was there when
they tried to baptise her. She vanished every time.
She had to be in league with the Unknown! She's no
doubt a lost soul floating in the Unknown even now."

Her body wouldn't stay lost. When it finally surfaced – like all bodies eventually did, it would be a sorry sight.

Would the girl's freckles still stand out against her skin, or would her face look like a washer woman's hands – as the Thrice Accused from the last moon's had – when she'd finally surfaced? Would baptism have seen to the erasure of even those marks of who she had been?

It would be unfortunate.

But it would be closure.

Odell's attention hitched on a face in the crowd. It could not be.

The apparition of a young woman sat not four tables away, a face like a mischievous angel, though one presently lined with worry. She held an unfamiliar, second ghost's hand in hers – a man's – her other hand lay below her breast upon her belly. The pair sat muted in voice and posture, like faded imposters unfit to share the bright canvas they were painted upon. Would this have been the woman's future, had Odell stopped the crushing opposition surrounding her? Love? Family?

Odell excused herself from the table.

She had to get *closer*.

She wove amongst the barrels and joined a queue – unsure what for, but uncaring. She craned her neck to better take in the vision.

Then the ghost-man spoke! Odell swallowed hard, sure she had been mistaken. "Come, Grete."

He tugged at the woman's hand, and guided her away with a hand on her lower back.

She'd heard them. And they wove amongst those gathered, solid and real.

Not ghosts.

Not Pabla la Presica.

Nor Ash.

But the resemblance had been eerie enough to send a guilty shiver through Odell.

Odell was suddenly face to face with the vendor at the front of the line, gaping and silent. "Sorry, I... I... " she turned back to the table she'd left – its party's disdain seeping out to create a vacuum within the happiness billowing around them. The man next in line leaned around her and took her place, so she was cut loose and spat back into the crowd.

She stood, jostled about, untethered. She couldn't go back to her table. *Could she?* Apparition or real, the woman Grete's appearance had brought pain, and a revelation. Ash had been robbed of the possible future Odell had just witnessed in tableau, and Odell had been party to the theft. And she had known it. She'd known she was cutting the girl's life short. But seeing the woman today, Odell knew *why*. With a tight hand across her own empty belly, Odell choked out a single gasp.

She could not allow Ash to have both.

Ash could not have reckless infamy in her youth *and* a long life of secure familial happiness. It was too much. It was enough that pious women Odell knew were afforded the blessing of bringing life into the world while Odell was left longing and barren. But for a girl like Ash to claim that blessing? No. A girl could be permitted a bright *short* life. She could not have Mystic excitement *and* the life Odell deserved, both. Odell would not let that stand.

Odell looked to *her life,* back at her table, then blinked hard to clear her vision – for there Ash stood, behind Bishop Gregory, dripping. Or was it Pabla?

This could not be – no one was reacting to the wet witch in their midst. Odell feebly clung to composure, her lips trembling. Then with her eyes closed, she shook her head as though it were a door she was slamming closed.

The apparition vanished.

Odell drew a deep breath. Sleep was all she lacked, not her wits. She would not be controlled by fear or fatigue. She had a right to be here. She was expected to be at her husband's side and she was a reliable, honourable woman – heaven knew he needed her – a good woman who would live the long life she deserved. And so, in a stupor – not quite knowing where the lines of what was real and what was imagined were drawn – Mrs Gregory returned to the good bishop's side.

ASH

Ash learned the queen's attendant was Yardena, a woman brusque in manner but tender in service, for which Ash was grateful. Although the woman insisted on feeding, bathing, and dressing Ash (and sometimes more than one of those at once), Yardena eventually accepted Ash's argument that the short measure of absence they were allowed would be best spent leaving Ash to lie down rather than styling her hair or lacing her corset.

Ash slept straightway and more deeply than she had since her parents' deaths, in part because she felt some semblance of safety, but she was sure also owing something to the medicinal nightshade Yardena had prepared for her pain.

It was on Yardena's return – too soon – that the poor woman met her real battle. Ash wanted no part of petticoats, corset or hose *after bathing* either. She justified the need for workable garments for her act, insistent the constraining flamboyance of the court was completely unsuitable for any commended show.

She didn't add that she preferred more comfortable attire off-stage as well – nor that she believed all women should – displaying prudence in which battles she engaged.

Yardena had outlined much of court etiquette lamenting Ash had missed an apparent class in the subject that morning. One such point Ash decided to take: Yardena was adamant Queen Valencia expected her courtiers and attendants to sport the latest fashions, and so long as Ash intended to remain at the pleasure of the queen, she should do as little as she could to warrant her *dis*pleasure.

They came to a compromise: Ash *would* wear a dress of Valencia's court – but without corset, petticoats or hose. She would roll back its sleeves from their design at the wrist to sit mid fore-arm. She would be permitted to gather its skirts back like an apron, tight around her frame, securing their surplus behind her waist. Her legs would be exposed to the calf so she could step freely without fear of tripping over her skirts and she would wear boots (she'd take any dry pair her size), not some ghastly court slipper. She would have no part of lace, pearls, or feathers being woven in her hair. Brushed and clean was more than sufficient.

"So many missed opportunities." Yardena ran her hands longingly through Ash's hair.

"Yours or mine?" Ash raised one eyebrow.

Yardena chuckled from her belly. "You're a sharp one. I've not met one with quite your purpose.

And even without the trinkets," Yardena fluttered her hands around Ash's head, "you may be too pretty for Her Majesty to keep around.   Oh fie! May the Mysteries untold share your will."

"What of my will?"

Yardena drew back, though not unpleased. "Or she may like that sharpness about you enough to ignore that face." Yardena held Ash by the chin, "All Untold willing."

Ash had thought herself fairly inconspicuous in her movements as she returned to the Presence Chamber. A masque-drama on the delicate relation between Mysteries and God had played out in allegory while Ash slept – some redolent piety relating how All Untold was available to all through God's mouthpiece, the basilica. Ash of course believed *anyone* might inquire of the Mysteries, and call upon All Untold.

Now, commended Minstrels were just finishing a double set. The court had appeared rapt in their attentions, but Ash's re-entry had not escaped *the queen's* attention.

"I see you *prefer* to appear in court half-dressed," said the queen, upon seeing her.

Ash pretended only now to notice her tailoring, scant comparable to the balance of ladies present – powdered, arranged, and barely breathing. "Oh, your Majesty, it is my understanding this is the first occasion a woman of the Mystics has appeared at your pleasure, and so it is the court's misfortune they know little of feminine Mystic costume!" The queen allowed herself a small look of surprise, but Ash saw delight too, and so continued. "Yardena convinced me to don thrice what I would have without her counsel." Ash winked. "You were wise to assign her, Your Majesty." Too far?

Apparently not. Ash thought she'd witnessed the queen snigger. She considered the tight curls beneath the queen's crown, the careful jewels around her bodice, the gold and silver brocade of her voluminous gown. Ash had the distinct impression the queen liked her own costume and was satisfied that Ash – though drawing significant attention – attracted admiration of a vastly different league.

"Indeed," the queen acquiesced. "I think it high time this day took a Mystic turn. Kynaston?"

Ash drew an anticipatory breath.

"Your Majesty." The Master of Revels bowed once from the waist. "Your Grace, honoured guests. At the pleasure of the queen: the Breath-stealing Banyan!"

Ash grimaced. Banyan emerged from a parting group of courtiers. His long cloak appeared heavy for all its embellishments.

Ash forgot all about Banyan when she saw Ren two alcoves away from the attention-centre – his dusky skin more pronounced amongst the predominance of fair faces about him. He was smiling at her. He was mouthing something. She read it well: "breath-stealing." Ren held his chin and lifted his index finger away from the hold subtly, so that it was clear at whom he pointed: her.

Ash shook off the distraction, though she took secret pleasure in it.

She lamented what Banyan did for the names of Mystics everywhere, but rejoiced that she could only look better for coming after him. She hadn't seen him since the night Wynn had dragged her out to see his "bullet catch," but she'd heard plenty word he was popular along the Western tract.

And now here he stood: Banyan. *Eugh.*

"Your Majesty, excuse me, I seem to have lost my head!" And then, inexplicably, Banyan created the illusion that his head had fallen from his shoulders only to be caught in his own hands. The farce required only a generous cape and stiff contraption within it that held its collar aloft while Banyan bent inside. There were gasps from the gallery and side chambers.

Queen Valencia frowned. Ash smiled. The queen found Banyan either disappointing or grotesque. Excellent. "You will have to do better than that," the queen stated.

Ash caught sight of Collier – the man who'd performed before her on Hughes' holding. Flanked by assistants, he stood a man made of props and finely-tailored clothing. And now, he blanched.

Something of the queen's reaction to Banyan had affected him. Interesting.

Banyan's head rose back to his shoulder (his cape drew in to those who watched closely). "But of course, Your Majesty."

"Your Majesty, please."

"But of course, of course... your Majesty." Banyan was bumbling.

He drew from within his cloak a semi-transparent carafe. It contained an amber liquid which sloshed as it moved. "Mayhap this pleases you better, your Majesty." Ash could see the sweat on Banyan's brow.

"I will not be drinking it!" The queen replied.

"Of course not, your Majesty. May I request a handkerchief from one of your ladies in waiting?"

"You may." The queen gave a small smile.

"Ladies?" Banyan directed his gaze to the entourage who curved about the queen at three paces from the throne, standing at equal distance to where the archbishop sat.

One lady drew out a kerchief and held it before her. An attendant retrieved it and carried it to Banyan.

"Many thanks," Banyan said. He returned the carafe temporarily to his cloak. His cloak really did look heavy. He brought the four corners of the kerchief up to meet each other so that the fabric square formed a pouch. He shook and preened at it with the other hand until it appeared inflated, and then he reached within his cloak for the carafe. Before the court, Banyan poured the amber liquid into the handkerchief, until the original receptacle was empty and entirely clear. The court gave polite applause, the queen among them. Banyan returned the carafe to the abyss of his cloak and capped the hand holding the kerchief with his other hand.

Banyan then pulled the handkerchief up into his hand – with no apparent sign of dampness – and with a twist of both hands, was cupping a dove.

There were cheers and applause for the bird.

"My handkerchief?" Called the lady-in-waiting.

Banyan held his chin in thought (Ash's least favourite of his moves), invited an unsure attendant to hold his dove, then held one index finger high – as though finally remembering where he'd placed the lady's possession. He then reached within his bulky sleeve and drew out the handkerchief with his customary fanfare.

From the ensuing applause, it was clear to Ash that gulls were not unique to farmlets or night shows upon holdings, but abounded in royal residences equally well. Surely seeing the kerchief *come* from the sleeve suggested where it had *gone* to begin with?

Ash missed the cave of her hood and its shelter for whispered curses. She refrained from being too insolent on the outside, but made ample curses inside.

An attendant brought the bird close to the queen, and she stroked its back. "A better show," she acknowledged.

"May we see the carafe?" A call came from the side chamber. It was unclear to the queen who had spoken, but Ash knew Ren's voice when she heard it.

"But of course! And see how it has transformed!" Banyan announced. He revealed the carafe – miraculously full of amber liquid once more. The gulls rendered applause.

"But can we *really* see it?" Ren stepped forward now, so that all could see it was he who made the inquiry.

"I'm not sure of the rules where you are from, sir, but it is considered impolite to request an inspection of a Mystic." Banyan smiled through his correction.

"I am pretty sure it is impolite anywhere, but for the queen, I assume you make exceptions? Have you something to hide?" Ren raised both of his thick, perfectly-straight brows.

"I... "

"As I thought." Ren made a small bow towards Banyan, then clapped in a way that paid no compliment.

"I see you are still with us, Besuto Ren, and part of the festivities no less. Have you changed your mind about offering us a show this day?"

"I will do as the queen pleases, your Majesty," Ren answered from a bow.

"Very well! Make a note, Kynaston! The next Mystic to perform will be Besuto Ren!" The chamberlain nodded and made literal note.

"I would have thought the balance of Mystics better for this one Besuto Ren's withdrawal, your Majesty," spoke Archbishop Fulton.

"Oh come now, Fulton, celebrating the world's Mysteries is no insult to God! I have heard no blasphemy yet, have you?" The queen's words gave Ash hope – perhaps rumours had failed to paint her fairly; this woman did not seem wholly ruled by either the basilica or her Privy Council.

"No, Your Majesty, I only suggest… "

"That is enough." The queen brought her hands into a delicate clasp. "Let us break for dinner." Definitely not a figurehead only, Queen Valencia appeared weary of men speaking for her and quite capable of correcting them when they forgot their station.

The Master of Revels announced acrobats would take the floor after the midday meal. Ash's eyes locked with Ren's. He shrugged, as though apologising for his earlier outburst. Ash folded her arms, and with her hand in the crook of her elbow pointed towards Ren with an index finger. "You – breath-stealing," she mouthed. Ren caught her words with one hand and drew them to his lips as though she'd blown him a kiss.

As far as distractions went, Ren was the finest kind.

ASH

Ash had missed the morning refreshments and now, seeing the spread laid before her was sorry for it. She'd taken some refreshment in her assigned quarters with Yardena – mostly by way of things popped into her mouth while bathing – but this meal was something else.

The queen sat at the head table spanning the length of the guildhall. Her taster stood at the table's end, having already tried all that the queen was served, but remaining present should any ill effects come late. He looked like a sentry in his position, but Ash knew better. Although the queen had been curt with the archbishop, it was clear they were now amiable and enjoying each other's company. The rest of the court and guests sat at tables in lines at right-angles to the queen's, each headed by their sponsoring Lord and Lady and peppered with affiliated gentry. So it was that Minstrels sat amongst nobles and Acrobats prepared to sup with duchesses.

Lord and Lady Hughes were hastily making the most of access to one of their own nominees; The Unflinching Ash. "We finally appear to have the opportunity to personally commend your show," Lord Hughes announced.

Lady Hughes tilted her head genteelly towards Ash. "Yes, please, show us how your palms fare, Miss Ash."

Ash presented her hands to reveal the ribbon-stick-marks, now healing.

Lady Hughes' face tightened in sympathy. "Twas a very good show. We look forward to seeing how you dazzle us all today."

"Indeed, we're glad you decided to join us." Lord Hughes' lips curled in, barricading a laugh. Ash appreciated the jest, despite it feeling quite soon. She shook her head to clear the memories of the lake.

"I'll say now what I couldn't risk tarrying to say then – thank you. Thank you for the commendation."

"You earned it." Lady Hughes punctuated her assertion with a decisive nod and Ash's heart swelled within her. *Mysteries tamed, she had.*

The meal began with an *apéritif* of apple confectionary. The small morsels were coated in honey, cinnamon and anise. Ash was still in the midst of deeply regretting how few of these were dispensed when she noted those around her were bathing their hands in shallow basins and drying them with crisp linen towels. It appeared she'd missed a step, and quickly amended her oversight.

The baron who had openly fawned over her sopping arrival had managed to secure a seat but one down and across from Ash, and offered his commiseration; "There's always too few of these, aren't there?" He wore a moustache that twitched when he smiled.

Ash smiled in thanks, for this baron had made light of her faux pas – even empathised with her eagerness to begin. "Indeed. I confess; I've never tasted anything quite like them and their smell alone made me forget my manners!"

"I'm sure you've washed yourself plenty and thoroughly already!" The baron's lips curled inwards with amusement at his own joke. She *had* arrived dripping. His lips' curl caused his moustache to become misshapen and distracting. Ash squinted at it with curiosity, then refocussed on the towel she held as she finished drying her hands. She was glad Ren did not wear a moustache, although she imagined he could make one look good. She smiled to herself.

Wait, if all were seated with their sponsors, that meant...

She glanced both ways down the Hughes' table. Then, someone shifted to alter her view and she startled to find precisely who she'd been looking for. Ren. He was close enough to have seen her conversation with the Moustache-Twitcher, but Ash suspected not close enough to have heard it. His face – which grew more addictive to her by the minute – reflected no jealousy, if he had.

The baron stretched his hand across the table, placing it closer to Ash. "May I break bread for you?" he offered. Ash looked around the table before responding, seeing the few female guests were being served by the male guests – perhaps to spare sullying their precious gowns – but for Ash it felt less like service and more like an insult. If the men were capable of breaking their own bread, so was she.

"I see it is the custom, but I am quite capable with my own hands." She realised the innuendo too late. There was nothing that could be done now, so she shrugged to herself and offered a feeble smile to the baron without any clarification.

The bread did not match Nicholas Baker's in its magic, but tasted good to a young woman who'd spent too long on the run and often on negligible fare. Ash helped herself to two bowls within arm's reach of both her and the baron – a vegetable assortment of purslane, herbs, fruit and goat kid from one, and a steaming rich broth from the other. Sweet almonds had been used to add creaminess to the broth in a way few inns or fry-houses on the tract bothered with. Ash appreciated the skill of the royal chef and ate with gusto. With every other bite she would remind herself to slow down, but she would immediately forget and catch herself inhaling her food again. She stole a glance towards Ren. He must have felt her eyes upon him, as he immediately turned his to her, smiled and lifted his plate in salute.

She tore bread with her teeth, briefly closed her eyes and hummed contentedly. When she opened them again, Ren was shaking his head in amusement.

It couldn't be helped; her love for food was a secret she refused to keep.

Ash was just feeling close to satisfied when the pork arrived. It came on platters in a nest of pears, chestnuts and sweet potato. She made room.

The baron leaned forward and spoke through the considerable din: "You have *quite* the appetite!" His eyebrows and moustache raised in flirtatious unison. Then he licked his lips, leaving no room for misinterpretation. Lady Hughes offered a crumpled expression of sincere apology.

It was time Ash nipped these growing attentions in the bud. "I think you should know I'm quite taken with someone else aaaaand... I'll never be a noble's inferior." *Perhaps she'd overdone it? Alas,* she shrugged, still chewing. "You'd be better off playing this game with... " Ash scanned the table and pointed with a nut, "...her?" Her nut of decision landed on a woman watching others eat, instead of eating. With unintentionally comical timing, the woman dabbed at the edge of her closed and empty mouth with a napkin she retrieved from her own sleeve. "Perfect, see! Now *there's* a woman who'll let you tear her bread." Ash winked.

The baron appeared taken aback by Ash's forthrightness but not yet deterred.

"No hard feelings?" Ash continued. "But let's not let a little thing like lack of mutual attraction stop us enjoying this fine meal!" Ash saw more food was coming. "Here now is dessert, is it not?" She inhaled through her teeth.

The baron gave Ash a look that suggested he was still (inconceivably!) undecided on how he felt about her.

Dessert was served – a fried pastry filled with tangy custard, drizzled in verijuice and sprinkled with slivered almonds. Mulled wine filled tumblers shared by guests. Ash refrained from partaking of these but not from the cubes of cheese on the platters beside them. Taking home a Seal today would mean she had no more need of Queen's Day. She felt sorry for her palate that this occasion should come but once, but relief for her stomach, which now protested her excess.

The tables were being cleared when Ash made another visual sweep of the top table, taking an inventory of tells. Though she should be safe in the palace halls, she checked her exits for good measure. She was startled to find two people's eyes firmly upon her.

Those of Queen Valencia, who appeared to have eaten little, and Archbishop Fulton. Whatever discussion had taken place while Ash had gorged herself, the two were in agreement. The queen looked resolute and slightly pained while Fulton... well, he looked triumphant. As the basilica's frontman within the residence, this spelled nothing but tribulation for an escapee witch.

REN

Ren excused himself from the table, summoned by
Kynaston's beckoning hand. He met the Master of
Revels beyond the head table, where they briefly
conferred as to what supplies Ren required for his
upcoming performance, as well as his preferred title
for address. Kynaston then invited Ren to remain
and enter the hall just after the chamberlain and the
acrobats next up. Ren nodded his agreement, and
clasped his own wrist above a fist in front of him as
he took up position – the acrobats flanking
Kynaston's other side.

This vantage point allowed him better
appreciation of how the ripples of the room radiated
from Ash's table. Ren was sure some watched Ash
for her beauty; others could not look away from her
unguarded manner and daring dress. Whatever their
motivation, all those surrounding her regularly made
checks her way. Ren imagined they were fighting
the urge to all-out study her, and would prefer to

never look away if they could help it. Or maybe that was just him.

Ren was not the only one who noticed Ash's effects, from afar.

"She amuses me already." Ren overheard Queen Valencia say, eyeing Ash across the hall. Even at this distance, it was clear Ash was eating at considerable speed.

Ren imagined the room falling away so that only the queen and archbishop remained. He honed his focus so he heard only them.

"I understand, your Majesty." Archbishop Fulton straightened his cutlery. "Though the discord surrounding her is significant, more worrisome, is her growing popularity. In repeatedly evading the guard she has attracted quite a following."

"But has she not been through more than one trial? What are the trials if their outcomes count for nought? She has passed the tests you sanctioned, and rightly earned some reputation for it. Shouldn't I be acquainted with what is popular within my own territory?"

"I respect your point, your Majesty. But what if that favour is aligned with one who strongly opposes how the territory is currently being run?" Fulton picked at a piece of flaking skin at his knuckle. "Bishop Gregory of Seeburg has observed a strong correlation between Mystic indulgence and rising rebellious factions. This girl-Mystic has set herself in opposition to you, my queen."

"Allowing the girl to perform sends a strong message that I do not consider her a threat. Stamping her out now will only stoke the fire of opposition."

Fulton lifted his chin and swallowed. "Then let her perform, but withhold the Seal. You send your message – that you are not afraid of a young Mystic's popularity – but you avoid the recklessness of granting immunity to someone who represents the face of rebellion."

"Your Majesty," Queen Valencia corrected.

Ren could not resist smiling at the correction.

"Your Majesty. My apologies, Your Majesty."

"You have been heard." Queen Valencia motioned for a server to clear her plate. "I remember well that another young woman's rise moved you to raise a similar voice of concern." The queen removed the napkin from her lap and placed it on the table. "Besides, what is a contest if it's decided before it's through? I haven't even seen what the girl can do!"

Fulton looked to his own lap, watching his napkin as he removed it and placed it on the table.

"But your concerns are noted."

Ren's throat constricted so abruptly that he choked his answer to Kynaston, who had told him it was now time to re-enter the hall.

Ren had thought Ash would be safe here. She had come this far – she was part of the exception, the standard-setting court, whose tastes and habits trickled down to influence many. Yet even in the palace, opposition remained. It nagged imperfect on the fringe of Ren's perception, an errant card from a mis-shuffled deck.

Ren could feel it – Ash was not safe yet.

Ren hurried to follow the chamberlain, drawing deep breaths in attempt to soothe the sense all was not in its correct place yet.

ASH

Back in the Presence Chamber, Ash winced at the contortions, turns and dives which the acrobats before her executed. Her own abdominal discomfort played a major part in her gut response to their performance. The queen seemed unaffected by such empathy, displaying a pleasant aristocratic smile.

Chamberlain Kynaston had been tasked with seeing that Ren was the next Mystic to perform. Would he come after this trio? Earlier Ash had assumed so, when she'd seen him standing alongside the chamberlain, but now she no longer saw him there. She cringed at a somersault which ended in two players doubled over.

A voice whispered by her ear, so close she felt the warmth of it, "It was torture to see glimpses of you eating that meal without hearing your commentary." *Ren.* Heat flooded Ash from chest to toes, while her head seemed to momentarily forget its function completely. All at once she wanted to turn and fold him into an embrace; thank him for being familiar and kind; smell his hair and skin and perhaps his clothes; touch his hand like she had under the bridge; draw one of his blades; and maybe ask if he'd ever considered a moustache.

Her faculties returned. Drawing a breath of discipline, Ash whispered that which was necessary alongside the best of the ideas that had assaulted her; "Thank you for being such a good friend to me, Ren, but you know I can't be seen with you now. I must do this alone, and I've risked enough already." She turned to take in his reaction. He was hurt, but mustering dignity. She was two for two in a single afternoon! "I don't mean to hurt you, but this is something I *must* do alone."

"I long ago gave up stopping you in that. Even when danger besets you." Did he appear concerned? Why? "Ash, I already understand, and agree. It is only in you dubbing me merely *friend* that I take offence." Ren squeezed her hand once – out of sight with the close-quarters crowd for cover – as though saying goodbye. It felt final, as though he was not only giving her leave to accomplish this thing, but ending a platonic relationship he could not bear.

Realising this, Ash caught his hand.

"Don't worry, Ren. I see kissing in our future."

Ren's preternatural stillness was broken only by him blinking once – very slowly, as though savouring a thought.

Then he said, "You read fortunes now?"

She whispered, "Oh no. As always, I read *tells*, and they're all pointing that way." She released his hand, dismissing him with a final hushed promise, "Friends first, Seal second, kissing *later*."

Ren drew a deep breath and grinned before weaving away and returning to the position she'd earlier found him in, alongside the chamberlain. He whispered something upon his return which she assumed was an apology. Ash smiled and imagined him saying, "Forgive me, I had to go cause a woman's heart to stumble before going on." It was likely he begged excusal for something far less romantic. Whatever explanation he'd proffered, Ash was touched he had taken the time to find her and whisper. She touched her ear at the memory of his lips so close as she watched him.

Ren applauded politely when the acrobatics finished their routine, then made small talk with the chamberlain – who appeared to ignore whatever it was Ren offered. Ash was impressed. Ren was making an excellent show of being unshaken by what had transpired between him and her. For Ash, the realisation of the depth of her attraction and affection for this man had, for a minute, caused everything to happen as though she were back in the water of the lake – buried in a quiet that pressed in all around her.

The full cacophony of the hall came rushing back as those close to her took up a familiar chant: "Besuto Ren, Besuto Ren, Besuto Ren."

The queen interlaced her fingers.

Ren stood at the centre of the polished floor. He'd erected an easel at the far corner of the performance space, nestled against a pillar and arch near the main entry doors – keeping whatever was propped for display on the easel a mystery to those in attendance.

He spoke to all. "As you know, my name is Ren," a few took up the chant of his new name again (*Besuto Ren, Besuto Ren*), but hush fell when he raised his hand to request quiet. "I bring to Queen's Day a simple show, and ask only that you watch very closely, so your eyes are not deceived. Your Majesty, I would ask your assistance, at your pleasure." Ren bowed deeply, then looked up to the queen.

Ash could see that Valencia, like most in the room, enjoyed Ren the performer. Ren's demeanour reflected a new air of confidence, which only lent greater appeal to his previous abundance of the same.

"How is it I may assist you?" she answered.

"I would ask that you draw me a picture. Anything you wish." Ren produced a piece of paper from an imperceptible pocket in his outer vest, followed by the same pen Ash had seen during his card trick upon hay bales. *That vest never ceases to amaze.* Ren unfolded the paper to four times the size it had been on its appearance. With one look at the sentries closest to the queen, Ren held the paper and pen out in an offer towards the lady-in-waiting at the queen's right.

The archbishop shifted in his chair.

The lady-in-waiting to which Ren had made his appeal received confirmation from the queen before making her approach. She took the paper and instrument and carried them to Valencia, who turned both over in her hands before beginning to write... or draw, by all appearances.

Ren stood facing the main entry doors, showing the queen his back.

"When you are through, your Majesty, please share the drawing with those around you – hold it up for the court to see – and then fold the paper up as it was before you drew your picture and return it to me." He of course meant via someone else's hands. The queen did as she had been asked, displaying a basic bird in flight over a lake. The lake was suggested by a cluster of three reeds and wavy lines across an oval. The ladies about her whispered, "Very good, Your Majesty," and the courtiers and attendants within range clapped politely.

"Her Majesty does good work, I hear!" Ren called towards the doors. The gallery and side-chamber occupants laughed appreciatively.

The same lady-in-waiting who'd made the first delivery crossed the floor again to present Ren with the queen's work, now refolded in quarters. Ren held the paper above his head, still folded, unseen.

"Here I hold a piece of artwork produced by Her Royal Majesty. I wonder if I should leave now and become a very rich man?" Ren made to tuck the paper back into his vest and raised his eyebrows playfully. "No, of course not! There is more to see!" He raised the paper once more and passed it between his hands in the air. "But first, we must take care of this!" Ren pulled and struck steel against flint before most of the gulls knew it had happened. The paper was alight in Ren's hands. As the flames licked closer to his fingers, he dropped the final glowing corner and stamped it out. There was no applause. Archbishop Fulton and a few courtiers looked mortified.

Queen Valencia remained reticent.

"Do not worry, Your Majesty," Ren assured her, "for I can see in my mind's eye what you drew, and will reproduce it for you now."

Ren backed towards the easel. The Archbishop leaned forward, no doubt claiming blasphemy. Valencia waved him away, but appeared to acknowledge Fulton's concern with a brisk nod. She then said, "His Grace is concerned you are claiming to read the mind of a queen, Besuto Ren. Is that your claim?"

Ren hovered near the easel, looked down for a moment in thought. *That was new.* "Forgive me, Your Majesty, for I misspoke; this is not my native tongue. I am about to *guess* what you drew."

Fulton sat back in his chair, dissatisfied but silenced at present. Valencia concealed a smirk. "Very good," she said.

Ren stepped behind the easel, and made a show of running his hands across the surface – the audience could not see, gripping the sides of the easel so only his fingers were visible. He looked out at the queen, back to his paper... and then finally, drew.

"Your Majesty, are you ready to find out how well I... guessed?" Ren called across the floor to the throne.

"I am ready. Let us see your artwork." She lifted her chin with interest.

Ren spun the easel on its legs so that all in attendance could see what he had inked there; displaying a basic bird in flight over a lake – a lake shown by a cluster of three reeds and some wavy lines across an oval to suggest water. A picture near identical to the queen's. But without a crease.

Ash smiled. He was good. She was uniquely positioned mid-hall to see as much, but the queen was squinting at her distance from Ren's prestige. "Allow me to bring it closer, Your Majesty?"

Valencia approved his approach with a hand of summons.

Fulton sat up and viewed Ren's approach through the side of his eyes.

The moment Fulton, the queen, and the ladies-in-waiting saw the image clearly was marked by their collective recoil. He had done it. He had known the mind of the queen.

The lady-in-waiting who'd twice assisted the queen from her place on the throne, came and took the finished replica from Ren at the queen's bidding. The queen grasped it and studied it in her lap. She looked up at Ren, then back once more to the copy – or restoration, she knew not which – and grinned. She laid the picture about her lap and led the applause.

Ren bowed low, then backed away.

"Very good indeed," Valencia conceded. "It is just as well you stayed."

A voice came from the side chamber. "Would you turn out your pockets?" It was Banyan. He stepped forward, in line with the pillar at the performance space's edge, and inclined his head in challenge towards Ren.

"But of course!" And Ren did. He pulled at the fabric within the faint seams of two pockets at the front of his vest until they protruded limp and impotent from his garment. The chant from earlier resumed, *Besuto Ren, Besuto Ren.*

His sleight of hand – and foresight – *impeccable.* Ash hoped kissing him was in her *very* near future.

REN

Ren was wary.

Chamberlain Kynaston had passed him a card calling Ren to a meeting in a side chamber. The chamberlain's nerves were clearly taut and the privacy afforded by the designated location demanded wariness. Privacy boasted a variety of sponsors – spies, thieves, politicians, attackers and paramours. Ren paused in his step, his thoughts caught on the last. Had he detected any clue from Kynaston to suggest an attraction? He didn't think so, but he'd learned from his time travelling to the Lough to be less reckless with the attentions he received from both sexes. If not Kynaston, might he be arranging an introduction?

Ren continued his approach, taking the turns noted on the card. How *would* he answer a proposal of courtship? His heart was taken, he knew that much, but what facts could he tender to clarify why? *Many apologies, but I am unable to entertain any pretence of romance, or even the promise a romance might develop as I am... infatuated with someone else?* Ren scoffed aloud.

It was more than that.

He was *devoted* to someone else, and intended to remain so.

Could he say that? Without qualification? There was no engagement.

But there *was* promise.

Of kissing.

Ren brushed his knuckles across his lips, dismissing the heat that flared upon them at the thought.

It was this dwelling upon promises and lips that saw Ren caught off-guard – though he'd wisely nursed caution earlier.

The first blow came from his right and was directed to his stomach.

Ren considered drawing his blades. Then he considered where he was, and thought it best to ascertain who he was dealing with first. He allowed his arms to be held behind him while a second hit evacuated all wind from his chest.

There was no sign of Kynaston. Four guards secured Ren, but instruction came from the shadows. "Nothing on the face." The archbishop stepped into the light. Ren was glad he'd given pause. "Besuto Ren." Fulton drew Ren's name out long like a lyric. "You forget yourself." Then Fulton nodded, and another man materalised beside the archbishop – the killbuck Ren had driven from the tavern, Segar.

Segar landed a punch to Ren's left kidney. Ren lurched, then straightened.

Fulton drew his face close so that Ren could see the pores on the man's nose, "Never... " Another drive from Segar to Ren's stomach. "Allege... " Segar pulled Ren's head back by his hair, "...to know the mind of the queen," Fulton finished.

Fulton and Segar took leave before the guards released Ren and dissolved into the dark halls whence they'd sprung.

Ren unfurled like a crumpled leaf and stood, waiting. Was it over? What was he expected to do next?

After smoothing his hair, re-tucking his underclothes, and gently exploring his injuries, Ren did the only thing that seemed to make any sense.

He turned back the way he had come to return to the queen's court.

ASH

The Master of Revels announced minstrels, who took up position in the gallery. The guests began to dance the Pavane. The vice on Ash's heart manifested again as she remembered her parents dancing the Pavane shoulder-to-shoulder. Partners took hands and led each other in circuit about the room – never facing one another, nor exchanging partners, simply dancing side by side. Ash leaned against a pillar, forlorn.

A man entered her frame of view.

The baron.

"M'lady, please join me for a round?"

"I'd rather not."

"But you will?" He was persistent, she'd give him that.

She thought of Yardena, who'd earlier attended to her. *What was it the woman had said as she'd unravelled Grete's braidwork from her matted locks?* Ah, yes. "The court will tolerate impropriety in your appearance *or* your manner, but not both. Be gentle with them." Considering Ash's brash rejection of the baron at the table earlier, perhaps she should muster some pleasantries – she wasn't giving up her hitched skirts. "One round," she answered.

As they stepped and paused, stepped and paused their way around the hall, Ash felt eyes upon her. It wasn't until she took the turn by the entry doors and made her way back towards the throne that she spied Fulton watching her. *Nothing but tribulation*, she thought, *nothing but tribulation*. The archbishop redirected his gaze to the musicians in the gallery and Ash sighed in relief.

"Do you delight in the chase then?" The baron asked, at her side. Eugh.

"Not often, and not today," she answered.

He was not deterred in expression, though he quietened.

She was surprised and impressed to see the entire company pause and bow, as the queen herself descended from her throne and joined the dance. With the chamberlain host as her partner, she glided amongst her guests, who all resumed their movements. *Good for her.*

Again Ash felt someone's eyes upon her. She gave her head a slight turn. There, behind her, Ren led the lady-in-waiting who had assisted in his show. He rolled his lips inwards, as though fighting the urge to smile.

Ash averted her gaze. "I heard her father was an excellent knife-thrower," she overheard the lady say.

"Is that so?" Ren replied. "I have heard she is very good in her own right."

Though Ash appreciated Ren's redirection, she failed to stifle a burst of rage. It was too common a tendency to remember only her father, and remember him wrongly. It felt like her mother's erasure repeated again and again. The minstrels switched tune and the dancers began reshaping their groups. Oh no, not the Galliard.

Ash saw the queen take leave. *Wise woman.* The queen returned to her throne, farewelled with bows by all those close to her, but the Galliard commenced around Ash before she could do the same. Trios of couples danced much the same as they had, only the males in each pair moved inwards along three spokes of a wheel to change places, and partners, before again fanning out into the dance. In a single turn, Ash found herself holding hands with Ren, her heart defiantly beating in rhythm completely out of time with the music. The rage subsided, reluctant pleasure supplanting it. She'd asked him to give her space, to wait a little longer. He smiled, for this association was pure innocence, not an attempt to ignore her request – neither he nor Ash could be faulted for it, nor could it be reasonably avoided. Ash gripped his hands and drank him in. *Soon,* she promised her heart, *soon.*

Wait. Was that a wince?

Ren was in pain.

Ash released him to the wheel and took her next partner. The lady-in-waiting who'd speculated about *someone's* father – now conversed with the baron. *Good, tempt him, please.* But before long, Ash was back with the Moustache, whom she treated with civility until the final notes of the Galliard played.

"Good dance," Ash said, with a small curtsy, then promptly backed away into the side chamber. Space be cursed, she needed to speak to Ren. Something was wrong. The baron followed, but so did Ren and the lady. The baron and lady stood between Ash and Ren, and the lady repeated her earlier insight to the baron, only confirming her object, plainly; "I hear your partner's father was an excellent knife-thrower."

That did it. The lady had gone and done it.

Ash leaned forward in mild fury. "My father, Alexact, was a juggler, foremost. It was *my mother* who threw knives. And yes, she was excellent."

The lady appeared to have choked on her insights, so recently tasty and worth sharing. They also appeared difficult to digest.

The baron interceded, "I believe Lady Ines only meant to praise your lineage, and Ash's answer I'm sure was only intended to enlighten us all, not give any offence." His moustache twitched in satisfaction.

"I am quite sure she intended to give offence," Ren said.

It was Ash's turn to bite her lip. The Baron and Lady Ines edged a step away, uncomfortable. Good. Ash made a quick assessment of Ren's carriage, attempting to locate the source of his pain. Ren caught her studying him, manoeuvred closer, then spoke in an aside. "What has come over you? I thought we agreed to wait… Restrain yourself!"

Ash ignored the jest. "Something is wrong." Ash's hands roved just over Ren's vest, studying his face in response. She settled on his back at the left, just below his ribs, and prodded lightly. Definitely a wince. "Ren! What is wrong?" Her words were a whisper, her thoughts a scream.

Ren looked up briefly, then rested his gaze on Ash's face.

"Always the truth." Ash locked eyes with Ren, insistent.

"I think it is safe to say… the archbishop disapproved of my performance."

Ash's chest inflated with her answering breath. "They beat you?" Her eyes flashed.

"It was but a warning. I am here, am I not?" Ren smiled. He reported having been suggill'd and *smiled.*

"You best not be downplaying what they've done to you." Ash threatened with raised eyebrows. "I'll need to see the extent of it later." Ash directed her eyes to the Master of Revels, who was readying to make an announcement, then spoke through the side of her mouth, "Sooner, if it swells terribly... or if you find blood in your urine."

"Oh, Ash, of honey-sweet tongue!" Ren smiled, his eyes on the Master too.

"Her Majesty will now honour us by playing a piece of her own composition on the flute." Any lingering dancers shifted their fanned positions in angle to greater appreciate the queen, who stood at the throne and raised a flute to her lips.

Ash was growing in respect for this queen more and more – even if the woman didn't eat enough. The archbishop, however? She felt no such feeling. His gaze was pointed, and though Ash did not flinch beneath it, she felt it like a weight upon her. He had a plan, and she must foil it.

ASH

After the queen's flute piece, a troubadour, and another dramatic ensemble – this time about Death and Judgement – Ash felt a shift in focus near the throne. Sure enough, the Master of Revels looked to her. Confirming Ash's presence, Master Kynaston made the announcement: "Your Majesty, Your Grace, honoured guests. At the pleasure of the queen: Ash the Unflinching!"

Why had she not been lined up like the other performers? Prepared? Asked if she required anything?

Ash dismissed her disgruntlement – she could see that her eyes' brief widening had purchased a smile from the archbishop.

He would not ruffle her feathers.

Ash took to the chamber floor in her modified dress. The bodice and sleeves, though more ornate and layered than her usual garments, were snug enough she could move freely. It helped to have her skirts gathered, though they too were heavy with detail and costly fabrics. She'd make it work. Frankly, it mattered little what she wore for the extent her face commanded notice. Though she'd authorised no cosmetics or adornment, she could feel her rapture shone – from her complexion, brow, hair and lips, she felt the glow. At the quietest of times, Ash imitated her mother's poise – which had so often translated as allure. It was upon a stage that Pabla and Ash both truly came alive, and Ash had known none grander than this – centre stage in the queen's court at witching hour. Ash channelled her mother's charisma and felt it draw down more potent for acknowledging her muse.

"Your Majesty, Your Grace, discerning defendants of the Mysteries that be! I have enjoyed getting to know some of you better today, and I invite your contribution this evening, for a Mystic's show is nothing without an audience!" Ash turned in place, her hands spread wide as though she would embrace all the courtiers and attendants if she could. They cheered over their applause in answer. Ash was grateful to be showing so late in the programme. The day's growing merriment (and inebriation level) clearly worked in her favour.

Ash warmed to catch Lady Hughes in her sights, palms pressed together, wishing Ash well. Ash pictured Grete and Wynn, Pabla and Alex, all in the same pose. Her radiance flooded the palace before she spoke. "I'd like to begin with a tale." And with that, the chamber gulls were hers.

Ash looked to the queen, weighing her liking of this opening; Ash had not forgotten whose approval mattered this night. Queen Valencia nodded over fingers delicately steepled in her lap. Ash continued, "Centuries ago, across a distant sea, there lived a man who enjoyed asking questions. He not only enjoyed it, he believed that we, as human beings, learn best by doing it. By asking questions, any man, any woman, or any group of people was better able to understand themselves. He was essentially a navigator of the human mind. His ship? The humble question." Ash made a charade of tipping a hat. "But for all his questioning, this man remained humble, and acknowledged if there was anything he knew assuredly, it was that he knew nothing."

She drew laughs for that. It appeared most were still following her telling, but more importantly, she still had the queen's attention. "The man sought to improve his entire city – a noble cause, if there was one – and so he went about it the way he believed best. Can you guess his approach?" Ash held her hand open, signalling for answers from the crowd.

Calls came from the gallery and floor about her: "Questions!"

"Indeed! The Questioner questioned. He questioned the social classes," Ash paused to read the room. "He questioned what was just," she was turning, and in her sweep sensed awakening ire in Archbishop Fulton, but she pressed on. "He questioned the government." Ash held her chin high, knowing the line she walked.

The queen brought her fingers into a firm clasp and twisted her head against her collar. Her facial expression confirmed Ash brushed close to the limits of her tolerance. Ash pulled away from her current line of oration; she could side-step further reference to a city's administration. Ash wished to tread carefully, but she was here to change things, not merely to gain a Seal for a single woman.

"The Questioner asked questions of all people from all walks of life. He even consulted – would you believe? – women!" Ash held a palm to her chest. "Because one of these women claimed an affinity with the divine, some called her a priestess... others... *a witch.*" Ash feigned horror, bringing the fingers of both hands to her lips. Fulton lurched forward on his demi-throne, his hand raised in objection. The queen did not grant him the floor. Ash wrapped: "Suffice to say, The Questioner's association with such a person did not... end... well." She drew out the final three words deep and slow. "For asking so many questions of so many people... The Questioner was executed."

"Give us magic!" came a jeer from the upstairs gallery.

Ash did not baulk at this censure, but instead blossomed in answer. "We must! We must get to the show! For The Questioner's execution brings me to it! The Questioner was sentenced to death by poison." Ash's eyes were only for Queen Valencia now. Although her lace ruff concealed her throat, the choker shifted with a hard swallow, her next blink was slow. Good. Ash had chosen well. She returned her attention to all.

"When I arrived upon the grounds of the royal residence this morn," Ash paused to allow the audience to remember her arrival – she'd not miss humour's window – and they laughed on cue, "...late, I confess... you could say I took a roundabout route." The laughter grew. In turning and casting her voice to all, she caught sight of Ren. He mouthed something. She knew what. She kept on, smiling. "And would you believe what I found, on Her Majesty's very doorstep?" She paused to allow speculation. "The very same poison that brought The Questioner's death."

In the margins of Ash's vision, she saw both the archbishop's hand shift within his pocket and the queen's slow blink. "Well, near enough. The poison The Questioner took allowed him to walk around – still questioning – until he observed his legs were growing heavy. When he lay down, he could no longer feel his legs. His students and the physician – they pinched them," Ash mimicked her words. "Nothing." Ash pointed to her own feet – scandalously exposed, "And then numbness slowly crept up, up, up... until all of his bodily systems were paralysed." The queen appeared pained. "But not his mind," Ash tapped her temple. "He was aware and questioning to the very last – even when death was imminent. Now this," Ash drew a flowering plant from beneath her skirts, "is like The Questioner's poison... only one knows even more quickly that they are poisoned, for its victims immediately appear possessed – thrashing upon the floor, confused, weak, dizzy, and quite incapable of holding their food."

More than one lady raised a hand to her mouth in silent horror. Others shrank back as though mere proximity to the plant might bring about its revolting symptoms.

"Hemlock, is one of its names; poisonous parsnip in SeeBurg; wild carrot or parsnip in Adhmad Thoir; false parsley in the Western Tract. I once saw a child dead who'd made a whistle of false parsley's stem." Ash averted her eyes, making a respectful study of the floor a moment.

"There must be a physician – or might we call the cook? Let us first confirm I hold what I say." Ash looked to the queen and her ladies-in-waiting. Valencia communicated with her eyes to a lady at her left, who signalled to a man in the side chamber.

"I can confirm it," he declared.

"I'll bring it closer." Ash did just that. Those around the man clearly did retreat on her approach now. The man hailed as a specialist dipped his chin and briefly eyed the small, white, umbrella-shaped flowers dotting the herbaceous plant in Ash's grip.

He made a clear pronouncement: "That is certainly lake hemlock, and she speaks true of its symptoms."

"Thank you, sir. Now, if false parsley were served in place of true parsley, how long would you say before its victim would succumb to its effects?" Ash asked the physician apparent, though her raised voice disclosed the dialogue for all.

"Before the end of the next course," he answered. Murmurs rippled through the retinue.

"This evening, I require two tumblers of ale." She looked to the queen. An attendant quickly scurried away.

"One last question, good sir?" Ash pointed at the physician with the plant in her hand.

The man frowned, listening.

"Which part of lake hemlock, if ingested, would most assuredly cause death?"

"The liquid within its roots, without question."

"Thank you," Ash said as she gave a shallow bow in the man's direction.

The attendant had returned with the tumblers. "And thank *you*," Ash dipped her head again. Taking the tumblers, she approached the throne. The queen drew a harsh breath that saw her chest rise upwards and back, away from Ash's advance. "Fear not, Your Majesty, it is only I who will drink one of these." She dared a wink. Valencia gave a small, disbelieving shake of her head, but there was a smile there too.

Ash placed the tumblers of ale on the first step ascending the throne. She laid the lake hemlock beside them. As she walked away, her back to the bishop, queen and throne, she made her pledge: "Anyone here may assist me now. A man or woman need only select a tumbler, snap open the root, and pour out the oil. Three steps!" Ash held three fingers high above her. She repeated them as she reached the end of the room, "Select a tumbler, snap open the root, pour out the oil."

There came no rush of volunteers. Ash waited. She thanked the Mysteries that Ren knew better than to raise a voice now.

"I'll do it." The voice was masculine and commanding. Its owner presented himself from the back of the crowd.

No.

Arsebeard.

"Very good." Ash smiled congenially. The man's soot-like mouth puckered with alarming anticipation. Instead of fear, Ash embraced opportunity. "Your name, sir?" *Deny me the answer here*, she dared.

The Seeker clenched his draw before relenting. "Segar."

"Ah, not a name I'd have guessed." Ash frowned, then she did something she'd mocked Banyan for. She stroked her chin.

Segar coughed and turned towards the queen, but said nothing.

"Please, Segar: Select a tumbler, snap open the root, pour the oil. And please, conceal your choice from all but her majesty and the archbishop."

The queen's aides took side-steps away from the throne in answer. Fulton and Segar exchanged a happy glance.

Ash remained facing the main doors of the Presence Chamber. She heard Arsebeard's steps cross the hall and to the throne. She heard a tumbler return to the polished step closest to the throne. She then heard multiple displacements. *Go ahead*, she thought. *Rearrange them as often as you count your dirty coin.*

"Are you through?" Ash called over her shoulder.

"It is done." Segar bowed, his arms spread wide.

Remaining a knife's throw from the throne, Ash turned, and spoke, "I am not an Illusionist, but a Mystic yes. In honour of The Questioner of our story, I will ask only three questions before I select a tumbler and drink to its bottom. I'll not flinch from its smell nor taste – no matter what comes, I'll drink it all."

Her audience buzzed.

Banyan interjected suddenly from the wings, "Your questions may not include 'Wherein lies the poison?' He was favoured with laughter for this condition.

"They won't," Ash promised.

The queen surprised Ash by addressing her next. "Are you quite sure, young Ash? This has the potential to be rather… wasteful. Not to mention gruesome." The queen had said it had *the potential* to be wasteful, illuminating profitably what Ash most needed to verify – begrudged Segar had not poisoned both tumblers; the queen lacked any tells suggesting duplicity. The trick should be fair.

"I am absolutely sure, Your Majesty," Ash said. And she felt no fear. Her old life would end here, one way or another.

"Your questions?" The queen leaned incrementally forward, intent. Fulton was less restrained, becoming suddenly and derisorily fervent in his attentions. Segar glowed.

"Your Majesty, do you believe I deserve to die?"

"No!" The queen spoke true.

"Your Grace," Ash addressed Archbishop Fulton next. "Do you believe God wills the death of women who claim to know anything of the Mysteries?"

"Oftentimes, yes, god wills it." Fulton spoke true.

Segar drew Ash's eye with one drawn-out nod.

Ash returned to Fulton. "My last question is also for you, Your Grace. Which tumbler would God have me drink?" Perimetric whispers abounded.

There was little demarcation between where the archbishop's lips ended and his reddened cheeks began. He pulled his lips back from his teeth and spoke slowly, holding himself very still all over, "The tumbler you think best." Bastard.

Segar folded his arms, smugness incarnate.

The queen gave no slow blink, there was no shift at the ruff, only an inhale and resigned smile. The stoic woman allowed not even a shadow of a tell to mark which tumbler contained the poison. The quiet stillness in the room confirmed the Seeker had managed to conceal his choice from the balance of the court. And Fulton? He appeared to be drawn out in elated prayer. They gave her nothing.

Nothing.

Ash straightened, holding her eyes closed for two heartbeats.

"Very well." Ash marched across the floor, her legs steady. Her hands did not tremble as she reached for her choice: the tumbler closest to Fulton. Its liquid gave a sinister glint as it sloshed inside. The tumbler felt warm in her hand. The chamber's collective inhale seemed to make the space in the room double. Still no tells from those upon the dais.

Grete's voice filled her mind then: Must you revel in risk? You can always withdraw, you know.

Without further ado, Ash sculled the liquid without pause. The wine was layered in strong flavours. Ash upturned the tumbler on the step and swivelled to face the greater hall. She waited for the nausea; to lose control of herself…

She felt no such things. She spread her arms wide. Resounding cheers answered her invitation, and unlike every other solo showing, she stayed. Ren was doubled over, one hand against a pillar, looking ill. Segar now allowed his shoulders to cave, slightly.

Ash turned back to the throne and gave a bow. The archbishop sat back in his seat and grimaced a smile. Queen Valencia nodded so deeply her ruff made indentations in her skin.

Well, that was lucky.

REN

It had become obvious. "The Luminous Collier" was the last Mystic on the Queen's Day register. After Ash's act, the queen and audience adjourned for a standing supper. Ren noted that Ash abstained – perhaps full still from the midday meal, or, he surmised, offended to have the break so-timed; Collier's act would be understood by all as the day's main Mystical event. Ren imagined Ash shared his assessment. Such a suggestion was outrageous.

Ren exchanged pleasantries with courtiers, always ensuring he could see Ash, who received attentions from members of a theatre troupe while holding an empty tumbler. Speculation and compliments abounded all around. Did a foreigner's levitation and transportation trump Besuto Ren's august sleight of hand or The Unflinching Ash's mentalism? Ren considered his opinion. Collier could make a table dance, and now was set to be the day's capstone. What would he offer? Would *the queen* deem it superior?

Ren caught Ash's eye across the guild hall. He gripped at his chest, then mimed wrenching his heart from it and offering it to her.

She smiled her small smile then – a subtle dimple tenting on the right side. How he strove to elicit that dimple!

He understood that having The Queen's Seal would not end some level of torment for any who cared for this implausible creature. Because Ash's performances always involved risk. *Always.* And her acts and the persistent opposition to them would garner worry for those who cared for her in years to come, he was sure. His heart would continue to be wrenched. But the Seal could *lessen* the risks. Even more, the Seal could help change things. Ash was not here to make one penultimate point and then stop, Ren knew. He hoped he would be permitted to see her keep making her point again and again and again.

Ash mimed back, pretending to take his heart from the air, and slip it into her vestments for safe-keeping. She gave the spot a pat and mouthed, "Later."

Ren shrugged acceptance at her needling, her singular dimple enough dessert for the evening.

Kynaston called. The large company followed the queen and her entourage back to the Presence Chamber.

Show time.

Collier's aides had just finished rolling two very large props out onto the floor. Typical.

Collier positioned himself between the throne and his staging, then rotated once. "My friends of the North! Your Majesty... " Interesting; addressing the queen second broke custom, and unfavourably. Collier continued, "This night I invite the Mysteries to attend us, and allow you the privilege of seeing their very hands at work." His accent was harsh. Ren hoped his own was not so distracting. Collier's phraseology also appeared to be learned by rote, mayhap explaining the queen's honorific being so regrettably inserted.

Collier bore some resemblance to Archbishop Fulton in colouring – similarly fair-haired and fair-skinned, though nothing suggested Collier's personal hygiene regimen involved abrasion at a ritual level. On the contrary, his skin was aptly... bright. Wherever he came from, the sun favoured his complexion instead of punishing it.

Ren looked to Ash across the hall, then to the queen upon her throne, then considered the pulse of the lake. Today was not to be Collier's. It was not to be Ren's. Change breached the shore. Ren settled in to watch a man's feeble attempt to stop it.

ASH

Ash closed her eyes a moment, instructing herself: *be polite*. But Collier wasn't making it easy. *Of course* the eburnean-skinned Mystic had two absurdly large props. *Of course* the prop that could be seen, uncovered in front of the other, was preposterously elaborate. The outrageously large piece displayed was a table. Collier motioned towards it. "First, my friends, I invite you to examine this table. Come, see it is ordinary in every way." Word. For. Word. The guy hadn't broken from his script of the last show Ash had attended. Good. Ash willed the queen to ask Collier a question – see how he fared with a deviation from rote.

One of the queen's attendants left the monarch's human halo to pace about the vast table. There was nothing ordinary about it. Ash could see from where she stood that its top was excessively thick, it had a central seam, and furthermore, it was fashioned with bevels and levels that obscured its true depth. The construction was finer and more elaborate than the blade box she'd known well as a youngster, but its purpose was the same. Ash knew hidden compartments when she saw them.

"What do you see, m'lady?" Collier asked the circling attendant.

"A very strong and heavy table, sir. It serves well that it has wheels," the lady answered.

"Thank you, m'lady. You may return to the queen."

Collier's men stood at attention either side of the table – well, one was a man, the other was but a boy. Abruptly, both mobilised. They moved to the second, larger object and lifted from beneath its curtain an additional prop, which resembled a coffin made up of multiple panels. Together, the pair placed the long crate on top of the table. Also from under the covered structure came a small construction. Steps, ha!

Collier ascended the steps, now aligned with the table, and lowered himself down into the crate, waving as he went. Then the man and boy unhitched the crate at its corners so that all of its walls fell open like a daisy's petals come morning, except these produced a bang. There lay Collier, face down.

Well, not only Collier, but the gulls didn't know that – nor, likely, did the queen.

Man and boy made quite a show of securing Collier's wrists and "Collier's" ankles in chains before lifting the crate's four walls and hitching them closed. Collier's chained hands... and the feet...

reappeared through breaks in the crate panels. Man and boy affixed the chains to the table. Hands and feet moved without the box.

The man and boy then moved to the prop still waiting, covered beyond. It towered over them both. They tugged at its covering, which fell to the marble floor, revealing a towering guillotine. Brassy, glistening and within a large rectangular frame mounted on wheels. Its design permitted both assistants to wheel it over the table – Collier's coffin-crate upon it – and line it up neatly over the table's seam.

The crowd convulsed and shivered in anticipation. The queen drew back. Ash now knew why Collier had paled to see the Queen's aversion at Banyan's first trick; it appeared Mystics' illusions involving the severing of bodies were not favoured.

Any realisation would have come too late for Collier; he was quite committed to this course. Ash played with her bottom lip, amused.

With the guillotine positioned over the crate, the trick approached its turn. But first, Collier's hand reached in its chains to undo the latch of the crate. Slowly, panel by panel, the walls of the crate fell back once more, only now with a guillotine hovering above. Collier's entire body appeared concave (by necessity, Ash knew), laying atop the spread-open crate and table, which together, were of significant depth. *Really, gulls, significant.*

Collier's adult assistant stood at the ready. Collier made as though to free himself, as if some mistake had been made and he had changed his mind.

The guillotine sang in its downward motion.

It appeared to cut him through. It did. That would be why a few screams echoed off the floors and pillars. One courtesan fainted and attracted a small ring of sympathisers.

The guillotine did *seem* to bisect Collier at his middle, and he (and whoever served as his legs) went very still.

Man and boy wheeled the table slightly apart to demonstrate the completed operation. *Come on, there wasn't even blood. And his garments were so loose.*

A muffled sob from the gallery turned to laughing disbelief as the legs on display moved. Ash could almost grasp the crowd's hope in its palpability: *Could it be? Collier was alive?*

Collier's arms moved too. He pushed the top-half of his torso up from the crate and looked over at "his" body.

Ash had seen more than enough and couldn't contain herself. "May we examine the table *now*?" she called over dubious audience mirth. The modest clamour subsided at once. Ash repeated herself. "May we examine that table?"

The elder accomplice stepped forward and briskly shook his head. Collier's raised a hand to halt Ash's advance.

"Your scepticism is noted, Ash," said the queen.

Ash suppressed an invasion of guilt in her middle. She and Ren allowed and even invited inspections during their acts because they did not rely on complicated equipment for their Mysticism. Her parents had maintained – out of respect for other performers – not to ask too many questions of them. Ash had always disagreed on this point. She held that true ambition thrived under scrutiny, and pushed a Mystic to new heights. She welcomed similar challenge to her own craft, so she could not be called a hypocrite. But what would people find if they did examine her? Ash read people and took real risks, not feigned ones.

Man and boy returned the table's halves together, raised the guillotine, and of course, closed up the box. Hands and feet were loosed from chains before vanishing within. Moments later, the prestige! The crate opened, and out stepped Collier, unharmed. A second guest fainted at Ash's left – a man this time.

Please.

Man and boy unhitched the crate so that it lay open to reveal itself empty while Collier took deep bows from his elevated position.

Meanwhile, someone suffocated within the bowels of the crate and table.

Ash could taste the air he breathed as if she were within the hidden compartment, stale and wet with his own vapour. She felt sick with memory and angry in the present all at once.

She rendered a slow clap, while open ovation surrounded. The moustached baron and two other lords tripped over each other, fanning the languishing guest.

Queen Valencia conferred with Fulton, her face thoughtful, her nods small.

Curses. The Mystic Seal would not be won without a fight.

ASH

Ash was pleased to see the final act of the day was not to be Collier's – that was something. After all of The Luminous Collier's props and parts had been wheeled away, Kynaston called a harpist to assume centre stage with an instrument as tall as its master. The harpist was a dark-skinned woman with hair streaming to the floor in small braids. She sat on the edge of a stool – pulled from its place by the chamber's wall – and held the harp's soundbox to her knees, its shoulder to her shoulder. There she began.

Ash thanked the Mysteries that her own worthiness was not to be weighed against this. The melody was so idyllic that she felt her eyes hastening to glaze over in repose. Her curiosity insisted she remain dedicated to a study of the harpist's hands. If Ash squinted she could almost imagine the strings vanished and the woman casting an exacting spell with her fingers, weaving and crooning sound-magic from the very air. So torn between tranquil escape and fascination, Ash forgot to breathe.

Her returning animation synchronised with Ren's, whose eyes she met across the room. His, too, were wet. As Ren had proven last time Ash observed him so moved, he was unembarrassed for feeling. He gave the smallest smile, then returned his eyes to the player and instrument.

Lalla Ekundayo was the harpist's name. She expertly plucked three complex compositions that charmed the court entire. The queen was no exception.

At the end of *Lalla* Ekundayo's performance, the shared trance over the court turned to shared stupor – as though all assembled had forgotten what had brought them together, what the day's agenda was mounting towards. Kynaston had to call twice, before regaining their attention, inviting everyone present to enjoy a recess while she deliberated. No doubt the queen perceived they all would benefit with some time to return to themselves.

Some were excused by their circle to relieve themselves, and others took up seats along the walls. The fainters were recovered, Ren was charismatically engaged with those around him, and conversations returned to the guillotine.

Ash watched only the queen. For all the presence and pomp of her ladies, the queen appeared to seek counsel from only one individual, and that was a man. Fulton had her ear, and his sour expression was avid. Ash knew such avidity well, and she mourned the archbishop's favour with the person who would so greatly influence her own fate.

A group of drunken courtiers tumbled into Ash's view. She repositioned herself to eye the continued exchange between the queen and archbishop. The queen's eyes narrowed. *Where had that tell been earlier?* She was relenting! *No.*

No.

Archbishop Fulton and Queen Valencia had come to some agreement.

This could not be good.

ASH

It was no surprise that Lady Ekundayo took The Musician's Seal. She accepted the queen's bestowal graciously, her curtsy practised and composed. Though her beautiful skin told of ancestors abroad, she was expert in the ways of the resident court.

This being Ash's first time within the royal residence where she could witness artisans being so honoured, she saw what carrying The Queen's Seal in actuality entailed: Paperwork, in short. Moreover, it involved the queen's own seal from her large gold ring being ceremoniously stamped into wax poured upon that paperwork. The prized document named the bearer in treaty with the queen, and recipient artisans were expected to attend their queen on short notice – a reminder it involved obligation, too.

It also involved protection, immunity... and hope.

Ash's throat had grown dry with hunger for a Seal of her own.

What mob would dare waylay a woman contracted as the queen's own? What intermeddler would dare suggest a performance unfit for any audience had the same proven fit for a queen?

While the Master of Revels called performers to the throne, Ash entertained fantasies of mentalist matinees in public squares, finding a dwelling to call her own, of tearing through SeeBurg bread...

Lady Ekundayo, Minstrels, Minnesingers, theatre troupes, Troubadours and Acrobats were called forth in groups to receive the court's applause and the queen's thanks. One among each group was invited to approach further and received The Queen's Seal.

No Mystics were called. Valencia was saving them until last.

The Breath-stealing Banyan was called to kneel before the throne. Besuto Ren came next, followed by The Unflinching Ash and, finally, The Luminous Collier. They four knelt in a line on the hard steps before Valencia and her many aides. Ash longed to reach for Ren's hand. To feel it within her grasp before knowing what the Mysteries held; to feel his fingers in hers now, on *this* day – which had been a good day, even if it belonged to the queen.

She did not.

Kynaston stood before a podium draped in fabric embroidered with the Queen of Mórlough's crest. It matched the mark that would be pressed into the wax. The Seal Ash *needed*. What difference could it possibly make to Collier, should he gain it? And Banyan – well, he was going home as pedestrian as he came, Ash knew that much. And what if Ren were to obtain the Seal? Ash did not want to wait a year to try for the Seal again... without Ren at her side. Forget the torture of further delaying them coming together, Ash doubted she could *survive* another year without the immunity the Seal afforded.

Kynaston read from parchment, "Her Majesty the Queen wishes to acknowledge that both The Breath-stealing Banyan and The Luminous Collier refused inspection by their peers, while Besuto Ren submitted to it and The Unflinching Ash's performance did not necessitate it. However," the master paused and allowed the crowd's hum of conjecture to subside, "Her Majesty the Queen also wishes to state she had not supposed two Mystics performing at her pleasure would chance mortal peril for Her Majesty's own entertainment."

Had it come to this? Queen Valencia was dismissing Banyan's decapitated-head deception completely and narrowing the field by two? He hadn't even been mentioned.

Leaving three contenders only; Collier, Ren... and Ash.

"His Grace the Archbishop wishes to state that mortal peril in no way equates to worthiness before the basilica, but that this day the Seal is awarded based solely at Her Majesty's pleasure."

Queen Valencia raised one hand and a ripple of corresponding signals succeeded in gaining Kynaston's attention so that he paused.

"While worthiness or accomplishment before God certainly does not always equate with mortal peril," the queen said, "it does this day, to my astonishment." Four Mystics knelt before her, but she met the eyes of only two, and one at a time, "Collier – you astonished me," then to Ash, "And you, Miss Ash, introduced me to a suspension of terror like nothing I've ever known – only to thrill at your triumphing unharmed."

The queen waved her hand to Kynaston, who resumed reading. "In the gay spirit of Queen's Day, the final Seal this night will be awarded in a ceremony that pays tribute to the Mysteries."

Ash noted Fulton bristled at the Mysteries, so honoured. There was hope yet.

Kynaston read on. "In these two chalices," Kynaston held his arm outstretched towards a male attendant, who carried in a small table and placed two stemmed, jewelled cups atop it, "Her Majesty the Queen has placed the two names of the two finest Mystic contenders this Queen's Day – The Luminous Collier and The Unflinching Ash." Kynaston stopped reading and looked at Ash. "The Unflinching Ash will choose the chalice with the winner's name inside it, unfold and read it, and thereafter announce for all present the Mystic to receive this year's Seal for the Mystics."

Ash straightened a little.

"Please, rise," the queen said.

No.

No!

NO.

Ash deadpanned a stare at archbishop Fulton, still at the queen's side. The game was up now, for she'd seen it all. His handsome features contorted into unmistakable arrogant gratification. Segar, within her peripherals, drew one finger across his neck, a promise.

She knew for certain then: that these pigs of men had ensured Collier's name was on both slips of paper. No matter which chalice Ash chose, it would be Collier's name she drew out as the winner. *A final show in gay spirit,* they said. Farce. The queen, archbishop and his lackey were playing games with her. And she was outnumbered.

So be it.

"At your pleasure, Your Majesty." Ash stood and strode to the chalices, retrieved the folded paper from within – the winner's name upon it – and popped it in her mouth. Like a bonbon. She turned for all the court to see, as she chewed and swallowed the winner's name.

"What is the meaning… ?" Queen Valencia started, and trailed off.

Ash came to her rescue, "My apologies, Your Majesty. I am so in the habit of ingesting one of two forthwith – I cannot say what came over me." Ash paused and looked pointedly at the remaining chalice. "But all is not lost, there remains the name of whoever came second."

The archbishop stirred in agitation. Segar took a step away from the ranks, before calming himself. A surprised smile grew to light the queen's countenance with admiration.

Her opposition had thought it fixed.

They had thought wrong.

Queen Valencia took charge. "Quite right, Miss Ash, all is *not* lost. Please, reveal the name of the person who came second." She dipped her head towards the remaining cup.

Ash replied, "We can't allow the discerning people of this court to doubt my words, I suggest Archbishop Fulton read out who came second. Is this acceptable to Your Majesty? For I still made the selection, as per your wishes." Ash rubbed her belly for effect, reminding the crowd where the winning name now rested.

"It is. Fulton, proceed." Was the queen masking amusement? Ash ventured she was.

"May I recommend an alternate course?" Fulton spoke to the queen, or rather, misspoke, for he had forgotten to address her correctly.

Queen Valencia's eyes narrowed. "I have given you the course to take. Go ahead." She gave the last in the sternest tone Ash had ever heard her deliver.

Archbishop Fulton slouched to the chalice and pulled out the paper. He unfolded it, and read the words upon it quietly.

Kynaston, oblivious to the convoluted sham that had almost unfolded, swept the paper up and announced loud and incontestable: "The Mystic who is honoured as second-best this Queen's Day, is... The Luminous Collier!" Applause rippled in answer. Collier wobbled slightly on his knee. Ren dipped his chin to his chest. Banyan was not worth inspection.

"Thereby, The Unflinching Ash is the winner, and so receives Her Majesty's Seal. Please render your congratulations." The Presence Chamber already boomed with their returns.

Fulton whispered wet and angry at Ash's ear; "You cheated."

Ash opened her eyes wide and answered; "You cheated first."

Kynaston gathered up the paper to be marked and presented, then halted. He had seen that the prepared papers did not bear Ash's name. To the backdrop of applauders unaware, he put things together, and smiled as he gave Ash a small bow of esteem.

Queen Valencia, knowing of the frustrated ruse, made her last announcement in that great hall for the day: "My welcome guests, this occasion has re-opened my eyes to the many gifts the Mysteries have bestowed upon the people of Mórlough, and which they have so generously shared with us all. I hope you are all as proud of the people we are as I am. Please enjoy the last dance, while I award The Unflinching Ash her Seal within my own chambers. To all, may the Mysteries untold share your will." She raised a hand in farewell. The revellers raised their hands in return, and bowed, speaking in chorus, "Mysteries willing."

As the queen led out, Ash following, she could not help but find amusement in Segar's beard failing to hide his cheeks turning red.

ASH

Ash sat at the tail-end of a long table covered in red velvet fringed at its hem in buttercup yellow. At the table's head, in a chair finer than all the rest, sat Her Majesty the Queen. The queen's chamber was dark, small and quiet in contrast to the great hall and festivities they'd left behind. The soft materials layering the table, walls, chairs and stools absorbed what little sound the current assembly made. They also gave Ash the impression she'd entered a wealthy giant's wardrobe. Everything was covered in fabric, and all of it freshly dusted so that it shone.

From what Ash could gather from the room's design, it appeared to be dedicated to political purposes. When one of the queen's ladies slunk through an adjoining door, Ash caught a flash of the neighbouring room. A bedchamber! Ash could scarcely believe she now sat at the heart of the queen's residence – on floors delicately spanning the public and private lives of Mórlough's monarch.

She and the queen were not alone. Filling the chairs between them sat a motley party of nobles and officers of government. Six guards attended the room's textile-rich borders, and two ladies-in-waiting stood just behind their ruler.

Archbishop Fulton sat at Her Majesty's right.

Although they enjoyed comparative quiet to the Presence Chamber's merry din, communications were open and alive, hissing between officers and nobility alike. Ash sat in silence, making her studies. The two ladies were educated, skilled in whatever pastimes took the queen's pleasure, no doubt serving as companions to Her Majesty as well as attending to her. It was disappointing to note that, even with these two alongside, the queen and Ash herself numbered, females were still greatly the minority in this room.

Valencia raised one hand to call for quiet. Discussions abruptly ceased and the scribe preparing new papers for Ash stilled his pen.

"Miss Ash," the queen laced her fingers. "You have caused quite a commotion among the privy council this night. We had reached a verdict that awarding privilege on the coat-tails of an inquisition – sanctioned indirectly by me – would set a perilous precedent for the realm. As you deduced, you receiving the Seal was not my first intention."

Ash drew a sharp breath and pursed her lips. She would not interrupt, she *must* not interrupt.

The queen continued, "It *was* my intention to instead arrange a most excellent marriage on your behalf, in lieu of this... political quagmire."

Ash *must* not interrupt.

"However... " Valencia held her index finger out in warning towards Fulton – whom she could see marshalling to speak. "*I* believe you proved our plans were made in error." She turned to address the archbishop, who did little to hide his contempt. "Fulton, I'll speak now to you. You are *not* my only counsel, and your insolence this night only confirms the prudence of taking auxiliary advisement. We shared intentions, and we might well again, but I *will* award this Seal to Ash the Unflinching." She signalled for the scribe to finish and slide the document to her. "This woman has overcome every trial against her – from her accusers within Mórlough, from the basilica who heard them, and this night, from two trials over which *you* presided most closely. Even you cannot refute that her failure to be found guilty suggests a great power shares her will."

"But what power, Your Majesty?" Fulton seethed. The fight was not over.

Ash cut in, before she could speak over anyone: "Your Majesty? Forgive my answering, but may I speak in my own defence?"

"You may."

Fulton sat back in his chair.

"First, in answer to your preceding offer of arranged marriage, Your Majesty – I am quite capable of taking care of the particulars of that myself, thank you. Though I appreciate you meant to offer me some social advancement to compensate for... withholding better protection from me." Ash's semantics were risky, she knew, but the queen did not appear yet enraged by them. "Second, I appreciate you have a large population of church-goers to consider in your decisions, but please know I have nothing against God-fearing, good people, nor their rights to worship what they may." She hoped the queen read between the lines there. "Third, these 'trials' you speak of – happening at the Lough's banks? Respectfully, Your Majesty, they are madness. Can you not see me here, before you? I am not without my faculties nor in any way possessed, yet I have been subjected to cruelties of which I'm sure if you understood in honest detail, you would never allow upon any subject within your realm, let alone good women who were not strangers to you." Ash paused and waited. The ladies behind the queen shared a brief look.

An officer mid-way down the table added his counsel: "Your Majesty, the only matter before us is whether or not this woman receives your endorsement. We cannot begin to explore the complicated affairs of the entire realm because one person has been inconvenienced by them."

"Amen to that!" added a marquis closer to Ash, followed by many raised voices in assent.

Ash needed to do something. She counted her exits... then realised she needed to do *something else.*

"Your Majesty, may I speak but with you, your fine ladies, and the six surrounding guards?"

That surprised her.

Perhaps Ash had mistaken the admiration she had seen in the queen earlier. No, she hadn't. It had been there. This queen wanted change too, Ash could feel it poised on its haunches in the hollows of the chamber.

The queen considered Ash's request. Fulton, fighting obvious temptation to oppose Ash, was sent a dare to do so in the queen's gaze. Dark and decided, Queen Valencia spoke: "Excuse us." She looked around the room at the dumbfounded surplus of men. "You *will* excuse us," she reiterated, insistent.

Chairs whined and groaned, footsteps fell. Ash's paperwork was left, completed except for its Seal, before the queen, the scribe scratched his neck nervously as he left. Fulton's parting stare promised the Seeker would find her after this charade was through. *Ash had to tie that man's hands... and rob him of his proverbial whip.*

Finally, only Ash and Valencia remained seated at the council table.

"Tread carefully, Lady Ash, I've extended rare liberties to you now." Then the queen smiled. "But I *am* curious."

"I only wish to speak more to my third point, Your Majesty, without rebuttal." Ash did not allow lingering irritation to seep into her tone, instead holding her chin high and keeping her voice level. *See how reasonable this request is; hear the reason in my words.* "Your realm is plagued by hysteria. Too many are ruled by fear and prejudice – singling out those different to themselves and seeking to do away with them. What is a witch, but a woman who understood something a man did not?"

The queen gave a tiny snort before quickly drawing back up her guard. She stretched both hands flat on the table before her, relaxing her shoulders enough that her incredible sleeves moved just a touch. "What of the confessions then? Witches who've professed their treason to basilica and throne both, by their own tongue?"

Ash answered, exasperated, "Extracted by way of torture, Your Majesty!"

The queen let out a sigh.

"The officer who spoke earlier is right, Your Majesty. We cannot begin to explore the complicated affairs of the entire realm now, in one night, but I hold to the hope you *will* explore them. There is no better time than now for an astute woman to investigate, and once informed... " Ash searched the tapestries for words, "...speak with confidence on behalf of the women she claims as half her people. Remind Mórlough that no God could approve crimes of hate being named acts of justice; remind Mórlough that you are guided only by that God and not by any *man*."

Ash could see she had struck some chord within the queen and read the tells aright.

The queen raised her chin but looked down. "I cannot make any promise to you now as to how or when things will change, but I can assure you I have taken your counsel, and will act upon it." Queen Valencia signalled for wax from an attending lady, then added her royal Seal to the paper before her.

"Ash the Unflinching. Daughter of Pabla and Alex," the queen held the paper toward Ash, who felt a pull in her neck to discover the queen had sought out a mere Mystic's lineage. "Trust that I take my responsibility to *all* of Mórlough's people seriously."

It wasn't perfect, it wasn't even a promise, but it was progress. Ash arose and reached for the paper, still held by the queen.

"Your Majesty, may I make one further request?" They both held to the parchment.

The queen's face crumpled in an exaggerated contortion of weariness and amusement. "Please, I cannot imagine myself stopping you at this point."

"Your Majesty, you never met my parents, I know. But you know their names, and for that I thank you. My request is this: I ask that you honour my mother's memory – a devout and good woman who died before you could see her... light – " Ash swallowed hard, " by awarding her an honorary Seal. You may not be able to stop mobs from stripping women down," Ash let a tear roll, buoyed by Ren's example of unabashed emotion, "and making a study of their naked bodies for a devil's mark. Nor may you be able to end all of the hangings, lashings, drownings and torture. But you can absolve one. Pabla la Precisa. My mother, who was better than this world, a world that is worse for her having left it." The tear fell from Ash's cheek.

Queen Valencia drew a sharp breath and sat taller. "Are you suggesting I know little of what it is to be a woman in a world that seems only to know how to be led by men?" Now Ash could see some fire.

"Quite the opposite, Your Majesty. I am suggesting you would care to learn of men in your service who have exceeded the directions you have given. For my Seal, I will render performances at your pleasure, always. For my *mother's* Seal, I will render fearless honesty."

The queen studied Ash, gleaning the full implication of Ash's promise. Valencia would gain an attending Mystic *and* a spy. "So be it. Marta, please call in the scribe," Queen Valencia said, releasing her end of the paper held between them.

Ash looked down at what she now held in her own grasp. She looked back to the queen.

"Thank you. Thank you, Your Majesty." Ash bowed deep and sincere. Progress.

ODELL

Pabla had been visiting Odell each night in her dreams of late. And in the daytime, besides. It had come time Odell settled the matter.

Though her husband was ignorant of the finer details of Mystic custom, Odell knew where Pabla had been buried. So she made her journey to the site – knowing a tombstone and grave would not confirm the resting place. Odell instead took her course towards an unremarkable ash tree, her only chaperone the apparition haunting her. Conventions be damned. This was for her, and her alone.

She stopped a fishing vessel's span before the clearing's edge.

Odell's accompanying ghost had appeared ahead, now standing by the grave. And the ghost was not alone.

Odell nearly crumpled, but steadied herself with one hand against an evergreen tree. Realisation bloomed within Odell. She recognised Ash, two men

Odell did not know, and Pabla's eidetic image as she'd appeared in the marketplatz.

Of course. They were both Pabla's girls.

In that moment, Odell could see, and more importantly, *feel*, the happiness these Mystics had could not be wrong.

Which meant Odell's father had been.

Odell silently wept.

When she saw their party taking leave, she wiped her face, and straightened.

She headed south, towards SeeBurg. She left the apparition behind.

REN

Ren smiled, leaning upon a tree. He watched Ash place the paper bearing The Queen's Seal of endorsement inside a simple Mystic's box. He knew it wasn't her own paper; it was her mother's. Ash knelt beside an ash tree in a cemetery in the North. Grete stood behind her, one hand resting on Ash's shoulder, the other loosely atop her growing belly.

"Come, Ren," Ash beckoned. He was anxious to not intrude, though he wished to be there. He believed timing was important.

"Do come," Grete called.

Ren came. Ash stood. She squeezed Ren's hand once, then used a gesture to ask Wynn for the spade.

"Wait. Before that, if I may? I brought something," Ren said quietly.

"Oh?" Grete asked.

"I brought a pearl." He revealed it from an invisible pocket within his vest. "I learned after we met, Grete, your name means 'pearl' in your tongue. Ash told me it was your idea to plant a tree with

Ash's name here, to mark this spot. You had no older sibling there that day to plant something for you." He pressed the pearl into Grete's hands, whose eyes welled as she held it. She added it to the box made of walnut, alongside Pabla's Seal.

Ren was moved by the gentleness of Ash's movements as she lowered the box and its emblematic contents into a shallow hollow, freshly dug beside the tree.

Grete lifted a fistful of earth and released it through parted fingers to garnish the box's surface.

Wynn lifted the spade that was leaning against the tree and began scooping soil back into the hole. Clumps of sod pecked out a hollow sound on the Mystic's box once, twice, and then hit soil. Ash took a turn with the small chest's burial. She continued with the shovel until all the soil was returned, with Seal and pearl laid to rest where they belonged.

Grete looked to Ren, smiling and crying at once. Silently she mouthed, "Thank you." then loudly, "Come here!" She pulled Ren into an embrace. "Please keep him, Ash!"

"He isn't an object I can own!" Ash barked a laugh.

"*We'll* adopt him if you don't," Grete said.

"Look, you seem nice enough," Wynn spoke to Ren, "but I must ask you to excuse my wife. In her condition she can be hasty in... "

"Oh stop, Wynn! Enough of my delicate condition!" Grete pulled Wynn in under her other arm.

Ren looked sheepishly towards Ash, who alternated between looking to the three of them hugging and watching the tree line.

Grete gently pushed Ren towards her younger sister while holding onto her husband, who kissed her on the top of her head.

Ren knelt beside the tree and raked the remnants of earth in the grass with his fingers, making the surroundings neat and complete. He looked to Ash for her approval, which she gave in a nod. She lifted the divot of earth they had removed earlier, and spread it over the site. They both stood, and Ash packed it down with her toes, then became still.

Ren placed his arm around her shoulders. The four stood a moment, woodnotes and the rustling of tumbling leaves the only sound.

"I feel like we should say something, you know? Now we're older, and have the time... " Ash looked to Grete.

"I'm not good at speeches." Grete shrugged.

Ash chewed her lip, then spoke out into the air: "May the Mysteries... or Gods... or whoever, whatever it was that received you, carry to you our love... and the knowledge that people are changing. People *are* changing."

Ren squeezed her across the shoulders. They all stood without speaking for a time, their reverence for birdsong their Amen.

"That was good." Grete spoke first.

"Thanks."

Then Grete said to Ren, "Will you join us for dinner then?"

"I would be honoured," he answered, his arm still holding Ash.

"As would I," Ash said.

They walked by the road. Ash wore her new cloak's hood down. The names and likeness of all those who'd earned the Queen's Seal had been published wide about the realm. Ash was recognised often for it, as well as for her miraculous escape from a watery grave.

Ren? He was still an unmet to most, but found he did not mind.

Pabla's name and likeness had been published too, and here, in the North, people knew who she was to Ash and what that meant.

Wynn and Grete were a few paces ahead, walking hand in hand. Ash leaned into Ren as they followed, his arm still around her shoulders, hers at his waist.

"I like that you spoke to them," Ren said.

"Oh?" said Ash.

"Yes. There is a word in the language of my home that means... you have a profound awareness of the Mysteries and that feeling causes a strong emotional response inside you."

"Just one word says all that?"

"Yes. I felt all of that when you spoke."

"I want to learn these weighty words you know from far off lands. I suppose this means we'll have to spend more time together... so you can teach me."

"Really?" Ren made no effort to hide his enthusiasm.

"Ya."

"Will there be things I receive in exchange... for this teaching?" Ren turned and looked at Ash beneath his protective arm.

Ash gaped at him, looking right back. She liked being this close to him. "What kind of things, exactly?

Ren laughed as he spoke, realising she had imagined things more scandalous. "Answers! I mean answers!"

"What answers do you need from me?" Ash frowned. Did he imagine she had slumped? Would she have preferred a more scandalous trade?

"Answers to my questions. First question – I need you to tell me what happened on Queen's Day – how did you read the tells? They gave away nothing!"

"I didn't."

"What!?"

Wynn and Grete smiled over their shoulders briefly, but carried on walking, not alarmed.

"You were willing to just throw your life away…!" Ren gripped Ash at her shoulder.

"That's just it. I wasn't willing, and I didn't… read the tells, I mean. Every other time I've taken what has appeared to be a risk, but it hasn't been, not really. I've always felt I've *known* by reading people. But this time, there was no telling from anyone there, yet *something* within me whispered which I should choose. I knew with my eyes closed. " Her eyes lit up as she explained. "And I listened to that voice, trusted it. It was like no other tell I've seen or heard. And it turns out it whispered aright!"

"So the Mysteries speak to you?" Ren said, not at all perturbed.

"Maybe."

"Or perhaps your parents do… " Ren offered.

"Or God!" Ash laughed. "Or perhaps I knew…?"

"Are you imitating The Questioner now? What was it?" Ren pulled away from Ash and held a mock thinking pose in tribute to the story she had shared with the court. "If he knew one thing, it was that he knew nothing." He beamed.

Ash ruffled his hair. "Well done – see how you learn from me? You'll teach me languages, I'll teach you history…"

Ren took her hand. "Really Ash, do you believe it? That truly knowing is knowing how little we know?"

"Maybe. But for the first time I *do* know *something*, and in a way I've never known something before."

"I think that is good," Ren said. "Now, another question." He stopped, holding Ash's hand so that it pulled her to stop also.

"Out with it then." Ash waited, smiling.

"When are we going to get to the kissing part? You said it was in our fu…"

Ash gripped Ren by his face, her fingers parting around his ears and into his hair as she pulled him close, stopping his inquiry with a kiss – a kiss built upon purloined purses, breath-stealing shows, birthdays beneath jetties and stories told while forest-bathing. Ren relaxed into the fulfilment of her Queen's Day foretelling, melted into Ash's yielding frame and eased his hands beneath her cape to grip her waist. A wagon approached and rolled by, and whistles and hollers erupted from it for sighting the two, so entwined.

This caused Wynn and Grete to again turn about. Grete called back, "Adopted!" while Wynn shook his head and turned back ahead.

And Ash and Ren's kiss deepened. Ren pulled back first, a touch breathless, to rest his forehead against Ash's. He spoke softly, his breath warm on Ash's lips. "I have imagined this kiss a thousand times. I had hoped to set a scene… "

Ash shrugged. "I wanted to sneak up on you."

"I am happy you did. This is better than I imagined."

"How so?"

"It is daylight."

Ash beamed. "Indeed. We have nothing to hide."

EPILOGUE

A performance was about to begin and each attending gull craved amazement.

Concealed by banners flanking the stage, two Mystics bickered.

"Could we not take it in turns?"

Ash grinned mischievously. "We *could*. But I think our current method is equally fair." Ash threw and caught a coin like a lake-fly. "You can even flip the coin, if you'd like." She offered the val for Ren's taking.

Ren waved her away. "No, you go ahead."

"You never know, maybe today's your lucky day and *I* will be the one to ready the crowd for *your* show." With a flick of her thumb, the coin left Ash's fist and spun through the air.

"Or we could really get them talking, and go on together." Ren's eyes followed the coin as it fell. Neither could catch it; it had to fall without either's shrewd interference.

"Ha!"

"The queen it is."

"Better luck next time, Besuto Ren." Ash clapped Ren on his shoulder. He caught her hand there, drew it to his lips, and kissed it. Ash twisted her wrist and caught his hand in her own, drawing Ren into a crush against her Mystic costume. She answered his kiss with some of what her lips had to offer, promising more later, in the way she leaned into him, their fingers intertwining.

Grete bounced her daughter at her hip atop the haybales, checking side-stage for confirmation of the show's order. "Please welcome..." Ren nodded in confirmation, "This year's recipient of The Queen's Mystic Seal..." Grete extended her arm, "Besuto Ren!"

Ren's swallow was visible as his eyes roved over Ash's face. She pouted as she said, "Shoo."

He bounded out from behind the banner in answer to whistles and applause, and then one loud complaint, "Where's your wife!?"

Ren didn't skip a beat. "The Mysteries share thy will, good man; the main event is to follow! Bear with me as she does?" Ren stole a glance back to Ash, who nodded appreciatively.

Grete smiled, dropping her arm. "Let the show, begin."

HISTORICAL NOTES

A variation of Ash's first act has been performed by Derren Brown. Ren's first show is inspired by a David Blaine act. All of the other acts resemble common tricks which have resurfaced time and time again on the greater Illusionist stage. Cutting a person in half, for example, has been done many times by many people – but perhaps by no one more notably than by David Copperfield in his famous "Death Saw" act, to which my depiction of Collier's character pays homage.

Elements of Ash's persecution and trials are drawn from all around our world, including the Trier Basque, Valais, and Salem witch trials. Unfortunately the bloodied horse, boiled stones, and "heretics fork" – like the notorious "baptism" trials – have historical basis.

Sadly, Ash's tale of a foreign philosopher who died by poison also has an earthly parallel – for Socrates was sentenced to death by hemlock in 399BC for heresy – one example of many who suffered for asking questions. Socrates championed oral modes of communication and his dialectic method of inquiry has essentially become today's dominating scientific method.

The Queen's judgement ceremony is inspired by a tale from the Jewish diaspora in which a shrewd rabbi outsmarts an Emir so that the Jews are permitted to remain in Cordova. The words "stay" and "go" were written on pieces of paper placed in bowls – words pertaining to the Jews continuation or exile. The rabbi ate one because he was sure both of the Emir's pieces of paper said "go." (A really accessible retelling of this tale is included in Susan Wise Bauer's second volume of *The Story of the World*).

Mórlough's Queen Valencia bears some semblance to our world's Queen Elizabeth I, who played a significant part in seeing performing arts advance from something belonging solely to vagabonds to its widespread reception and the sophistication of its form.

AFTERWORD

My father has always nurtured a fascination with magic and a good show. He took us as children to shows; he put on shows; he stocked our home library shelves with books filled with curiosities, capturing spectacles and wonder.

I came to understand many magic acts feature female "assistants" (who often perform the real magic, I hasten to add), women wielded like glittering trophies.

It was after attending such an international act that *The Unflinching Ash* began in embryo. I had attended with my three daughters, and their heads were spinning as they marvelled at all that this male magician had done. Mine ached with all the woman had done that they had *not* seen.

I knew I wanted to be part of creating a new narrative.

I could not believe male dominance in magic was so pronounced, still. I began wondering what a world like ours would look like, if things had begun to change sooner. I began thinking about what it would have been like if a gutsy female illusionist had succeeded in making her way long ago... and then my thoughts snagged on how that story would be told if such ambition was born during a time of mass hysteria.

So many stories about witches end with women tortured, trialled or straight-way executed because they did something entirely reasonable although perhaps thought different; they provided contraception to others, had a way with animals, or consumed herbs someone thought unseemly, met together unconventionally, or most dispassionately, experienced a seizure. These stories were not always of women, but mostly so.

I wanted the fight to be won there, at the front line.

Although Houdini was to rise to prominence later, magic and illusions had been thriving around the world for centuries – with varied reception.

What was clear to me was that no female magician in any era has ever risen to distinction comparable to the bevy of male magicians who are household names. I'm sure you've heard of Harry Houdini, Penn and Teller, David Copperfield, David Blaine, and Siegfried and Roy. Can you name one female magician? If I gave names to you, would they resound with matching familiarity? What about Dorothy Dietrich, Misty Lee, Kristen Johnson, Ning Cai, Debbie Leifer, Eusapia Palladino, Frances Willard, Ariann Black, Mariko Itakura, Faye Presto, or Lisa Menna?

So in Mórlough we find an alternative world and history where I imagined a war was won for women – and for anyone who is different or little understood – like those wars we are still fighting now; a war that might have led to a different world than ours, where talented, untamed, mystical women can be respected and remembered with equal distinction.

May we all keep fighting for our right to be seen, to be different, to receive equal opportunities and pay to perform, and always too for our voice to be heard in the who, when and how of our relationships.

Prejudice is an old beast that seems to rise no matter how many times it is slain. We simply must rise each time it does.

ACKNOWLEDGEMENTS

Thank you to whoever in the Mysteries sends me a guiding voice.

Thank you to my three growing young women, for building block-cities, exploring bush, rearing animals and reading books while your mother taps away.

Thank you to their dad, who works a 9-5 while I work for an artist's wage – my husband of almost two decades, Haki.

Thank you to my dad, for exposing me to so many shows but never doubting I could make my own magic.

Thank you to the many "Gretes" in my world, by blood and by choosing. Thank you Ashley Woodward, for keeping me writing, astute editing, and always teaching me through your own way with words. Thank you Sarah, for being the most talented and generous fan and friend a writer could wish for. Florence Hartigan, for walking your parallel road with matched endurance – always encouraging me along on my own. Rachael Craw, for saying she couldn't wait to get home and read more of my book – it's an honour to have you in my corner, you've been an incredible support. Many thanks too, to Emma Abrahams and Anne-Marie Amende, for reading version after version of *Ash*, alongside these superlative ladies.

Thank you to Nicola Santilli, for challenging me to make this story stronger before being snapped up and away from me by a different publishing house.

And thank you to YOU, dear reader, for taking a risk by purchasing this book.

ABOUT THE AUTHOR

Before writing books, Angela studied English and Film at the University of Otago, taught full-time in schools, owned an art gallery, and reviewed books for trade publishers. She lives with her husband Haki in Northland, New Zealand, where she devotes her non-writing hours to home-schooling three chatty daughters who have inherited a fierce love of words from their mother.

www.angelaarmstrongbooks.com

Made in the USA
Monee, IL
29 September 2021

79049444R00215